True Tales of a Fictitious Spy
Hungarian Gulag Grotesquerie

Ferenc Aladár Györgyey
and Paul Sohar

with contributions from
György Faludy,
Gyula Illyés, and
Zoltán Nyeste

Györgyey, Ferenc Aladár and Sohar, Paul
ISBN: 978-0-7443-2112-8
True Tales of a Fictitious Spy: *Hungarian Gulag Grotesquerie* / Ferenc Aladár Györgyey and Paul Sohar – 2nd ed.

SynergEbooks
948 New Hwy 7
Columbia, TN 38401
www.synergebooks.com

Contact the author via email at
sohar.paul@gmail.com

Printed in the USA

True Tales of a Fictitious Spy

TABLE OF CONTENTS

FOREWORD

In the second half of 1949, I was shadowed by plainclothesmen wherever I went, night and day. There was no doubt in my mind what lay in store for me. In preparation for the inevitable, I began reading the classics of Hungarian prison diaries. Most of them were put to paper in the fortress prisons of the Hapsburg Empire in the nineteenth century. From one of them I gleaned a precious bit of information that was to haunt me in the coming years: how to write with one's own blood when deprived of ink. Unfortunately, I could never put this method to use, because I never felt like writing when bleeding profusely, and later when I had a chance to write I was so emaciated I could not have squeezed enough blood out of my body to write two words. Hungary's unsuccessful bid for independence in 1848 resulted in a large crop of prisoners who were generally kept in moldy old forts, usually a dozen to a large, rambling room where they passed the time playing cards or chess, re-fighting old battles, and writing their memoirs. If they felt like smoking, the guard filled the pipe and lit it for them.

The law-enforcement methods of nineteenth-century absolutist monarchies were so different from those of twentieth-century totalitarian systems that on reading these books I began to wax nostalgic about the good old days. There was nothing these memoirs could teach me about my own times....

There was nothing there to prepare me for Recsk, the most notorious and cruelest institution of the Hungarian penal system in our country's history. The number of those tortured and starved to death there was by far the highest of all the prisons. It was built and instituted exactly according to the Soviet model, down to the network of stool pigeons, the political officers sniffing around for conspiracies among the walking dead. Everything was reproduced from the shape of the guard towers down to the size of the back door of the kitchen. While Recsk was in operation, it was the most closely guarded secret of the entire system. When our prison mate, Gyula Michnay, managed to escape, the whole big apparatus of the law enforcement system was put on his tail, and when he made his report on Radio Free Europe in 1951, the official statement from the Rákosi government denied the existence of any penal colony or camp in the country.

After Stalin's death a new government came to power in Hungary. One of the first decisions of Imre Nagy, the new Prime Minister, was to abolish and demolish Recsk. Before they were set free each group of prisoners were warned under the pain of ten years' imprisonment never to talk about Recsk once they were outside. But the explosive nature of Recsk was clear to us as well as to him. The majority of the 1300 surviving prisoners were allowed to go. Most of them were not afraid to talk, and they had plenty to say, just like the survivors of the various show trials who were liberated later. We were well aware of the fact that we had an important message to convey, to enlighten the rest of the world, just as Voltaire had in his time, and our work was not without results. It turned out that the propaganda barrage of the system had failed to deceive the population.

Even though this is the eighth book about Recsk that I have been asked to introduce, I am glad to do it, because I had been watching it develop from the sidelines and cheering it on. I came to know Aladár Györgyey quite well at Recsk. Under those conditions, his dry humor amused me at times, but his writing ability was only revealed to me when, as editor of a Hungarian literary journal in London, I received a delightful chapter from this excellent book which bore the unmistakable evidence of considerable literary skills. I immediately became a fan of his and urged him to send more, but the other chapters were very slow in coming. I was worried that we would never live to see the completion of the book – or a free Hungary where such a book could be published.

I consider myself very fortunate that I did live to see both of these fervently hoped-for eventualities come to pass, and now my good friend Aladár has a book here that describes the absurdities and unreality of the Communist world in a very realistic manner, a book that is completely free of self-pity, yet full of self-deprecating humor, a book that deals with matters of great gravity in a nimble style, a free-floating, colorful book that takes chances and yet manages to maintain itself on a literary level; in short, a book I can wholeheartedly recommend to the reading public, whether in the original or in this new, expanded and eminently readable English version.

György Faludy

THE UN-COERCED CONFESSIONS OF A SPY

The Collaborator Interrogates the Author

"I, Ferenc Aladár Györgyey, hereby revoke all the confessions I was often compelled by circumstances beyond my control to help fabricate about my activities during my eight-year-long career as a spy between 1948 and 1956. Now that I am retired and most of my alleged confederates have passed away, I finally feel free to tell the world the whole story in my one and only true confession."

Aladár Györgyey – and from here on we will drop the first name, just as it was in prison for some reason where he was known by his less common and somewhat comical-sounding middle name – is a gaunt man in his eighties with a slight stoop that gives him an air of modesty not entirely at variance with his character. His thinning, silvery hair still testifies to the dark mane whose loss so upset the dashing young man he was a half-of-a-century ago, at the time of his arrest as the enemy of the People's Democracy of Hungary, the subject of our discussion. We are sitting in Yale Club, a quiet oasis in midtown Manhattan; between us on the table – right beside our glasses of Chardonnay – sits a sheet of paper with the above little statement scribbled on it. We are looking at it with a deep sigh of satisfaction having just hammered it out in cooperation as the first step in the arduous process of finalizing the English version of his adventures – and misadventures.

His impish smile invokes the irrepressible spirit of the unwitting (anti)hero who animates his stories about his prison experiences, which were published over a period of time in various émigré periodicals and finally collected helter-skelter in a book in Budapest after the regime change. The unedited book was a great success there; so what's to stop it in New York? The formidable task of translation? And of course collation and unobtrusive annotation? Well, let's get to work on it. Having translated two volumes of poetry and two books of children's stories I feel about as confident about the job as he does in the role of a spy. That's why the sigh of satisfaction; in spite of all the odds, we forge ahead.

"It is not only a great relief but lots of fun to finally tell the truth," he says with his usual deadpan expression that must have infuriated some of his interrogators. Then he takes a cautious sip of the wine before retreating into the depths of the faux-renaissance armchair to explain:

"The spies of fiction are given a glamorous life, full of adventure and excitement, a life to go on forever even as they drive off in a Maseratti into the sunset with a bottle of Dom Perignon in hand, surrounded by a bevy of sexy ladies. For them the danger of getting caught is only something to play with and eventually to foil, but for many of us real-life spies the story starts with the arrest."

It's a good thing words do not carry in this cavernous place, but he still looks around to check. Old habits die hard.

"For us there are no thrills, no adventures, no fast women or fancy living; for us there is only punishment, almost as if we had to pay for the free ride the fictitious spies enjoy. For us there is only one half of a spy's life: the wrong half, the one that starts at the prison gate."

Yes, I nod and observe that the number of spies of his kind who share a similar fate varies greatly with the ebb and flow of political upheavals; communism, a social experiment on an unparalleled scale in history, required the transformation of numberless ordinary citizens into enemy spies (under the aegis of "intensifying the class struggle") by the simple expedient of arresting them.

"I was one of them," he reaches for his wine with a decisive hand as if to claim his just compensation, "and so the lopsided spy story I offer to the world is not a unique one, except in its stark contrast to the legends created by popular entertainment. And I maintain that it is a true spy story! After all, what could be more real than eight years of imprisonment, filled with deprivation, humiliation, and torture?"

Indeed, turning logic on top of its head is not the exclusive privilege of dictators; it is called irony when it is done with a wink and a blank look of innocence, a look of curiosity that is ready to take in whatever strange things life might offer.

"But how do you feel now, after having survived those events by almost a half a century?" I wave my hand vaguely in the direction of the stately windows and the richly stuccoed thirty-foot ceiling.

"Old and tired."

"But how do you feel about the book?"

"Tired and old."

His voice is brittle with resignation and defiance, but his eyes cannot hide their sparkle. They tell me he has just pulled off another prank, like the ones that used to enliven his young years and even helped him bear the barbs of prison life. But more about those later.

Our only problem is what to call his story. The Spy Who Went out into the Cold? The Life of a Half Spy? Half the life of a Spy? The Unforced Confessions of a (Quasi) Spy? The possibilities are endless but, since Aladár's modesty compels him to turn the spotlight away from himself and to other interesting characters he had run into as a spy, we decide to present them all like exhibits in a wax museum. A grotesquerie.

* * * *

Aladár can never resist a joke, he spices his conversation with the same kind of mock-serious pronouncements as he does his writings, but I believe his claim that the stories in this book about the Stalinist gulag system in Hungary are true. And not only true but tried as well, and well-honed on grateful audiences, because these were the kind of stories other prisoners liked to hear, the kind of stories they would exchange whenever they had a chance to talk. It seems that when physical suffering numbs the mind it's not all numbness but hunger for nourishment. An empty mind is as painful as an empty stomach. Isolated from the world and suffering from deprivation, discomfort, and constant humiliation in the gulag system, the inmates thrived on the only form of mental stimulation available to them, the spoken word, the stories their fellow prisoners had to tell. Of course, whenever they met someone new, the subject of the story would be the "business" that had brought him into the system. The subsequent interrogation, torture, and eventual humiliating defeat (signing the confession), were all too familiar, and nobody wasted time talking about them.

That was why early on Aladár had made the unfashionable decision not to include the gory details of torture.

Another thing: in that situation, some inquisitive and inventive minds would sometimes take the opportunity to expostulate on a pet theory concerning the grand design that governed all political events behind the scenes. Aladár says he could fill entire libraries with the convoluted lectures he heard delivered to captive audiences, but they fell mostly on deaf ears that let the intricacies of the carefully-constructed visions pass through them without leaving a trace. So don't ask us to retrieve them now.

Instead, let us reproduce here a few of the stories that they could listen to without hearing their stomachs growl, without feeling the soreness left by the last beating, without hearing the curses of the guards who were never far beyond earshot.

So let us pretend the guards are not looking. We can drop down on a tree trunk or an upturned bucket, maybe even light up a cigarette – more likely an anxiously-preserved stub – and tell a story.

"And please," Aladár insists, "spare me your sob stories, I want to laugh. In a dire situation nothing makes you feel human again as fast and as effectively as a little laugh. But it has to be a laugh not just at the other fellow but at ourselves, the guards, the judges; the whole world. And its illustrious leaders. A good laugh can even tame the devil, far more effectively than tears. Tears have never hurt him, but a good laugh can trip him up, and his pratfall only crowns your laugh."

One would think that the absurdity inherent in the interrogation – which was more like a writing team collaborating on a cheap adventure novel, pulp fiction – would naturally offer itself as an endless source of humor, had it not been for the fact that in every case one member of the team had his imagination vigorously prodded along by physical means. Humor is not enough to conjure up these grotesque stories; the effort also requires a big dose of irony.

The dictionary definition of irony is saying the opposite of what one wants to say in such a way that the truth shines through. And that was exactly what the spy-initiates were forced to do as soon as they were thrown into the system, starting with the initial interview and the coerced statement that condemned them. And then it continued. Perhaps, being innocently accused, condemned, punished, is the purest fount of irony. It is forced upon you when you sign your confession with trembling hands and eyes half shut, by swollen eyelids. It gives you a certain amount of ironic satisfaction then to announce with a straight face to your new prison mates, yes, I am here as General De Gaulle's personal secret agent. And then irony becomes a mask that enables you to deal with a life your sheltered upbringing had failed to prepare you for. Irony then becomes second nature to you, and so does the wink that goes with it.

It is only in retrospect that you can laugh about such experiences, but by that time you would want to laugh about the whole business, and – as Heinrich Heine observed somewhere – it would help to see some of the especially active participants of the story hanging by the neck from a nice big oak tree. This pleasant sight has never been granted Aladár, but something even better has: Hungary has been liberated and the rule of absurdity abolished. Many of the perpetrators of the gulag are still around, living and well, some of them on government pensions and some of them in ministerial positions, but now they all have to live under the rule of law; they are no longer law onto themselves. And that is more than the former prisoners could hope for even when they were furtively laughing among themselves at their tormentors.

The funniest thing was that the only time the sadistic rulers of life and death in that world had their comeuppance was when they were tripped up by their cronies on the same kind of fabricated charges that they were so good at making. When László Rajk, the bloodthirsty Minister of Internal Affairs, was arrested, convicted, and executed as an agent of the Yugoslav government, the whole country was laughing. Finally the murderers were turning on one another. He was the only high-ranking Communist butcher who had even been brought to justice. His own kind of justice.

* * * *

As far as this book is concerned, do not expect a comprehensive picture of the gulag system; Aladár is not one to paint the big picture, to construct the grand edifice of an all-inclusive theory; it was enough for him to see his stories elicit a smile on the faces of his fellow prisoners, or, later, from his readers. He offers no solution to the world's problems, only an insider's view into the crazy house of mirrors that was the Communist-Stalinist justice system.

We might as well admit here that the only real spies Aladár had ever encountered were prisoners who spied on their fellow prisoners for the secret police. They were a sorry lot, possessing none of the glamour associated with their (part-time) profession. All the other fellow inmates were make-believe spies, encouraged by their investigators to make up tall tales, like little children in kindergarten, to tell lies, the bigger the better. These in turn imparted an impish-lighthearted feeling to Aladár's stories and eventually shaped the levity of their tone and the laxity of their organization.

Thus, each chapter in this book is a story by itself, but now in this English version the stories are arranged in chronological order for the sake of clarity, starting with Aladár's arrest and his being swallowed up in the system by the jaws of Sixty and progressing all the way to Recsk, the lowest circle in his tour of hell. In some of the chapters we decided to let him relinquish the lead role for a mere supporting part so as to highlight some of the interesting characters that animated this theater of the absurd.

In one chapter we even let another member of the cast speak up; Zoltán Nyeste's bittersweet eulogy of Paul Jonás, concentrating on his friend's foibles, allows us to memorialize two colorful personalities (both of whom went on to make distinguished careers in the USA) in one guest chapter. And Faludy's witty poems; one about his first interrogation, the second about a Soviet overseer, and the third about an evening of philosophy at Recsk (all of them written on the spot, in his head! And preserved in his or a fellow inmate's memory! And until his recent death at age ninety-six he was Hungary's oldest, if not best, living poet...) provide excellent literary illustrations (sorry, no photos are available to document life and death in the gulag); however, his ruminations about Recsk, written shortly after his release in a more somber mood, can best serve this book as an epilogue without it being trivialized by the generally detached tone Aladár was striving for and the collaborator was trying to recreate in the English version.

And it is this mock-serious tone of levity that allows us to present this sketchy chronicle of Aladár's travails as a grotesquerie. No insult is intended except where it applies. Aladár did not seek out the grotesque, but we really can't say it was the grotesquerie that sought him out either, as it did the three above-mentioned prison mates who were too serious about socialism for their own good. It just happened to swallow Aladár up almost by accident. But perhaps that was the most grotesque thing about the eight-year-long derailment of his life.

* * * *

The other parts of the Epilogue give the outsiders' perspective at the time from two sources; that is from outside the prison walls but from inside the larger prison that was the whole country, the whole region under Soviet rule. One of them is a poem by Gyula Illyés, "Tyranny in One Sentence", written in the early 50's to describe the terror that gripped even the general – not-so-free – population outside the barbed wire fence.

Needless to say, unlike Aladár's narrative, these additional contributions are presented without embellishments or deletions and with respect for the Hungarian original, well within the scope traditionally accorded to literary translation.

Names have been left unchanged to honor the innocent victims of persecution. This honor roll is necessarily limited by the scope of this book, and we apologize to those who were not included. Unfortunately, no names can be named when it comes to the guilty, because most of them managed to remain anonymous, except for the public figures. Their exposure would not surprise anyone.

* * * *

One more thing, a glossary of persons and institutions named in this book that may be unfamiliar to some of the readers:

AVO: State Security Division of the national police force under the Ministry of Internal Affairs. Later it was turned into an independent agency, directly under the head of state, as AVH, State Security Force, but the acronym AVO stuck. Recsk was run by the AVH, but by that time the AVO acronym had entered the vocabulary as a word (pronounced as ahvoh), and its members were referred to as something like Avo-ers, or AVO-men. This institution held sway over life and death for the Stalinist period as the representative of the Soviet occupation army, the true holder of power.

Internment: Imprisonment for an indefinite period of time without trial. In Marxist-Leninist jargon the final phases of the class struggle required the isolation of class enemies from the rest of society. At first the enemies were the aristocrats, industrialist, owners of large business empires, officers of the defeated army of the previous regimes, etc, but later the leaders and the more active members of the Social Democrat Party were also singled out for this distinction after their party had been swallowed up by the Communist Party in a forced unification. In some cases the interned received harsher treatment then those convicted after a trial. If the forced labor camps had been allowed to run their full course as in the Soviet Union they would have proved themselves to be as effective death camps as their Soviet model. A ten-percent attrition rate can make the routine ten-year sentence a death sentence, as the mathematician and writer, Solzhenitsyn, pointed out.

Mátyas Rákosi: Stalin's Hungarian henchman, the effective head of state in various capacities until 1953.

László Rajk: The Minister of Internal Affairs, Rákosi's faithful henchman until his downfall in 1949 due to Stalin's distrust of anyone who had spent the war years in the West instead of being with him in Moscow.

Gábor Péter: The head of AVO, AVH, the key witness against Rajk.

Captain Thompson: Fictitious character, agent provocateur, played by an AVO officer who later got arrested himself.

Noel Field: An American Communist working for the Quaker Refugee Relief in France during the war.

Sixty: AVO headquarters at Andrássy út 60, Budapest; an apartment house used for a similar purpose by the local Fascist organization during the war.

Buda-South: Former army base in the outskirts of Budapest, converted to an internment camp.

Kistarcsa: A small suburban town where political prisoners were kept for trial and/or before being sent to more permanent accommodations.

Recsk: A small town in the Mátra Mountains northeast of Budapest, but later the name came to denote the notorious forced labor camp located nearby.

Várpalota: A small town southwest of Budapest, best known for its coal mines.

Gulag: This word, popularized in the West by Solzhenitsyn's famous books, "One Day in the Life of Ivan Denisovich" and "The Gulag Archipelago", was unknown in Hungary where the German lager word lingered in its new, Soviet version of the same idea.

Kulak: a word imported with the forced labor camps from the Soviet Union where it originally meant an overseer on a large estate, a hated figure in the village. In Hungary there was no equivalent position, and the word – and the accusation – was loosely applied to well-to-do peasants, with slightly larger than average holdings, necessitating the occasional employment of hired help.

Uncle: A friendly, informal form of address applied to any older man in Hungarian, denoting only age difference, not relationship or position. Apart from elderly African Americans, the term in English was used only in reference to Stalin as Uncle Joe, maybe because the English-speaking World was not under his rule, but in Hungary such an appellation would have been unthinkable.

Paul Sohar

SIXTY
THE GATES OF HELL

By 1948, life was regaining its irrepressible pace in the streets of Budapest in spite of the marks of the recent war. Unfortunately, I cannot lavish a long, loving description on my last glimpses of my beloved City, because it was eight o'clock in the morning, and I was in a hurry to get to my classes at the university, oblivious to my surroundings, when I felt a weighty hand descend on my shoulder from behind. It turned out to belong to a heavyset man with a Hitler mustache who immediately addressed me in a brisk, businesslike tone.

"Mr. Görgey?" he asked.

My name is spelled with two soft g's, Györgyey, but the hard *g* version of the name is better known, as it was worn by the military leader of a war against Hapsburg tyranny exactly one hundred year earlier. I was fairly used to people making that mistake.

"Not quite," I answered wearily, "but very close."

But that seemed good enough for my interlocutor who went on without hesitation:

"I arrest you in the name of the working class."

I took a quick look around to see the toiling masses. Indeed, everyone looked very busy. Only the two of us were standing idly by, he and I.

"But what for? I happen to be in a hurry..."

"Only as a material witness. Won't take more than a half an hour."

A taxi was already waiting by the curb.

"Csengery Street number so and so," he said while sticking a huge handgun in my ribs after we had settled in the back.

"What a relief we're not going to No. Sixty," I remarked with the savoir-faire of a man of the world, referring to the infamous AVO headquarters at Andrássy Boulevard No. 60, affectionately known as just Sixty.

"Of course not, Mr. Görgey," the man with the Hitler mustache assured me, slipping the gun back in his pocket.

If this had been a scene from a film, it would have shown two men completely at ease and with trust restored between them. It would have had to be redone, it didn't fit in the scenario at all.

It soon dawned on me that the grim No. Sixty was at the corner of Csengery Street, only two minutes away from that fatal spot. Two minutes! This jerk was lying to me. Giving me two-minutes' worth of false hope and precarious peace of mind. There's not much I can say about the third occupant of the car. He was just driving, without saying a word. Like the sea captains of old, he seemed interested only in doing his job, navigating the car through the perilous streets of Budapest. The rings of fat on the back of his neck seemed laden with a heavy sense of responsibility.

My conjecture turned out to be entirely correct. The taxi pulled up to a side entrance of No. Sixty. The uniformed guard at the door was expecting us.

"How did it go?"

"We have Görgey under arrest," was the triumphant answer.

Then up to the third floor. They led me to a corner room, Andrássy Boulevard on my left, Csengery Street on my right. I was ordered to stand there facing the windows. However, I was not able to enjoy the view; the shutters were all closed.

There was a uniformed guard posted at the open door behind me. Then a continuous flow of people started in the corridor, as if they had all been waiting in line to see me. Well over a hundred men passed by to inspect my back and ask with great excitement:

"Is this Györgyey? Is Györgyey finally in custody?"

It seemed the whole building of No. Sixty had been looking for me. The good news had probably reached Moscow by then.

Alternate waves of terror and vainglory washed over me, and probably would have overwhelmed me completely, had it not been for every fifth voice persistently mispronouncing my name in the same hushed tone:

"Did they get Görgey?"

It didn't take me long to figure out that the endless line of curiosity seekers consisted of my arresting officer with the Hitler mustache and four of his cohorts, who were taking turns in building up my self-esteem. Of course, that was not their purpose. Soon I came to wish they had stuck to this kind of psychological torture when they started to use the more conventional, physical kind.

I didn't know it at the time, but that bizarre charade in a corner room of No. Sixty marked the true beginning of my career as a spy, which was a fanciful adventure drama worked out by my interrogators; in other words, pure fiction, but the eight years while it lasted were pure hell – albeit, punctuated by some very human encounters reminding me that I was still alive, even if not very well. The incidents recorded in this little book have none of the thrill one would expect from the adventures of a secret agent but they do give glimpses into a world now rapidly vanishing from memory. Admittedly, the result is a kaleidoscopic picture that, nevertheless, serves to flesh out with personal experiences an era now known only in abstract, ideological terms.

CHARLES DE GAULLE'S TOP SPY

Before we go deeper into the socialist prison system, let us step back from the gates of hell, let us go back in time by just a month or so, to an incident that seemed inconsequential – if puzzling – at the time, but, as the AVO was quick to point out after my arrest, constituted an important instance of my interaction with the Enemy, one of my major accomplishments as a spy.

Perhaps I should be grateful to the AVO for rescuing the true significance of this seemingly innocuous event, this missing link from the missing half of my life as a spy, from the half that I had either totally missed out on or allowed to become inaccessible to my memory. The incident is set forth in its entirety in this chapter, and the reader is free to decide how much fun and glamour I was having as a secret agent before my arrest.

Espionage is a peculiar business, and we spies come in all varieties. A layman would suspect nothing out of the ordinary when we go to work. Just look at the deceptively innocent way I received my assignment: there I was sitting in my modest little room in Budapest in the year 1948, studying for my exams at the university, when the bell rang. The visitor at the door was a stranger to me, a stocky young man with a moustache and a furtive look. He marched right in and, after inspecting the walls, sat down and began whispering in French.

The great coups, plots, and conspiracies of history rarely proceed without a hitch. In this case one initial difficulty we had to deal with was my lack of French and English and his lack of Hungarian and German. We probably had Latin in common, but somehow it didn't occur to us to resurrect a dead language for the purpose of oral communication. Most likely, it would not have been up to the demands of a modern-day conspiracy. And since he was to be my "contact" with the enemy, let's call him K for short.

As a conversation of sorts slowly developed between us,

based on our common European background and the few words I gleamed from scraps of Verlaine, it emerged that he was indeed from France and at the end of the war he had served as an officer in the Gaullist Forces. Another fact that came to light was that he had been given my address by an idiot friend of mine, Zuard, who had gone to study in Paris on a scholarship and failed to return home. It was not idiotic of him to shirk his duty as a citizen but it certainly was to have forgotten that you don't send foreign couriers from France to your friends in a country where the flag of civil liberties is held high in the clenched fist of the Gestapo or the AVO and that fist is eager and willing to smite traitors.

If anything, the language barrier between us was growing as the meeting progressed and soon became insurmountable, so far as I was concerned. I couldn't understand a word he was saying. Monsieur K's face clouded over with frustration, and finally, staring me in the eye, he struck the table with the palm of his hand and carefully enunciated the word: information.

Maybe he was asking about hotels, I thought. I tried to act out the bombing raids that destroyed most of the hotels in the otherwise hospitable Hungarian capital... At that time the ravages of the war were still all around us, and even a foreign visitor didn't need a guided tour to find them...

Monsieur K. waved me down: "Non, non, non!" He finally said something I understood perfectly well. Non. After all, Paris is like second home to most of us Hungarian sophisticates.

Then he imitated the noise a steam locomotive makes with puckered lips, elbows working, eyes blinking. I ran to the bookshelf and grabbed an old railroad timetable.

Monsieur K shook his head. I tried to reassure him that the date of issue (1941) was irrelevant; the postwar railway schedule had not yet been established. Most people just went out to the station and caught the first train that came along, whether it was yesterday's train coming a day late or tomorrow's coming an hour early....

Monsieur K again attempted to catch my eye, and then

suddenly kneeled down on the rug. My first thought was that, as a last resort, he was about to seek divine guidance in prayer. But he had another idea. He started to draw parallel lines in the rug with two fingers, two pairs of parallel lines, one narrower and the other wider. Then he fired up the engine again with his lips and looked at me in a fury of frustration.

That was the turning point of my career; if I had called the rescue squad to relieve me of the presence of this raving lunatic, as I was sorely tempted to do, I would have missed my opportunity to enlist as De Gaulle's personal spy and would have lived the humdrum life of an average man. And history's colorful tapestry would now have a gray spot where my story is depicted.

That critical moment was irrevocably gone when K's eyes suddenly lit up when he caught sight of a French-German dictionary on the shelf. He riffled through the pages feverishly, and soon our communication lines were firmly established.

It turned out that the parallel lines represented railway tracks, and the crucial bit of information he wanted from me was whether Hungary was going to switch from the narrower European gauge to the wider Russian gauge track system so as to facilitate the unimpeded progress of Soviet boxcars toward Western Europe.

A fictional spy, like James Bond, has it easy. His creator poses the problems and feeds the answers to the superhero. But a real-life spy like me has to think for himself. And with regard to the question put to me, I didn't know what to think. I wasn't really sure if I understood the question, let alone how to supply the information.

"*C'est relatif,*" I answered, confidently demonstrating my Western-European cultural background. I dropped down on my knees next to him.

The only way one can intelligently weigh the issues in question is by finding a basis for comparison. One has to look at examples of both systems side by side to come up with a solution to the problem. The Russian wide-gauge track is only wide if it is demonstrably wider than the Hungarian narrow-gauge track next to it. Since I had traveled outside of Budapest only on two short excursions by rail, I had no idea whether the Hungarian railroads had adopted the Russian system.

We did not stay at an impasse very long; I was not entirely without resources. I decided we should examine the facts before us, and for that purpose I took my visitor to the closest railroad tracks I knew of, located at the nearby terminal of the suburban railway system, affectionately known by its acronym HEV. On the way though I felt it my patriotic duty to offer good Hungarian hospitality to the distinguished visitor in the form of a glass of beer. We dropped into a pub where one glass led to another and then to slivovitz, plum brandy, and slowly the dour expression on K's face thawed a little. I could see that as an officer of a great colonial empire he could not permit himself a smile; nonetheless, his mood improved noticeably.

It was already dark when we arrived at the HEV suburban railway station. We set about examining the rails by the light of matches. We even tried to measure the gauge by stepping over from one rail to the other without touching the ties. The experiment was hampered by several falls which we sustained. Finally I decided that that particular track was neither wide nor narrow.

Unfortunately, I was unable to communicate this conclusion to my fellow investigator, because I had left the dictionary in the pub. And it was just as well. K seemed to be satisfied. Suddenly he staggered to his feet, shook my hand warmly, looked meaningfully into my eyes, and then disappeared in the dark. I remained standing on the tracks, musing over our experiment, and then headed for home. A couple of times I tripped over the railroad ties but eventually made it home without any serious problem.

I never saw Monsieur K again. Men like him just appear on the scene, do their job, and then silently melt away. They are the unknown soldiers of history, for whom no tears are shed and whose heads are unadorned with laurel wreaths. I doubt if he was ever informed of the eight years his friendly little visit cost me.

Of course, I am only scratching here the opaque surface of the invisible half of my life as a spy, the half that stubbornly resists my attempts to penetrate it, and was only revealed to me after my arrest.

In the next few weeks, I entertained my friends and drinking companions at the university and on social occasions with the amazing story of my strange visitor. When the eagle eye of the AVO turned on me with the result of my arrest, I was not even surprised. The guardians of public order and security did not find any humor in the visit. It did not take them long to unravel the details of my crime, tracing the tentacles of the conspiracy all the way back to its source, General Charles De Gaulle, my spymaster and my direct controller.

A little creativity and corporeal persuasion in the hands of those dramatists of the AVO went a long way. On my own, I would not have come up with such a story from the bare facts as presented above. Moreover, I could not have been so drunk as not to remember the main aspects of my meeting with my courier; after all I did walk home on my own. Alcohol indeed can loosen the tongue, but I still find it hard to believe I was fluent in French under the influence. I still don't speak that language. But the AVO must have known a lot more than I did.

After all, everyone knows that in the murky, topsy-turvy world of espionage nothing is what it appears to be; what appears to be an ordinary stray visitor to a layman may indeed be a high-ranking intelligence officer. It required vigilance and hard work on the part of the AVO to sort out all the facts of my case.

Thus my stay at headquarters at Andrássy Boulevard no. 60 was short. In two weeks I found myself in the Buda South internment camp, shorn of my hair and somewhat emotionally, mentally, but mostly physically traumatized. I was assigned to room No. 74. I stopped in the middle of the cavernous room and introduced myself to the fellow inmates gathered there. The headman of the room stepped forward and inquired about the case against me.

"Espionage," I answered modestly. I expected my future

roommates to be impressed, but they acted rather blase about it. It turned out there were already at least twenty spies in the room, so I was nothing special.

"Who did you work for?" Somebody asked, and before I could answer a sour-faced gentleman with a moustache answered: "Probably the British or Americans... Spies like that are delivered by the truckload every day..."

"Well," I tried to hide my peevishness by controlling the tone of my voice, "if you must know, I happen to be a French spy."

There was an immediate change in the air. I was informed that there were only four French spies on the whole floor, and I was the first one in the room, a welcome addition. The sour-faced gentleman turned to me with a friendly smile:

"Young man, I am Ágoston Ófalussy, and I am glad to make the acquaintance of a representative of the Deuxiéme Bureau. My Uncle Bandi, my late granddad's brother, lived in Paris for years..."

To my great regret I was compelled to correct the kind gentleman in a few words, rather coldly delivered:

"I had nothing to do with the French intelligence community. The indictment against me says I reported directly to General De Gaulle."

That was only the beginning of the pleasant aura of adulation that surrounded me from then on. There's no denying it, great historical figures thrive on that feeling. They may be willing to sacrifice their lives for their country, but they expect their fellow countrymen to recognize them in the street. My fame quickly spread throughout the building, people in the corridors pointed me out as the single known Gaullist spy. My room was proud of me, older inmates sought out my opinion concerning the restructuring of postwar Europe. I had no illusions when about our situation. It was clear that the US would rise in power and influence, but I did not believe American spies would affect further developments very much. There were hundreds of them in the camp, they were a dime a dozen, without much respect or prestige. But I was unique.

And in demand. It was not my fault that my natural (and well-earned) reticence soon came to be mistaken for the modesty that often accompanies the self-confidence of unique individuals, especially when I sometimes consented to give my opinion on the great issues facing the world.

My position was secure, because the miffed De Gaulle was living in self-imposed exile at his estate at Colombey-les-Deux-Eglises. He most likely had his political representatives who worked on behalf of his return to power, but when it came to foreign affairs I was his sole secret agent.

Some time or other everyone has to face competition. I must confess that I was not the most prestigious spy in the camp. That honor deservedly belonged to Vince who represented Switzerland. Once he had gone to a dinner where the Swiss chargé d'affaires was the guest of honor. Even though he did not exchange one word with the diplomat, he was hauled in by the iron fist of the working class as a dangerous agent of the Alps. Vince was enormously proud of his status. We became good friends, because, as he said, we higher-caliber spies had to stick together, so long as the proper pecking order was observed, in which he definitely took precedence over me. After all, he had a whole country behind him, while I had but a single individual directing me. His unseemly pride prevented him from seeing my point, that Switzerland was a very small country, and De Gaulle was not just an individual but France itself. Our dispute was settled in my favor when fourteen years later my general and his country found each other in a happy reunion. In the short run, however, Vince trounced me when a year later they brought in a waiter named Füge as a Gaullist agent.

I don't know how this could have happened. I am sure my general had nothing to do with it. Clearly it was a clumsy mistake on the part of the security forces. Füge had indeed lived in France for a while, but so did a lot of other people. Just because someone serves up garlic bread and escargot in smaller bistros, that doesn't entitle him to be called a spy.

Needless to say, I regarded the fellow as an impostor and

refused to have anything to do with him.

Vince professed his continuing friendship, but his cooler manners betrayed the fact that his estimate of me had suffered. He warmed up to me again when Uncle Bazsi, an illiterate night watchman, was brought in as a Swiss spy. My friend was on the brink of a nervous breakdown at the news. I tried to make him feel better by speculating that Uncle Bazsi had probably misunderstood the charges against him, and in reality he was not a Swiss but a Swedish spy. But then, shortly afterwards Uncle Kálmán showed up, having been charged with the crime of selling the secret of DDT to the Swiss imperialists by making available to them a sample of the cheaper domestic generic version.

"This is not fair! This is industrial espionage!" The outraged Vince bellowed.

I tried to produce a conciliatory smile.

As time passed more and more Gaullist spies were turning up. That charge still retained its prestige value, and being the first, I also retained my privileged position as De Gaulle's top spy in the eyes of every prisoner in every prison where I was accommodated.

The rest of my career consisted of a steady but protracted decline. A spy's fate follows a familiar pattern: a fleeting moment of fame, trail-blazing rise into the spotlight, followed by the usual meteoric drop back to earth. From the heights of glory there is only one way to go: down. But there is no need to feel sorry for us; we only get what we bargained for. We are willing to give up the quiet pleasures and comforts of the average middle-class life in order to shine, no matter how briefly, in the limelight on the stage of history.

This is the total extent of my activities as a spy, and, in comparison, the rest of my career is hardly worth talking about. I am living in the USA as a citizen of that country in spite of the fact that, according to my statement to the AVO, my intelligence work on behalf of the Americans was rather minimal. But I have my memories, the delirious feeling of being one of the movers and shakers of history, armed with an unlimited amount of secret power. And for a long time I had the reassuring feeling that I had my General's unstinting support. His career moved on to new heights, and I was rooting for him. That is not to say I agreed with all his policies, but there is no need for complete agreement between a top spy and his controller for successful cooperation. The secret connection between us always filled me with a warm feeling. Even when he resigned I was not worried, I knew that France would turn to him again in an hour of her need.

Now he's gone. Beyond recall. He left me alone completely and irrevocably. The dead have no need of spies. The Deuxiéme Bureau has no file on me. Charles De Gaulle has marched from center stage straight into the pages of history, and I am alone now, without a patron, without a future, like a Mata Hari ineligible for pension.

* * * *

"Charles De Gaulle is dead, France is a widow!" said Prime Minister Pompidou at the funeral ceremony.

But what was there for me to say? Indeed the mournful event left me feeling like an orphan. Strage as it may sound, but these were the thought going through my grieving mind: During my slowly lengthening life span I have been a student, cook, quarry worker, coal miner, librarian; however, on the side, I also pursued a profession that secured my place in history. I would have felt like a grain of sand on an endless beach, washed away by the waves of time, had I not been privileged to be top spy for Charles De Gaulle. Now that the flowers and the wreaths have long wilted on his grave I can confess that the spy network I operated for him consisted of myself alone, and my activities on his behalf involved nothing but the shameful betrayal of my Hero in the confessions concocted for me by the AVO.

If France is a widow, I am an orphan now. It's easier for those who work for large organizations, such as the CIC, the British Intelligence, etc. The headmen, leaders may come and go, but the organization remains standing like a fort which the spy can always look to as his home, a place where he can turn to when he must come out of the cold. But where can I turn now that my General is gone?

A PLUMP SNOW-WHITE AND THE RHINO WHIP

As it turned out a few months later I was not quite finished with Sixty yet. Or rather, it was not finished with me. I was yet to enjoy the hospitality of the place on a return engagement. It was a command performance in front of the big cheese himself, and I must say I made the most of it.

My off-stage co-star in the show was Kornél Sigmond, whose role went way back in the past and continued to contribute to the dramatic developments; therefore, I must sketch out some earlier events preceding the time the curtain went up at Sixty.

According to the arduous AVO investigation, this story had its roots in the Public Opinion Research Institute where Kornél had worked under its founder and director, the famous Prof. Harkay-Schiller. I had worked for Kornél for a few weeks in the late forties.

The crucial role public opinion plays in a nation's development is indisputable. It is the force that rules in a democracy: it can not only pass and set aside laws, but it can install and depose governments. Although the will of the people does not prevail in a dictatorship, it cannot be totally ignored. But the important role the Institute came to play in Hungarian history had little to do with the work done there; it involved something else that only the vigilant eyes of the AVO could see below the surface.

Kornél at that time was about twenty-five, a lanky young gentleman of great modesty, a praiseworthy trait people tend to retain for life. So he may be shocked to see his name in print now, but he will not deny his significant contribution to history. His tall figure was topped by a long face with a chin that jutted out at an aristocratic angle. Even though not exactly an Adonis, he enjoyed the reputation of a Don Juan. Kornél was the only man I knew who had been sexually abused by not one but two female members of the Soviet Army. We looked up to him with great respect. Those two women had demanded from him at gun point what we could not manage to give away even after lengthy and arduous courting.

We often saw each other, more often in cheap pubs than in the institute where he lectured. At that time he held an "oligarchic" political view, inspired by ancient Greek philosophy. Essentially, our friend believed that leadership was the preserve of a select few with the proviso that he, too, would be included. That was why he accepted a job in the military officer training program at the College of Arts and Humanities in 1943.

"Let us remember we're talking about crawling in the mud. That being the case, it makes more sense to me if I am not the one who crawls around on his stomach, but the one who gives the order to others to hit the ground," he explained in his erudite manner. In his class, however, neither he nor his subordinates engaged in any physical activity that might have advanced the cause of the war to final victory.

This episode of his epoch-making career will have to be explored by a younger generation of historians; let me just mention here that the final exam, monitored by officers on active duty, turned into such a fiasco that it is still observed as a day of mourning in the Military Academy. Needless to say, our friend was relieved of his duties on the spot.

The Armed Forces were represented by a young eager-beaver lieutenant who, instead of letting Sigmond conduct the exams in his own way, started to butt into the proceedings. In an arrogant manner he kept questioning us: the parts of a rifle… individual initiative under fire… airplane insignia… Melancholic silence. On discovering such depths of ignorance, the officer, his face drained of blood, turned to Sigmond:

"What the hell did this class study all year?"

"Map reading," our leader replied coldly. "No victorious war can be fought without maps."

A strange, deep grunt escaped the soldier's lips. As if playing the role of the proverbial sergeant in a film comedy, he rushed to the blackboard and drew the sketch of an airport.

"What's this?" he asked Kornél.

"A *bürü*."

"This is a sign for an airport!"

And then he scribbled a few more glyphs, snapping questions.

"And what is this?"

"A *bürü*."

Again a hoarse grunt bubbled up from his throat. (Later Sigmond explained that he was applying psychology: by the constant repetition of the word *bürü* he was trying to hypnotize the lieutenant into drawing those markings. And why *bürü*? It is a beautiful old Hungarian word, though he didn't know what it meant.)

The examination degenerated into a scandal, but from the perspective of all these years it seems unnecessary to speculate how the slip-shod training of Hungarian college students in military theory influenced the outcome of the Second World War.

But I am digressing from the subject at hand. So let us skip forward to the late forties, to the years following the end of WW II, when the Public Opinion Research Institute (let's call it PORI) played a crucial role in the events then shaping Hungary.

As an impecunious student I, too, signed up to canvass public opinion. Kornál immediately gave me a job. The questions we had to ask were partly political (who's going to win the election?), partly marketing oriented (what shoe polish do you use?) from individuals of our own choosing.

My work, chiefly centered around Károlyi Park in the center of Budapest, brought me numerous acquaintances. My supervisors did not so much object to my new contacts as to my selection of interviewees.

"Ninety-nine women and one man out of a hundred questioned?" asked Kornél.

"Who wants to talk to some Joe Blow when…"

My boss remained aloof:

“We have to question a cross-section of the population!”

A new methodology was introduced and from then on we were assigned to specific districts where we had to canvass at selected addresses. I considered this approach totally unrealistic. We received forty *fillérs* for one questionnaire which, in those inflationary times, was not enough to cover streetcar fare – and so I decided to fill out the sheets without harassing of the public unnecessary questions. I don’t think I was the only one who had arrived at this solution; thus, Hungarian public opinion had come to rest on the shoulders of just a few of us. Unfortunately, there’s always someone to throw a monkey wrench into a well-oiled, smoothly-running machine. Our supervisors soon caught on to our diligent efforts and I at once became an unemployed pollster, albeit enriched with experience and memories. On one such memorable occasion we celebrated something I can’t recall now, somewhere in the nearby hills of Buda. We must have enjoyed ourselves, because we did not notice the lateness of the hour, so much so that we had to climb over a fence in order to exit to the street when we staggered out of the place late at night. I had the bright idea of bringing along three bottles of refreshments for later on. While teetering on top of the wrought-iron pillar I was enjoined by the worried voice of Prof. Harkay-Schiller from below:

“Just watch out for the bottles, dear colleague. They might break if you fall!”

I don’t remember how, but I managed to descend without drenching the sidewalk with our precious grape nectar.

We got on a streetcar headed for the Pest side. From the murky past the honest Hungarian faces and thirsty lips of the conductor and the driver still stand out in my memory; the contents of the three bottles were gone after just a few stops. Then the streetcar started skipping the other stops. Kornél convinced these erstwhile uniformed employees of the Transport Authority to take us directly to our destination. Having an intimate knowledge of public opinion gave him considerable influence over it. Trampling the bureaucratic schedule under its wheels, streetcar No. 61 was well on its way to Pest and to a happier future at a dizzying speed. If Kornél had not called for a halt at the sight of a favorite pub we could have become the perpetrators of the first streetcar hijacking in history…

After that our paths diverged. While PORI took off on its short, meteoric career I went back to my studies. The subsequent emergence of the People's Democracy condemned my historic role in the fledgling field of opinion research to stagnation. I had already been passing the time in the Buda-South internment camp for a half of a year when unexpectedly I was taken back to AVO headquarters, not only for a short visit, but as a house guest.

"Who else could have employed me as a spy?" I asked myself in the unmarked car, having already been classified as General De Gaulle's personal secret agent. Very soon my first interrogation by the expert staff of Sixty was though to reveal something else that should have weighed heavily on my conscience, in addition to the clandestine information gathering: the high position I had occupied in PORI.

"But please," I explained, "I was actively employed only for a few weeks, I filled out a few hundred questionnaires and then I got laid off; I had no choice but to chuck the place for good. All that happened at the time the institute was being set up, and I have no idea what went on later."

My defense was judged to be religious-bigoted and revisionist bunk by the two AVO interrogators, and the atmosphere of trust, in which they initiated the interview, suddenly soured between us.

"The fact that you were not there, or hardly ever there, is irrelevant. This fascist coordinating organization enthusiastically offered its services to the imperialist camp. Their chief henchman, Sigmond, fled to Paris, but we've captured all the rest. Including you!"

I refrained from mentioning that I had been nabbed much earlier and in connection with an unrelated case. I had no idea Kornél had defected to the West, but I showed no sign of surprise. The silence was suddenly oppressive in contrast to the wild hammering that had prevailed previously during the day. Change was in the air. The food which had barely qualified as such earlier (dishwater in the morning, two peas for veggies at night, with less than a quarter-pound of bread), suddenly improved. The portions were still minute but they tantalized the palate with actually enjoyable tastes while leaving the stomach aching for more. The basement floors housing the holding cells were being renovated, and for that period only the most diabolical enemies of the people, the most prominent figures involved in the most dangerous conspiracies were accommodated at AVO headquarters. Reputedly, there were only six of us in the basement; thus Maki (a fellow PORI researcher and co-conspirator) and I made up 33% of the total prison population. A teacher named Vermes was the third, the others I did not know. The light load made it possible for Gábor Péter, the dreaded head of AVO, to interrogate each one of us personally. To the younger generation the name may mean little, but those who lived through those times will still feel an uneasy shiver of terror run down their spines at the mere mention of that name.

It was in the middle of the night that they dragged me off my newly-built bunk. A plain-clothed AVO-man led me through strange corridors to a splendidly appointed office. Three men were sitting around the desk, Gábor Péter in the middle, a heavyset dignitary on his left, and the third I don't remember now.

"What's the matter, what are you afraid of?" asked General Peter with anxious concern. "Did they beat you by any chance?"

I ignored the first question; it was purely rhetorical. The way I looked, having been awakened from my well-earned sleep in the middle of the night at AVO headquarters, standing there with my two hands holding up my shapeless trousers in the absence of my confiscated belt, I could not possibly propose myself as a model for a statue of unflinching bravery. However, the second question presented a problem… Suddenly

I thought of all the kings and potentates in history who had been kept from the truth by their evil courtiers. My chronically childish brain immediately decided to let Gábor Péter in on the truth for the sake of those who might come after me, no matter how dangerous it may be to myself.

"Not now," I answered truthfully, "but yes, they did when they first brought me in. Brutally…" I added for emphasis.

"You probably deserved it," said the General, forever demolishing my faith in the innocence of great leaders.

It will disappoint future historians that after this profound exchange of views my conversation with that personification of evil descended to the level of such mundane problems as the quality of the blankets, the meals, and the new bunks. But Mr. Vermes, the grade-school teacher had done much better. This very modest man who hadn't a malicious bone in his body had been persecuted by Comrade Varju, the village party secretary. The charges against the teacher were nebulous (just like ours), but for some reason he was hauled in front of Harum al-Rashid himself. The patient teacher was able to convince Gábor Péter of his innocence, and he was released. Unfortunately, this victory of justice turned into a fickle mirage back in his village where Comrade Varju would not relent. In a few days the teacher was back in the iron hands of the security forces, and this worthy man was to spend the next few years in jail.

After this intermezzo we had another session the following night. The atmosphere was frigid and I was beginning to fear that corporeal intervention was in the wings. As a peace-loving person I was ready to do anything to avoid such an eventuality. My brain was already paralyzed by visions of raised fists and truncheons when suddenly a casual question brought its gears back into operation.

"What do you know of Kornél Sigmond's sex life?"

The banality of evil. Yes, it's the banality that gives human dimensions to even the most hellish situation. I was suddenly awake and myself again. Apart from the two Russian women I knew nothing of the subject, but I could not let my ignorance sabotage the investigation.

“Well, as to his sex life, it was kind of strange.”

In spite of the lateness of the hour a burst of sunshine instantly flooded the interrogation room at 60 Andrássy Boulevard.

“Speak up! Give us all the facts without reservation!”

“Kornél Sigmund enjoyed abusing the wiggling, snow-white flesh of plump women with a black rhino-skin whip.”

“Let’s hear all the details!” The request sounded almost friendly, and my interrogators leaned back in their chairs.

“I did not personally witness the whipping,” disappointed groans greeted my earnestly truthful words – the only ones in my story that contained a kernel of truth – and I rushed on with my narrative, “but on one occasion when visiting Kornél to return a bunch of notes on Renaissance paintings…”

“Skip that part,” the chief waved aside my preamble. He could not have been less interested in the notes even if they had involved the blueprints of a new submarine to be built by the People’s Democracy, and if I had been delivering them on orders from my French operatives. Obviously he had no appreciation for my efforts to create an atmosphere. But I did not let this spoil my performance.

“Before I could ring the bell the door popped open.” At this point I made a dramatic pause, not so much to crank up the tension but it occurred to me that I had never been in Kornél’s apartment, I didn’t know exactly where he had lived. What if I were asked to produce his address? Must not give them a chance to ask such embarrassing questions. Better keep the focus on the salient points. With that in mind I plunged into the rest of the tale:

“A disheveled lady in an agitated state ran past me. Her white blouse was in tatters, and the part of her body thus left uncovered showed reddish welts going down from her neck toward the breast area. To be strictly truthful I must add she wasn’t so much plump as full-bodied and curvaceous.”

“Not a chick but a regular jelly-belly,” remarked another AVO-man.

I nodded in agreement and went on.

"I stumbled into a room not knowing what to say or what to do, so shaken I was by the scene I had just witnessed."

"Perfectly understandable," observed the interrogator.

"In the middle of the room I saw Kornel with a black whip in his hand. The rhino skin had a sheen… For a while we were just standing there, both of us embarrassed. Finally my friend started to speak in a hoarse voice: 'I hope… that is, I wouldn't like you to misinterpret this scene'. But what was there to misinterpret? I turned to him asking: 'Tell me, Kornél, do you beat all your women?' 'Only symbolically,' he protested. 'But this is sadistic,' I admonished him. 'I saw the marks of your whip!' He gave me a sorrowful look: 'It slipped a little… Even a connoisseur can make a mistake sometimes… In any case, this is not a real whip… only a little souvenir."

I wrenched myself out of my reveries and turned to the AVO-men.

"It sure looked like the real thing to me. They don't sell anything like that at a dude ranch in Hungary's Hortobágy."

"They sure don't!" was the general consensus of my interrogators.

"From that time on he avoided me. He asked me as a gentleman not to speak about the scene to anyone. And I never did, except now, and also when I noticed him in the company of a jelly-belly type of woman at the institute or the university. In such cases I spoke to the potential victim in confidence about the incident."

"Quite right," said the chief investigator.

"And the dark hair. I don't think I mentioned her hair. As far as I know he never whipped a blonde!" I added for the sake the truth.

We parted on the best of terms. Two days passed before they summoned me again. The room was practically crowded, but only the two earlier AVO-men spoke, the rest of them seemed to be observers.

"Györgyey, listen carefully, this is a very important question. Think about it first, then answer to the best of your knowledge. A lot hangs in the balance. Perhaps even your release…"

I nodded gravely but did not disrupt him with questions of my own…

"Well, suppose a dark-haired woman with a snow-white jelly-belly… you know, with soft white flesh, were to present herself to Kornél Sigmond in Paris, offering her body for whipping… what would your friend give for that? What would he be willing to do for such an opportunity?"

"Anything! There's nothing in the world he wouldn't do for that," I answered without a moment's hesitation.

The next day I was taken back to the internment camp. My brief part on history's stage was over. In the ensuing years I often tried, with forgiving compassion, to picture in my mind a French comrade of the female sex who, for ideological reasons perhaps, may have appeared at Kornél's dormitory room, with her silk (or later nylon) blouse strategically ripped so as to offer her soft shoulders or other body parts for whipping. Perhaps, more than one made the attempt, and I hope they did not neglect to bring with them the so essential rhino-skin tool.

The infamous No. Sixty continued to swallow up its victims for several more years before it was closed down and then transformed into an office building by later regimes of the milder, "goulash communism" persuasion, in order to eradicate any signs of earlier brutality. I never saw the inside of the building again until much, much later, after the collapse of communism, all forms of communism, when it was turned into a museum of terror, "The House of Terror", documenting both the fascist and the communist organizations that used the building and abused the prisoners housed within its walls. The walls are silent now, but some of their captives are still around and able to speak. And speak they must before their story is entirely forgotten.

TORTURED RHYMES

by György Faludy

Alas! Alas!
Whacks and kicks are still alive
in my aching ass!

Will this ever pass?
A ten-year sentence means the end!
Alas! Alas!

My body aches for hers
but for years I will not see
even visitors.

Siberia!
What's the use of pleading
with Beria!

The tundra calls;
it wants my frozen fingers and
my frozen balls.

And the AVO pack!
They all had a hard on while
whacking my back.

Alas! Alas!
In the noose my neck will tell
the weight of my ass.
If I ever go free,
I'll denounce this wretched pack
in my poetry.

(The AVO men kicked me around on the floor and then had me stand against a wall for 24 hours; that was when I came up with these lines in my head; 1950) – Footnote by the poet writing about his experiences in the same building.

BUDA-SOUTH
THE RAG

The first circle of my descent into the hell of the gulag system of the Hungarian People's Democracy – if we regard No. Sixty as its gateway – was the internment camp of Buda-South, a complex of nineteenth century structures, originally erected as a military base, back at the time of the Hapsburg Monarchy and appropriately named after the last ruling Hapsbug Emperor and King, Karl – or Károly in Hungarian. Strangely enough, as serious as my case was, it was not brought to trial, not at that time. At the end of an intensive introductory course, spent without daylight and with very little sleep, I was simply interned by administrative order for a period of six months, renewable indefinitely; that is, I was removed from normal society as a threat to it, together with other dangerous elements.

Although still in a daze, I felt alive again, almost redeemed, when I could see daylight on my way to the camp. It's amazing what a little sunlight can do; it felt like a discovery. As a rookie, I had to spend the first few days in the Reception Building before my assigned place was decided upon. The inmate in charge of maintenance was Uncle Bodo, an elderly peasant, who had been interned as a "kulak", a concept directly imported from the Soviet Union and imposed on us by our liberators. Generally, the word came to mean a well-to-do peasant whose property aroused the envy of those in power in the village, but in the absence of such a candidate any unlucky peasant would do; the local authorities were assigned a certain number of "class enemies" they were supposed to produce as an evidence of their zealous pursuit of the "class struggle."

Uncle Bodo was not a bad sort, but he harbored the mistaken notion that the newcomers, starved and physically abused as they were, would benefit from hard work. Scrubbing floors would do wonders for us; after the nightmare of No.

Sixty, it would restore us in body and soul.

I had never been much good at cleaning. And with my hands and arms still sore I couldn't work up much enthusiasm for the job. Fortunately, as the old barracks building was not a national monument and didn't have a fancy in-laid parquet floor, there wasn't much damage I could do. Bodo was not exactly a slave-driver, but he kept stalking me with obvious impatience. I could sense from the expression on his dark face that he judged me to be the most inept laborer he had ever employed.

"You and work don't seem to get along very well together," he remonstrated with me finally. "Put your back into the job! Wring out that rag real good, then mop up the dirty water and wring it out again! Don't be afraid of straining your muscles! If you do it with feeling it will all come out shining like Salomon's balls!"

I just kept pushing the rag around silently. What could I say? That I was a Gaullist secret agent and not an ordinary house servant? Or else tell him, no I wasn't a spy either and I'd been unjustly arrested? And that the scrubbing of Buda-South Barracks was none of my business?

I really didn't want to hurt his feelings. He was a decent sort, and he had also been brought in without just cause... So I pushed the puddle of water on the floor from side to side a few more times and then wrung out that dirty piece of scrap he honored by the appellation of rag.

The word "rag" covers a multitude of sins; it's a concept open to a great variety of interpretations. Some rags still bear the marks of their previous incarnation and could serve again as a T-shirt, shorts or towel, but some others do not lend themselves to the easy identification of their original function. They are obviously parts of something else, whether they are black, gray or brown and shaped into square or oblong pieces, frayed at one or both ends, ripped in the middle or with ribbons hanging out of them… The possibilities are endless. A rag doesn't have to come up to the level of a rag rug to qualify as a rag.

The rag I had been given for the job of restoring the floor of the reception building to its original glory, however, did not fit into this seemingly all-encompassing concept. It was a flimsy piece of fabric with an unyielding line of stitches in the middle, bearing not a clue as to its origin. Its smell was overpowering even when soaked in fresh water. It reminded me of a dead eel, which had been exterminated by machine-gun fire and allowed to rot for a week as a deterrent to other errant eels. That thin, dirty, narrow strip of scrap did not qualify as a rag by any stretch of the definition.

At last, Bodo turned to me:

"Why don't you go and dump that dirty water. I wonder what will become of you." He was shook his head.

On that point we were in complete agreement. I, too, had grave misgivings about my future, but for the moment I decided to follow his advice and headed for the restroom.

I spent what little time remained of the afternoon sitting on a bench, without any further attempt at cleaning. Uncle Bodo acknowledged my quitting for the day with noticeable relief and had no more words for me.

"Time to turn in the tools!" A little later Bodo announced the end of the shift; it was evening. "Place them in the left-hand corner. I must say the floor is a lot cleaner. Watch where you go, you guys, let's not track water over the dry parts!" He cautioned one of my mates.

Suddenly there he was, next to me, looking into the bucket. I expected him to commend me on its cleanliness, because I had rinsed it out very thoroughly.

"Well," he snorted, "where is the rag?"

"The rag?"

"Yes, yes, the rag. The rag you were trying to wash the floor with!"

"Oh, yeah, that rag. When I dumped the dirty water it went with it, down the toilette. It looked just like sewage."

"Did you flush it down?"

"Yes, of course. What else do you do with a toilette bowl?" I looked at Bodo. Was he joking? Crying for that piece of garbage? I was lost for words.

"Listen to me!" He started yelling at me. "The rag is government property. How are we going to account for it if you toss it out? Not enough that you flub the job, but then you squander government property...."

The poor man staggered out of the room with a ruby-red face, on the verge of a stroke. I knew he was not going to report me. He, too, was only an interned, except he had his values all mixed up. It was painful for me to realize that I had arrived in a world where words took on meaning different from what I had been accustomed to. Where a rag that's not a rag can become a rag!

And that was only the beginning. Later, in the forced labor camp of Recsk, I had several occasions to recall Uncle Bodo and his rag with nostalgia when, looking at one of our freshly expired inmates, the guards explained to us that the interned did not have to be accounted for– if they died, it was good riddance.

Before I was transferred to more permanent quarters a few days later, two other noteworthy events took place: I had another run-in with him Mr. Bodo and lost my mane, the proud adornment of my youth. Although the two events were intertwined, I could in no way hold Mr. Bodo responsible for my shocking loss.

The first event was preceded by an unexpectedly pleasant interlude. It happened the next day when I was taking a pail of wash water outside to dump on the ground instead of the toilette so as not to risk losing anything as precious as a rag. Straightening up after emptying the pail I found myself facing two women. They were waving to me from a window not more then fifteen feet away. I immediately took a liking to one of them, the one with dark hair, strong chin, mischievous eyes, and thick, sensual lips.

"Where are you from?" the lips were shaping the word behind the glass pane.

"From No.Sixty."

"What are you in for?"

"Espionage."

The two heads rocked from side to side in awe.

"Did they beat you?"

I raised the palm of my hands to show the black and blue marks of hematomas.

"Oh, you poor man," the luscious lips were saying. "And your hair... your nice head of hair!"

"What's wrong with my hair? Is it all messed up? Sorry, I don't have a comb."

"No, no," both of them were laughing. "It'll have to go! Too bad!"

That was when Bodo showed up. "Have you gone mad?" he screamed. "If a guard catches you, you get 39 days in solitary for playing *fidi*."

"What the hell is *fidi*?"

"What you've just been doing." And he pulled me back into the building.

"But they can't punish me for that."

"What d'you mean they can't?"

"I have not been given the camp contract to sign yet."

"My Good God!" Bodo sighed. "You sure take the prize for stupidity."

A few days later in my new quarters, I realized indeed how stupid I had been. And how lucky I was to have got away with a quick game of *fidi*. That was when I learned what the solitary was all about. Some people spent months in there, starved and half frozen. I ran into some members of Conspiracy No. 6018 – the number referred to the number on the internment decree – such as Jonás, Sztáray, Benkő, who surfaced in the camp like rattling skeletons when Dreifusz, the camp commandant, let them mingle with the rest of the interned.

Compared to that, losing my hair was just a minor indignity, the kind of thing that made up our daily routine in the camp. I looked like a plucked chicken when I walked into Room No. 74 to introduce myself to my future roommates. But they were not in much better shape, either.

ONE DAY IN THE LIFE OF ALADÁR GYÖRGYEY AT BUDA-SOUTH

Dawn was breaking in faded yellow tones. Instead of the blood-red crown of the sun a 25-watt bulb was pouring its light on the denizens of this one-time barracks room. Aladár Györgyey, a seasoned Gaullist spy but a rookie in the room, i.e., a prisoner of less than three months standing, was waking up to another day of his life in Buda-South internment camp.

The room commandant, Pál Magyar, an interned infantry general, packed up his gear with measured movements. "Time to rise and shine!" he hollered as he folded up his straw mattress; and then, with toothpaste, toothbrush and towel in hand, he led his ragtag troops in a charge toward the washroom. There were several other positive-minded interned individuals in his wake, and soon the faucets were gurgling with the ice-cold Budapest water.

Aladár was in no hurry. By then two regimes had branded him a dangerously destructive blot on society, and he wore that mark with dignity. What's the use of such zeal? he was musing. Actually, it was excessive zeal that had led to Uncle Pál's arrest. The general had no use for politics, he was not a war criminal, he could have retained his freedom for another couple of years even in the new regime. But it was his excessive zeal that had landed him in trouble. As fate would have it, his neighbor, the local party secretary liked to throw orgies...

"Naked women were romping around in the bushes," as Uncle Pál later related with great indignation. "They were carrying on right before my nose, no more than thirty feet away. After a while I couldn't stand it anymore. I grabbed a shovel and chased them away. And I filed a complaint with the police. Next day they picked me up and took me to AVO headquarters in Szeged. I've been inside ever since."

"You should've grabbed your glasses instead of a shovel,"

observed Aladár on first hearing the story. This worthy old soldier was the only one in jail for his objections to feminine curves.

The zealous ones returned from the washroom. Aladár ambled out and found a sink available. Next to him Ape was doing his ablutions. "Ali," he whispered, "a re-shuffle is in the works. The lights were on all night in the office."

"Just a false rumor," Aladár shrugged, "but to tell you the truth, I wouldn't mind it. I'm in good company, but my situation is untenable."

"What do you mean?"

"Cards! I don't have a moment's free time. All day long at the cards. I'm fed up with it, and there's no end in sight. This is not how I used to picture the life of a political prisoner in the pink nursery of my innocent youth."

The card game we played was the best bloom in the field of penal logic. The Ministry of Internal Affairs had strictly outlawed card games, but it was all right to play with cut-out card boards bearing colored numbers. The Jack of Hearts was taboo, but there was no objection to a red numeral eleven. Four different colors, from one to thirteen – that was our special prison game.

Old Man Pali Magyar was carefully watching Aladár when the latter was first introducing himself in Room No. 73. Afterwards he pulled aside the newcomer.

"Young man, can you play bridge?"

"I'm familiar with the rules, and I've played a couple of times. You see, I put in some time as a cadet firefighter."

"Then sit down, we've been waiting for you. The regular fourth is in the hospital."

How come I didn't suspect anything, Aladár had kept asking himself ever since. Only three out of sixty played bridge? And my predecessor in the hospital? From then on every free minute was taken up by cards.

Aladár consumed the caffeine-free (guaranteed!) black soup and one half of his bread ration. He was ruminating on the last bite when he was startled by a voice used to issuing commands: “Let’s get to work, the cards are waiting!”

Picture the long table in the middle of the room. Around it the interned are reading, eating, rolling cigarettes, and the General’s brave troops are playing bridge. The mattresses, some filled with straw only, some more like the real thing, are lined up folded in half along the walls. The big room is more than a little smelly, but not that cold. Sixty bodies can produce plenty of heat even in the winter. There’s no glass in the windows, only cardboard tacked to the war-ravaged frames.

“One spade,” the General announces.

Aladár takes a look around. Old man Szalay is considering his bid. The General refrains from urging him on even though the other is only a colonel. But at least one third of the room is “under his command”. His men are sitting around on their sacks, smoking and yapping.

When his gaze strays over them he probably can’t help recalling that portentous dawn when the two Molnár brothers appeared on his doorstep and asked him to form a new government. The whole thing took only a few minutes, but one’s life can be changed in a dizzyingly short span of time.

“One heart,” Szalay decides.

Oh yes, the conspiracy of Széll Kálmán Square. “Old soldiers can only make good night watchmen,” the younger Molnár was wont to observe. These veteran non-commissioned officers spent their nights guarding warehouses, and at dawn they converged on a pub to take the chill out. The first shot usually unloosened the tongues and the second the brains. By the end of October a well-built young man joined them, paying for several rounds of drinks. “We ought to take over the government,” he suggested casually, “we have to put a stop to this.” The veteran sergeants objected, but only in feeble and polite terms; after all, the one buying drinks enjoyed certain privileges. “You want to take up arms against the Soviet Army?” they asked him doubtfully. Finally it was resolved that in case the Soviet troops pulled out and the regime collapsed by itself, they, the night watchmen of Széll Kálmán Square, would intervene, but only in order to stave off a possible fascist coup. "There'll be a great need for responsible and thoughtful men, and we shall be there!" This after the fifth round of brandy on the first day of the conspiracy.

"What d'you say, young man?" asks Magyar. "We're waiting for you."

"Two spades," Aladár answers.

"I assume you don't mean the Culbertson two-spade convention," the General is deeply concerned. "This is valid only as an initial bid."

The next morning the cabinet posts in the new government were assigned. In case the present ministers resigned, the Foreign Ministry was to be taken over by the kind-spirited but very flamingo-like Molnár, while the Ministry of Industry was to be Joe Balinkai's responsibility.

Old Nyerere was filled with enthusiasm. This scrawny, sickly little old man was an interloper in the group, being neither a soldier nor a night watchman. He was unemployed. He went under this nickname because his voice reminded people of, *nyerere,* a supposedly ancient Hungarian musical instrument according to those familiar with that instrument (but, not being a musicologist, Aladár cannot vouch for this derivation of the name). He was only hanging around for an occasional free beer. The generous young man – we might as well call him an AVO plainclothesman on a mission of entrapment, in other words, an *agent provocateur* – was treating him to rum.

"I'll take over the Ministry of Internal Affairs, including the National Police."

"That will require a sizable force," the AVO-man remonstrated, "it's heavily guarded."

"How many?" asked Nyerere examining the deep burgundy-colored shot glass.

"Two thousand!"

"*Gemacht*! I'll bring them in from that housing development, from Albertfalva," and he drained his glass. Another round was in order; the extravagance of the AVO knew no bounds when it came to the unmasking of the enemy.

“Aladár, are you there?”

“Three hearts,” that was a good way of getting out of the game.

“Nyerere was the weak link in the conspiracy,” maintained Simak, the tanner, who was also a civilian. He used to sit at a nearby table sipping his plum brandy for breakfast. He was an innocent bystander, as he often complained in prison.

“For one thing the old man could never hold down a job. He was permanently unemployed.”

“He used to work at archeological digs, on a temporary basis,” the younger Molnar, the one without any resemblance to a flamingo, defended his fellow-conspirator.

“How many digs can you name in the last thirty years? I don’t think there were more than three in the area. The longest one lasted three months. And that was the time Nyerere was moved to Albertfalva, to a welfare apartment. He hardly knew two people, let alone two thousand,” Simak went on.

The AVO, too, had a problem coming up with two thousand names. Nyerere’s circle of acquaintances turned out to be rather small, being limited to other pub regulars who occasionally bought him a glass of beer, but whose names eluded him.

“Deal, Aladár, we’re ahead by three.”

The only thing missing was the head of the conspiracy. On prodding from the plainclothesman, the name Lajos Szalay surfaced. Several of the veteran sergeants had served under him.

The emissaries, the two Molnár brothers and the provocateur, wasted no time going directly from the pub to the colonel’s apartment. Szalay opened the door, still unshaven and in his pyjamas, so they thought it only polite to get on with their business.

“If the government collapses by itself,” they recited in a chorus, “we will have to maintain law and order. Colonel, sir, would you accept the supreme command?”

Good old Lajos was a courteous gentleman. “Under no circumstances!” he answered. “This is madness, probably a provocation."

The eager young provocateur did not seem disheartened. "That's all right", he said gallantly, "let's go out and take a leak."

On the way back to the bar he came upon a telephone in good working order.

Then things moved fast. Before the colonel could finish shaving and the Molnar brothers sipping their drinks it was all over. By ten o'clock they were all sitting at AVO headquarters, including Simak who had claimed no post in the new government.

"Two spades," Aladár announced, looking anxiously at the cardboard numerals. "Why did I say that?"

"Let's get out! Time for your walk, out!" The assigned trusties were howling into the room.

Aladár was glad to throw his makeshift cards on the table. With a casual movement he even managed to mix them in with the others. The General swung open the boarded-up windows.

The interned of the fourth regiment were peacefully circling in the huge quadrangle of the Károly barracks. At first they passed in front of building occupied by the third, the kulak, regiment, where melancholy peasant faces peered out at the strollers. Their melancholy had multiple components; before 1948 very few people had heard the word kulak, and the denizens of the third regiment barrack could see little correlation between the internment decree and the farms they owned. Some of them were indeed wealthier, but most of them were just average peasants, and some had never even set foot on anything but paved ground. If the local Party secretary didn't like somebody he would denounce that person as a kulak. But the problems arising from these overzealous act were soon corrected in the internment camp; the blacksmiths, carpenters, plumbers, etc. were transferred to the first regiment, which was made up of skilled workers.

Now they were passing by the bathhouse where Bill Bullenstein and his colleagues were cleaning the windows. Bill yelled over to Aladár:

“We’ll have hot water tomorrow!” The craftsmen of the first regiment were feverishly working in this badly damaged structure.

“They say the new, fifth regiment will be housed in there,” said Gecser, the stone-carver, to Aladár. “Dreifusz is going to gather up all you cosmopolitan intellectuals from the fourth regiment and dump you here, and we, the proletariat, will have it a little easier.”

“Possible,” Aladar was musing, “quite possible.” Gecser was no dummy, and he never was a stonecutter. He functioned as the barber of the outfit, and that was how he had earned his title. But some people called him a lumberjack, claiming he felled each strand of hair one by one, but others swore he carved them off.

The walkers had reached the second regiment, the women’s section. The members of the “weaker” sex were appearing one by one, at first hesitantly but then in droves. Gecser, Aladár’s tour guide started to ppint out the more important personalities.

“You see that apple-faced kitten in the military gear? It’s good stuff, from the old army. The woman is okay too, her name is Lisa Görög, she plays *fidi* with Ludányi.”

By that time Aladar knew all about *fidi*. One smoothed one’s hair down with a stroke of the left hand: you look good to me. Right hand: I love you. Both hands: I’m madly in love with you, and so forth. But of course, he didn’t have much hair, nothing but short stubble was sprouting on his head. He looked quite bald and felt quite naked after losing his thick, dark mane.

“That’s Klári Püski-Smidt, up on the second floor. A political chick! She has beautiful big eyes, you can see them even from here.”

“And the older one next to her?”

“Mrs. Péter Hain. She’s in here on account of her husband, though they weren’t even on good terms.”

“And the one on the third floor? She keeps waving and playing *fidi,* but I can’t see who she’s playing up to.”

“To you, it seems to me.”

“You crazy? I don’t know anyone here, and my hair’s gone.”

“You poor fool! They have no use for your hair. It’s that hoe handle they’re interested in.”

Aladar was ready to dissociate himself from that uncouth Gecser, but new questions came up. Wending their way in front of the first regiment they passed by a group of what looked like regular civilian gentlemen, chatting.

“Who are these strange birds?” asked Aladar. “And what are they standing around for? How come they don’t rate a police escort?”

“The one in the black overcoat is Jenő Diner, he leads the seminars. Of course, not officially, because, in addition to a college diploma, he also had a plant. He was a capitalist. The official head is Tyukodi, a veteran Communist. But don’t ask me what battles he fought, I don’t know. Supposedly he played a role in the 1919 Hungarian People’s republic.”

“It was a Hungarian Council Republic,” Aladár corrected him, council being the equivalent of the Russian “soviet” word.

“It’s shocking,” Gecser went on, “the trivialities you educated, smart people can argue about. The story is Tyukodi hasn’t said anything that made any sense: I swear he denies having any brains on purpose. It may be dangerous at those seminars to let them know that you know what you’re talking about.”

“Lectures, seminars, for prisoners?”

“Yes they have them. But only the working men are allowed to participate, and some idiots actually believe they can get time off by listening to the hogwash from Szabad Nép, the daily rag of the Party.”

“Gecser, you are slowly becoming an intellectual.”

“Well, I’ll kick the habit if I ever get out of here. The third guy, Kapocs, the former secretary to Prime Minister Ferenc Nagy is the present secretary of the first regiment. As far as I know he doesn’t open his mouth at the seminars. But why don’t you wave back to that chick? No fooling, she’s playing *fidi* with you.”

"Absolutely not."

"Come on, run your hand over your head!"

Aladár raised his despondent eyes up to the window on the upper floor, and did as instructed.

The woman went crazy. She started jumping up and down, nearly broke the window blowing kisses, and then she started pulling on her hair.

"You see, Gecser, she makes fun of my haircut."

"Hell no. In the language of *fidi* she's saying she's gonna pull your hair for ignoring her."

Aladár got busy playing the game. So, my life is not over yet, he realized. When the woman turned sideways he recognized her from her strong chin as the girl from the reception building.

He quickly brought Gecser up to date on the previous encounter.

"Well, you see, you jerk, you have a *fidi* partner. Women's taste is inscrutable."

The whole world had suddenly changed around Aladár. A woman who liked him even with his hair shorn off!

"Gecser, what do you think she's in for? Espionage or just for trying to cross the border?"

"She'd infected too many of her customers and working without a permit."

"What d'you mean?"

"I saw that chick at the infirmary getting shots. They only check on those with a permit, but they lock up the ones with VD."

"Gecser, you insensitive brute, how can you say such a thing?" and Aladár kicked his mate in the foot.

"Why? Did you think she was a virgin? It comes out in the examination and everybody knows about it in short order. In any case, you can't expect a nice young lady to jump in your lap when you get out of here, you idiot! By that time this chick'll be all cured and ready to squeeze all the pent-up energy out of you."

Aladár, overcome with noble indignation, broke away from

Gecser. The exercise period was over and the trusties were corralling the fourth regiment back inside.

The afternoon had got off to a good start. A big kettle of bean soup was delivered, and the general was busy receiving the bread rations for the room. The bridge game was cancelled.

Beans! Aladár was examining the rust brown stew. "It's thick," he observed with relief. Bean soup divides the population into two camps – according to Bill Bullenstein.

Bill had a job in the bathhouse; he was a poor fellow without a family, a member of the Vizy conspiracy.

"Aladár," Bill had explained, "there are two kinds of people, apart from newcomers, of course. One kind gets a food package from home and can skip the prison slop, at least as long as the package lasts. They stuff themselves with ham sandwiches and chocolate bars. I don't blame them for it, because they let me have their share of the bean soup, the best on the prison menu. It's packed with energy and fills up the stomach. But then there's the other kind," and here Bill raised his voice aggressively, "who take their share of the kettle and then guzzle bacon from their care packages. And then they roll a cigarette using the tobacco smuggled in with old socks."

Aladár knew all about that kind of tobacco, and also about brandy inside a condom suspended in milk. Aladár's parents were becoming adept at preparing packages, except for the brandy-in-the-condom trick which they had not learned about. The tightly compacted tobacco they managed to send in, however, amounted to three times the allowed ration when loosened up for rolling.

"Human beings," Bill went on, "can be divided into two groups. The bean-eaters and the bean-guzzlers! Only those in the first group qualify as serious political prisoners, because they are willing to share. I rarely ever get to taste sausages from home. Only those who were arrested with me or who come from my hometown are willing to share theirs with me."

Aladár Györgyey was from Budapest, a place too big to inspire local-patriotic patronage. Its contents quickly consumed, the bottom of his tin cup gleamed at him as if mocking him with its emptiness. He was still hungry. He started to circulate in the room until he bumped into Imre Fábri, the Jewish kulak, a rich peasant. Imre spoke a north-country dialect, and his tanned face combined folksiness with intelligence. He handed out his half-full tin cup, smiling kindly at Aladár, who gratefully gobbled up the remains while listening to the on-going conversation. Laci Virágh was questioning Imre.

"You survived the Nazi death camps, so tell me, sir, is our Buda-South as bad as Auschwitz?"

"I'm sorry," Fábri smiled, "this is nowhere near as bad." The disappointed Virágh took a step back, and Imre went on. "But I've lived through a lot, and, based on my experience I have a feeling this is only the beginning. Mark my word, things will get a lot worse. More like in the lagers. Just mark my word, Virágh, they will!"

A worried Aladár finished his soup while watching Magyar, the old general, dispatching some of the candle-lighters with blankets for loafs of bread. They were picking up the bread ration for the room. He felt sorry for them, the old bastards: in spite of being a Gaullist spy he did not look down upon those arrested for lesser offences. But, on the other hand, these trivial cases tended to lower the standards of the camp...

Their story had some unique feature. It seemed the AVO kept the cemeteries under surveillance, especially around All Souls' Day. Room 73 had among its residents (fortuitously or by design?) two individuals who had paid their respects at the grave of former premier Gyula Gömbös. One of them, Tibor, even confessed to his crime. "Back, before the war, I was out of work, and I asked the Prime Minister for help. And he got me a job. This was in the thirties, and now when I happened to see his grave with nothing on it, I put a candle on it and lit it. I owed that much to the man."

The other member of the bread delegation denied having any right-wing connections, especially as it concerned the founding father of the Axis Alliance. "My uncle died on the Russian front. I always liked him, but he has no grave here and probably nowhere else. I happened to see this abandoned, uncared-for grave so I lit up a candle on my uncle's behalf."

Was it true or not? Aladár asked himself. Had there been any connection between Menyhért Kiss, a lathe-machine operator from the outskirts of Budapest, and Gyula Gömbös, the Fascist premier of Hungary? Who could tell? Certainly not the AVO.

Aladár ran into Bill Bullenstein in the washroom. "You're just the man I was looking for," said the unshaven, moon-faced visitor. "I'm here for the bread, but the divvying up will take hours yet."

"I thought of you at lunch," said Aladár. "We had beans."

"We don't have time to discuss the virtues of beans now. I have a business proposition that should interest you."

"Sorry Bill, but I finished the last of the grub from home yesterday."

"That's not what it's about. In any case, I never scrounge from newcomers. I'm talking about a whole different subject. Literature!"

"Literature?"

"Listen to me. Man does not live by beans alone! You know I receive no packages from the outside so I suffer from the lack of literature in addition to the lack of food. Klanovsky finally got out and I inherited a volume from him. You know how it goes. A book is in demand in proportion to the number of murders and sex scenes in it. If your book is like that you may get people to sign up for it in advance, and in return, you get a book from each of them, which you can peruse while your book goes through the list. Once they sign up, it's a deal, and they have to stick to it."

"And what do you have? Christie? Colette? Or some hard-boiled mystery?"

"From Klanovsky? 'The Pilgrim's Progress' by John Bunyan."

"Bill, you're raving mad. It has no murder, no sex in it. This guy journeys from the city of perdition into the celestial city. It's as boring as hell."

"You're telling me? Klanovsky was a hermit who lived in a cave. You know what happened. Cardinal Mindszenty was on his way to that place to give a sermon, but before he got there the AVO picked up Klanovsky."

"Yes, I know the case. We have someone here connected with it. He says he knew nothing of the sermon, he was only picking cherries nearby, and the AVO picked him up."

"I can see why the AVO got suspicious. There are no cherry trees in the area."

"Well, this guy is a village administrator not far from Budapest, and he picked the cherries somewhere else, but somehow got caught up in the crowd. He had not only the cherries but his train ticket to show in evidence to the investigators, but it didn't do him any good. He never saw the basket or the cherries again."

"Stop talking about fruits, it makes me hungrier, and I'm running out of time. You will act as my agent in Room No. 73. Spread the word about Bunyon, what a page-turner it is. Drum up a little publicity, and you'll get one of the books I receive in advance."

"Sure. You'll probably surprise me with Tasso's 'Jerusalem Delivered'."

"Sorry, I haven't run across a copy of that, but you're a friend, and I'm counting on you. Tell them, the city of perdition is some kind of Sodom, and in the celestial city the hero fools around with virgins and on the way there he commits a couple of murders."

Aladár returned to his room. He heard someone clear his throat behind his back. He quickly darted to one side to avoid the Spinach-Rat. This man was named after the green jacket and breeches he wore. Plus the fact that he diligently ratted on his roommates and then scrounged cigarette butts from them. Luckily, he had the habit of clearing his throat before speaking, a warning sign that gave him away. It was hard to tell whether he only squealed on those who refused to share their smokes with him or everyone. He always reported those who had chocolate smuggled in their food package. He wasn't really dangerous, he didn't meddle in politics.

Aladár suddenly had an idea, and he stepped back.

"Listen," he said, "Bill Bullenstein, the fellow in the bathhouse, has a terrific porno thriller. It's packed with murder! A pilgrim's progress! Try to sign up for it."

The Spinach-Rat remained standing in the middle of the room, lost in thought, his mouth open. Had someone actually spoken to him? Well, only a newcomer, but still...

The General finally returned with the loaves and divvied them up carefully. It was getting dark out, supper time. They started ladling out cabbage soup, and Aladár could have had three cups of it, but he wasn't that hungry.

A game of cards was cut short by the call to turn in. Aladár lay his tired body down on the straw mattress.

Hardly ten minutes had passed before rude voices suddenly interrupted the quiet of the night.

"Leave me alone! Stop molesting me! What's this? What the hell's going on?"

An interesting scene was revealed in the light of the yellowish 25-watt bulb. Old man Kucor, a kulak, was standing on the edge of his mat, wearing black cotton shorts and holding a hole-riddled army blanket in front of him like a Venus of Milo, suddenly turned modest. Standing next to him was a thin, trembling, bespectacled prisoner who had arrived only the day before.

"This man here," Kucor was barely breathing the words while pointing a finger at his neighbor, "molested me!" And he almost dropped the blanket as he was nervously scratching his round head, covered with graying stubble.

"Beat the hell out of him! A queer! Disgusting!" Several residents were rising angrily from the floor.

"Hold it for a minute!" General Magyar yelled out. "What's the story? What's happened?"

The accused was nearly in tears.

"Please," he pleaded, "I'm sorry, but I can't help it. I wouldn't have tried anything... but the old man... when we turned in... was making eyes at me."

For a few seconds there was total silence. Every eye was on the old kulak. Scarlet-colored potato nose, varicose veins hanging in lumps from his bare legs, shock mingled with incomprehension on his face. First he's accused of masterminding a conspiracy, he's arrested, and now this...

Slowly a ripple of snickers wove its way across the room and soon grew into a storm of laughter, with people rolling on the floor and slapping their thighs.

"Order! Order!" yelled out the General. "This is no laughing matter." But then he broke into a smile, too. "Get your stuff and move over to the door! Right now! The rest of you get back to bed and keep quiet!"

The light went out and so did Aladár.

Altogether it had not been such a bad day, he was thinking. He picked up a girlfriend (or she picked him up) who liked him even with his hair cut off; the food package from home was gone, but another one might be on its way; the rumored reshuffle might liberate him from the endless card games, and he could spend his time playing *fidi*. That remark of Imre Fábri worried him a little, but he tried to quiet his fears. "After all, we are in 1949, how much longer can this madness go on? Maybe another month... or two... or three... Or is this it? Are you, Aladár, facing the rest of your life here? No, that cannot be…"

* * * *

As a Footnote: the name Cardinal Mindszenty mentioned above may not ring a bell for some readers. Religion, especially as represented by the Catholic Church, was perceived as a rival ideology and, therefore an obstacle in the way of the communist ideal reaching the hearts and minds of the people. As the head of the Church in Hungary, Cardinal Mindszenty was targeted by the AVO for surveillance and later removal in a carefully orchestrated show trial. A lot of others, only vaguely connected with him, were swept up with much less ceremony. Thus, the story of the hapless cherry-picker.

CHEFS WITHOUT A SPOON, OR THE IMMORTALS OF HYPERBOLE

The room recently reserved for a newly-picked kitchen staff of Buda-South internment camp was still empty. And peaceful. The solitude and the silence were an unusual luxury and quite conducive to meditation, except for the fact that something worried me. I had been assigned to the job of chief chef, and I didn't know how to cook. No wonder, it was with mixed feelings that I looked forward to meeting the members of my staff.

The first one to enter was a young man with a bulbous nose. He tossed his sleeping mat on the floor and started sniffing around nervously like a mouse starved for cheese, then finally he turned to me:

"Are you a cook?"

"With a diploma," I said somewhat distraught. Was I already under suspicion?

"Oh, with a diploma... how interesting..." he stuttered painfully.

Nothing is as effective as a piece of paper. This insolent fellow was humbled in a few seconds. Now it was a timid hand he stretched out toward me.

"Budai is the name," he said, "István Budai, actor."

I had never heard his name but I gave him a gracious nod.

"From the town of Debrecen. I used to do summer theater." He sat down on his mat in a corner.

We sat there, quietly taking each other's measure. The upper corners of the room seemed to hold his attention for a while before he finally got up to examine the paint job on the empty walls.

It was obvious I'd have to make friends with him. I depended on him: as a friend he could teach me to cook but as an enemy he might denounce me, and I'd lose this terrific job.

"Care for a smoke?" I held out my tobacco pouch.

He turned to me, and I saw the incredulous but happy face

of a mouse about to gobble up a piece of cheese. Before a yes left his lips his hand had already grabbed the pouch. Sitting down next to me he started rolling a cigarette.

"Where did you get your training as a chef?" I asked.

"I was a chef at the Golden Bull." he said casually, referring to the best hotel of Debrecen, and lit up.

I noticed my hands were shaking as I tried to join him in the smoking ritual. What if everyone here turns out to be like him? What was I going to do among such seasoned pros? The Golden Bull was the pride of the whole country, not just Debrecen. It had been described in loving details by famous authors who would make the proverbial detour to enjoy the renowned cuisine of its kitchen... I had read about it, and now my diploma seemed like a worthless piece of paper in comparison.

"Oh, yes, the Bull was famous for its restaurant," I stuttered. "Wouldn't it be nice to dine and wine there to gypsy music instead of rotting away in this miserable, stinking joint."

"You're telling me!" sighed Gyulai. "What are you in for?"

"Espionage, conspiracy," I recited the old list of crimes. "And you?"

"An awful affair. The charge was smuggling human contraband. Actually, there was no smuggling, all that happened was this john offered me a wad of dough if I could introduce him to some guy who could get him across the border. By coincidence just that day I had heard of some crook who was transporting these jerks across, so I decided to get them together."

It was fascinating how many different ways he could say "man" or "person".

As the story unfolded, he had set up an appointment on behalf of the escaping party with the bloke running the operation. "I only went there to grab my commission. The john didn't want to part with his money until he met the smuggler in person. When I got to the cafe they were both there but sitting at separate tables, and the place was crawling with plainclothesman types. I decided to beat it out of there, but they both jumped to their feet hollering: ’Grab him!’ With that the whole place converged on me, some twenty detectives. ‘Where’s the smuggler?’ screamed one of my customers. ’Where’s the defector?’ screamed the other. And then they just looked at each other.”

“You lost me,” I said.

“Both of them were plants! That’s my luck! Not only the border hopper, but the smuggler, too, were AVO agents.”

I gave him a nod of sympathy. That was indeed singularly bad luck. It would have been enough for just one of his customers to be an *agent provocateur*.

“So that’s why I’m here. Is there justice in this world?” he asked raising his hands toward the ceiling dramatically.

He was still holding this pose when the door opened and a man entered. Apparently overcome by the scene he addressed us in a tinny falsetto voice.

“Lajos Kukucs, the restaurateur of the Stutz Hotel of Kőszeg, at your service.”

Budai’s face now took on the expression of a mouse in a trap, as he slowly lowered his arms and turned toward the newcomer.

Kukucs was a man of average height with a round head, like an overgrown baby. He was not fat exactly at that point in his life, but it was obvious he used to be and would soon again be fat, AVO permitting. He rolled his dark eyes at a dizzying speed.

Budai stepped closer to greet him. Every muscle of his face seemed to converge in his horn-sized nose.

“István Budai, from the Golden Bull of Debrecen!”

The room vibrated with electricity. After the actor introduced himself they both remained standing stiffly, gaping at each other. A slight twitch rippled through Budai’s face now and then. Kukucs’s eyes rotated at an ever-increasing speed.

I stepped back, automatically yielding to the pressure of the explosive atmosphere. The two gastronomic champions of the country were fighting an undeclared duel, and there was no room there for someone with a mere diploma. There was no point in even mentioning it.

But before the two titans could clash the inmate commandant of the regiment, Jancsi Kisházi, appeared at the door.

"Kukucs, you jerk," he yelled in a jolly tone, "you left your stuff downstairs, hurry up and get it before someone else claims it!" He cast an appreciative glance around the room like Napoleon might have when (before the fire!) looking for proper quarters for his soldiers in Moscow. "It's a nice little boudoir, isn't?" he said as he left.

Kukucs slapped his brow, almost poking his eyes out in his frenzy, and ran out screaming: "Oh, my stuff!"

I was left alone with Budai who collapsed on his mat, his face turning an ashen hue. "It's all over for me!" he moaned hoarsely.

"How come?" it seemed to me I was the only one who had something to worry about.

"Don't you see? This gent is the manager of the Stutz Restaurant. He's going to have me booted out... Didn't you see his face?"

"Sure I did. It was impossible to miss. But why would he want to get rid of you?"

"He's going to report me, that I can't cook. Did you see his eyes, the way he looked at me? He probably knows the owner of the Golden Bull, he'll catch on to me...He's up to no good, this monster...." The actor's eyes flooded with tears.

"Get hold of yourself!" I yelled at him. "Kukucs is no monster, he's just upset. Actually, he seems like a good sort. Why would he denounce you? And what's this about you not being able to cook? You, the chef of the Golden Bull!"

Budai buried his face in his hands. His voice sounded as if it were coming from a tomb:

"My mother was a cashier in the Bull. She used to bring home leftovers... I... I can't even cook scrambled eggs."

What a relief! So I was not the only impostor here. In the few minutes I had spent with Kukucs I formed the impression that I had nothing to fear from him. While Budai was doing his theatrical sob-sister act I rolled myself another cigarette. There was no longer any point in sharing tobacco with him, I figured I'd better save it for Kukucs when he got back with his gear.

Just at that moment Charles the Fifth stepped out of a painting by Velasquez and into the room newly reserved for the newly-picked kitchen staff. The resemblance was inescapable, even though he was somewhat bedraggled and burdened by a cardboard suitcase fastened with twine. He had a huge loaf of bread tucked under his long, lantern jaw. He was out of breath and eager to dump his stuff on the floor. Before he could open his mouth Kukucs returned. The latter, too, unburdened himself of his belongings and when he turned to me, I extended a hand toward him.

"Aladár Ferenc Györgyey, a student of the College of Liberal Arts and Humanities."

Kukucs grabbed my hand, obviously relieved. Budai cast anxious glances at us from his mat.

"It's my pleasure," said Kukucs smiling like an uncomfortable baby. "I like intelligent people who are not ashamed of their education and don't try to push their way into a job by talking about fancy restaurants."

Budai was visibly having the shakes, but I felt challenged to bolster my position. "I have a chef's certificate," I announced.

Desperation suddenly overshadowed Kukucs's soft face. But before he could answer, Charles the Fifth started to speak from the other end of the room. He had a halting German accent which was further mangled by the long, narrow slice of bread he was munching on. He cut the slivers from the middle of the loaf and when he popped one in his mouth it was obvious he had nothing but metallic brackets on his gums, the remains of one-time dentures. They did a poor job on the bread, leaving long streaks behind, like a broken lawn mower.

"Certificate, so what? No one can eat a certificate!" He took the slice out of his mouth and raised it like a weapon above his head. "I was the head cook in a French POW camp. I cooked for seventy thousand prisoners. Certificate, so what..."

But the slice he was brandishing suddenly broke in half.

With a muffled curse Charles the Fifth started collecting the crumbs from the floor. The rest of us were silently surveying one another. Budai was the first to regain his composure.

"POW camp, so what! Horsefeathers! Mister, you're looking at a group of prominent chefs. Look at this gentleman," and Budai rose from his mat pointing at Kukucs. "Mr. Kukucs was a restaurant manager at the Stutz Hotel. You get that?"

Kukucs rolled his eyes appreciatively at the actor. And then as a token of his gratitude he grabbed the scrawny boy by the jacket and dragged him to Charles the Fifth.

"Meet my fellow chef from the Golden Bull. You ever heard of the Bull? To hell with your Froggies! Everyone knows how poorly they fed the prisoners. What kind of shit did they make you cook?"

Charles the Fifth put aside his tortured bread slice and rose to his feet without any hurry. The long, narrow face, the dark Spanish chin radiated determination. I had the feeling he was no coward. Kukucs and Budai relied on each other for strength; that's what gave them their voice. But Charles the Fifth had inner resources.

"Listen to me you Mr. Kukucs. And you, too, Mr. Budai. Listen to what I have to say. You'd better watch out if you try to play dirty with me, if you try to screw me out of this job. I must have this job, because I am hungry, and I need to eat, and if anyone...."

Jancsi Kisházi poked his head into the room again. "Györgyey, come out for a minute, I have to speak with you," he said. What's happening, I worried on the way out. They could not have discovered yet that I was no cook!

"Györgyey, I understand you were promised the job of head cook. Look, I don't want to disappoint you, but Dreifus doesn't like to see intellectual types in leading position, not even in this elite regiment. Would you mind if Kukucs got the head position and you'd be second in command? After all, he was a restaurateur."

"Of course," I agreed quickly. I really didn't want to be the head of anything. And then I added: "I expect Kukucs will do a great job. His boysenberry sauces are well-known among chefs all over the country."

Kisházi gave me a suspicious look. I returned to the room. I had expected the others to have devoured each other, but as soon as I stepped in I sensed a different atmosphere. They were engaged in an animated conversation and rolling cigarettes from a tin container held out by Budai (the brigand had his own tobacco!), but seeing me they shut up. Especially Budai was worried.

"What did the commandant want?" inquired Kukucs in an emotion-tinged tone.

"Who cares what he wanted, let me just warn you, too, I don't give a hoot about the commandant I'm just warning you, if you try to screw me out of this job..."

The irate Spaniard sounded like he could go on babbling forever, and it was my job to stop him. Besides, I could see the two chefs and the actor thought the commandant had inquired about them.

"First of all," I'd decided to take the bull by the horn, "my name is Aladár Ferenc Györgyey. What's yours?"

"József Longaver," answered a still suspicious Charles the Fifth.

"Listen, Longaver! Nobody wants to screw you or your grandmother's fanny. I can't put up with this constant mutual suspicion. After all, we're all political prisoners, so let's behave with the dignity befitting our position. Why can't we trust each other? We're all in the same shit together, so let's stick together and help each other."

Budai extended the tobacco tin toward me. Although this was not the kind of help I had in mind, I accepted the offering.

"Kisházi only wanted to know who I'd recommend for head cook."

This was a slight exaggeration, but I might as well earn Kukucs's goodwill for my concession to the commandant. "I recommended Lajos for the position, he's well qualified. After all he managed a famous restaurant."

Kukucs stepped over to me and wrung my hand without

saying a word. His eyes were rolling in tears. Longaver also shook my hand. "You're perfectly right, Györgyey," he said, "we have to stick together and help each other. I concede others may cook better than I..."

"I can accept that too!" Budai seconded the motion.

I felt the general thaw among us made it possible for me to fess up. Kukucs was obviously with me, Budai was no threat to me, and Longaver didn't' look like a stool pigeon either.

"Listen fellows," I started, "my friends, I have to confess I don't know anything about cooking."

The sepulchral silence was underscored by Longaver's rhythmic chomps. An astonished Budai wanted to know:

"But you said you had a chef's certificate!"

"Yes, I do have a certificate," I replied with aplomb instead of sobs like Budai, because I was determined to play the ingenious swindler who entertains the gaping audience with his secrets. "I do have a certificate but I can't cook. I enrolled in a course but didn't attend the classes!"

"I'll be damned! The way you went on about your certificate, you had us all fooled. Mister big shot who got his certificate handed to him by Augustus himself!" Budai suddenly started throwing his weight around.

His audacity shocked me even more than his allusion to the Roman Empire. Kukucs, the restaurateur, Charles the Fifth, the cook for thousands, continued to regard me with silent sympathy, and this self-important ham…

"Listen, Budai! First of all, stop acting so boorish, you're among gentlemen!" The other two nodded in agreement. "Second, it's high time for you to explain your credentials as a cook. Third, what about Augustus?"

Budai cringed again. "I was only joking! Augustus was the Roman emperor and great chef."

He could see I still didn't understand.

"Don't you know about him? You a university student! Augustus. The Roman emperor, famous for his feasts!"

"Lucullus!" The name finally dawned on me.

"Of course!" Budai agreed, and then looked around. "And

how do I know these gentlemen won't squeal on me?"

"We've already discussed that subject!" I replied. "Don't forget that these esteemed colleagues will instruct us in the art of cooking. Speak up!"

"I can't cook!" Budai announced simply, with his eyes on the floor.

"And I will not teach you guys to cook!" Kukucs groaned.

Professional jealousy?

My chief chef pulled himself up. "I will not teach cooking to anyone… How could I? I've never cooked a meal in my life!"

For a minute we all stood there petrified. The food dropped out of the Spanish King's mouth and the metal brackets continued to grind away empty. Budai was again the one to break the silence:

"Kukucs, you louse! What was that big talk about cooking? Hotel Stutz indeed… You make me laugh!"

Budai was not a magnanimous winner. I had mixed feelings about the situation: on the one hand, I was glad I was not the only phony cook, but on the other, I was beginning to worry about the proliferation of impostors and the lack of real talent among us. But Kukucs regained his composure. His baby face took on a new hardness, and his eyes rolled with injured dignity instead of fright.

"I was indeed the restaurateur of Hotel Stutz," he yelled at us. "I had a lease on the whole place. But I didn't cook, I only played the fiddle. I had an excellent chef. I wish he were here, Mr. Horvath. His cooking was out of this world."

"Let's bring him in!" proposed Budai.

"You played the fiddle?" Charles the Fifth had a fresh light in his eyes.

"Did I ever!" Kukucs's spirits suddenly lifted. "My wife was cashier and I was the maitre d'. When the guests loosened up a little I'd grab the fiddle from the band leader and I played for the regulars. You wouldn't believe how people loved it!"

"I played the accordion!" Charles the Fifth announced, pushing the loaf under his chin.

At this point, I was beginning to get seriously worried.

"Longaver, I hope you're not trying to tell us that you only played music in the French POW camp?"

The subject of my inquiry swallowed hard, and then started to hiccup uncontrollably.

"Oh' no, no, no…. in the camp I didn't have an accordion! But I was quartered right by the kitchen building," he answered coldly, "and I watched the cooks go in and out, the fat bastards, and me almost starving to death. I'm determined not to face that kind of situation again. It's true I cannot cook, but our barracks were indeed right next to the kitchen, and the camp had seventy-thousand prisoners."

Not even Budai was gloating any more. For minutes we were all quiet. The shocked silence was finally shattered by Benő Sós. Flinging the door wide open he howled: "Welcome to the leading chefs of the country! Let collective cooking forge our way into socialism!" and he stopped in the middle of the room.

Sós was a little man with a big head and merry eyes. In his tattered blazer he gave the impression of a ship owner from the 17th Century who, in addition to slave trade, engaged in a little piracy on the side, and, given the opportunity, would also sell small-pox-infected blankets to the Indians. The way he winked at us from under his bushy eyebrows I felt he was catching on to us.

"What's the matter?" he roared. "How come you guys are sitting around like dry bird shit in the sun?"

We took turns introducing ourselves. Kukucs of Hotel Stutz, Budai of the Golden Bull, Charles the Fifth of the seventy-thousand-strong POW camp. I did not mention my certificate.

"Fellows, I'll be honored to assist a team of such illustrious chefs, and all for the glory of a socialist future. I too filled a key position in the restaurant and entertainment industry. And I'm sure my experience combined with yours will move the economy of the country forward…"

Key position in the restaurant industry? What could that be? Perhaps the head of some big catering company delivering lunches to factories. Charles the Fifth stopped chewing. He was eyeing Benő with suspicion, thinking the latter must have obtained his position due to his Communist affiliations. But Benő's manners, the way he was sputtering the slogans of the regime, contradicted any such supposition. I felt it was time for me to regain the initiative.

"Benő, we are happy to have an expert cook among us. The sad truth is none of us can cook worth a damn and we need someone to teach us."

The others didn't seem to approve of my bold approach; Budai was practically yelping from fear.

"Aaaaaaaaah!" Benő bellowed, and then made himself comfortable on a chair. "So that's how it is with you, my dear fellow chefs. Well, well, well! I will share with you the benefits of my vast and varied experience."

Finally! I thought with relief, finally here was someone who could teach this bunch of amateurs to cook.

"And where was it exactly that you filled that key position?" I inquired, changing the tone of conversation to casual. Benő took off his jacket, and, after flicking an invisible speck off the lapel he carefully folded it.

"I ran the cloakroom in the Fecske Street bordello," he said with becoming modesty.

After this things picked up speed. The next person to arrive, Sanyi, did not even claim any qualifications for the job other than the fact that his fiancé was in the female regiment and he was hoping he'd be able to see her more often as a cook. Bill Bullenstein (he acquired this sobriquet as a raconteur of detective and cowboy stories), Nándor and Rozsomák also proved to be totally inexperienced in the art of cooking. On being asked to account for their presence among chefs, they explained they had applied for kitchen help's positions but those were already all filled.

Jancsi Kisházi showed up again. He rubbed his hands together with satisfaction, looking at us. "Glad to see my cooks gathering together!"

Well, just wait until you taste the first meal, I thought, but when he beckoned with his eyebrow I followed him out to the corridor again.

"Györgyey," he turned somber, "I hope as an intelligent fellow you will understand that Benő Sós is the brother-in-law of the commandant of the 4th regiment, and we have to make him the assistant to the head chef. You don't mind, do you?"

"Not at all!" I said with relief. I really didn't relish the idea of any responsible position in this outfit. "Benő is a first-class expert, he's well-known in cookbooks for his filet mignon recipes.

Kisházi glanced at me with the kind of pity usually accorded to mental patients. I returned to the room where Benő was in the middle of the story of his arrest.

"You guys know how it is. If you want to flee the country they catch you as a defector, but if you want to sneak back they arrest you as a spy. That's just exactly what flashed through my mind when I was stopped at the border on the way back from Vienna, loaded down with lighter flints. 'Stop and identify yourself!' the border guard howled at me."

I stretched out on my mat and lit up a cigarette, painfully aware of the fact that with so much excitement going on the week's tobacco supply wouldn't last me beyond another day.

"I dropped the merchandise," Benő went on, "I gave my name and said I was on my way to Vienna. I asked him if he was the Austrian border guard. The fellow burst out laughing and informed me that Austrians speak German. So I said 'How come?' 'You idiot', he answered, 'didn't you know that in Austria they spoke German?' And I replied by saying in that case I really didn't want to go to Vienna, because I would not be able to speak to anyone. And, putting on a heavy country dialect, I explained that this was the first time I had left my village in my entire life. My voice was cracking, I was all choked up with sobs. The border guard was ready to let me go, he even gave me directions to the local railroad station. I was just about to ask him for the fare when the lieutenant showed up. Letting me go was, of course, out of the question. It didn't do any good for the guard to explain I was but a misguided, stupid peasant lad. In the next moment I felt a slap on my face that almost sent me flying into Austria."

Every ear perked up suddenly. The mention of the slap seemed to have touched a sore point in everyone present, even those who had not been following the story.

"Get this, the lieutenant recognized me. It so happened that one day I was substituting for the doorman who had the day off, and as part of my job I had to bounce this very same officer out of the cat house, because he was drunk. Now he fell upon me and beat the hell out of me... Had I let him in to see the girls, I'd be sitting in my favorite cafe in Vienna...."

I turned to Longaver. "József, tell us what's brought you here?"

With a somber expression he removed the slice of bread from his lips and caressed it with his eyes as if saying a fond farewell, for however short a spell.

"That's something I'd like to know myself. I think I'm a spy. Actually, I don't think so, but they do." He angrily waved his hand and started to lift the slice again, but his anger burst out of him. "Horseshit! They don't really think I'm a spy either. So what the hell am I doing here?"

I handed him my tobacco tin. For a moment he looked undecided between the smoke and the snack for a minute, but finally put the slice down and rolled a fag. From behind a filthy blanket, Kukucs's eyes lit up. "Spies! I'm up to here with spies! What's a spy compared to me? I'm responsible for the transportation of whole armies!"

An audience started to gather around him. Charles the Fifth was merrily puffing away. Benő was busy pulling hairs out of his nose with tweezers. Gyulai was wistfully watching the smoke rings. Kukucs sat up, rolling his eyes, visibly relishing the attention. With a decisive movement he produced a piece of paper from his coat pocket.

"Yes indeed, for the transportation of whole armies! I wrote down the internment decree verbatim." Having unfolded the slip of paper he intoned the words:

"The internment of Lajos Kukucs is well justified, because

it is reasonable to suppose that he intended to transport the Hungarian Army to the West.'"

Benő, with the manners of an experienced surgeon who can lecture while performing surgery, was deftly wielding the tweezers in his nose. "Some people smuggle cigarette lighters, others flint stones for the lighters or saccharin, and there are those who smuggle whole armies. I think I've got it!" With a lightning jerk of his hand he snapped the tweezers away from his nose and holding them up he triumphantly inspected a hair stalk, invisible to us but obviously of major concern to him, and then he sneezed like a trumpet.

"That's about it," Kukucs confessed, "the only difference is that I never laid eyes on the Army. For one thing, Hotel Stutz is located on the border, the other, these high-ranking officers in Budapest conspired to defect to Austria. As a guest one of them might have met me in the restaurant and figured Kukucs was okay, you could count on him, and so he wrote my name on a list. So they brought me in..."

His cigarette burning down to a butt, Charles the Fifth reached for his bread again, but then he changed his mind and started to tell his story:

"It makes some sense that Kukucs is here." The subject of this remark snorted at that, but the other continued: "You have no reason to complain. An army is serious business. How many soldiers in an army? The Hungarian Army may be twenty thousand or sixty thousand strong. It's a lousy army, but it's an army. But it is true I only smuggled lighter flints and saccharin. And then the Italian dentist came."

Italian dentist? How did he figure in the smuggling operation? Even Benő put down the tweezers. Budai remarked: "You're telling me? You should have seen that Italian woman dentist I used to know! What a slut! How she could bite!"

I looked at the actor, but I couldn't picture the scene. Not only because Budai had an exceptionally ugly mug, but the whole idea...

"Budai, did she bite during treatment?"

"Let me roll a fag! Thanks. No, she wasn't the one who was

the dentist but her father. What a chick she was! She positively adored me! Every time she saw me she wanted to jump into bed!"

"Shut up, Budai!" Benő waved him aside. "Mr. Longaver, the jewel of the Franco-Hungarian culinary industry, our chief chef, was about to say something interesting. How did that case go, my dear colleague?"

Charles the Fifth shot a suspicious glance at him. Between bites he related his story in his improvised Hungarian that's impossible to reproduce, though it added much drama to his delivery.

"I'm not a Hungarian citizen. Never was. I'm an ethnic German from Vojvodina, Yugoslavia, and when the Germans came I was drafted into an SS unit. I didn't like the SS, and when we captured seven of Tito's guerillas who had been my childhood friends, I helped them escape. When Tito's army recaptured my town they murdered my parents and brothers before the seven guerillas got home and had a chance to tell them I was an okay boy. That was when the Tito people sent word to me that it was all right for me to come home, all was forgiven. But I preferred to stay in Austria after my stint in the French POW camp. I pursued my profession as a dental technician. But we were short of food. So I made a trip to Hungary, smuggling lighter flints and saccharin, and it worked out fine, I was already on my way back with flour, sugar and lard, and would have made it across the border, too, had I not heard about an Italian dentist staying in the neighboring village."

"What a beast she was!" Budai was muttering to himself, smoke rising out of his eyes. "Her breasts were as big as a pillow each."

"These Italians go from village fair to village fair, pulling teeth for the peasants. They work without diploma or pliers, using nothing but their hands. And they do it in a flash, without any pain. I always wanted to learn this trick. Now I thought if I have this guy pull one of my teeth I can observe him as a professional and I could catch on to the trick. Maybe they used some kind of a liquid painkiller or something."

"But József, what tooth did you want to have pulled?" I asked suspiciously.

"I still have two wisdom teeth!" he snapped back at me with insulted dignity, opening his mouth wide towards me. All I could see were metal frames and bread pulp. "I only needed one, because I am in the same profession. At that time I still had my bridges. The porcelain teeth were later all knocked out by the AVO. Well, anyway, it was a good idea, but the village was close to the border, and there was a raid, and we were all rounded up, the Italians and I. Unfortunately, I never saw them again, though how I wished I could have been in the same cell with them, so that I could have learned their secret, but the AVO separated me as a spy. For two months they kept beating me, and I was so hungry, but so hungry..." Charles the Fifth took a quick bite out of the bread. "And now I'm here as the master spy. They made me sign a confession listing airfields, troop movements, everything, all the secrets I had passed on to the enemy..."

Having finished with his nose, Benő started to fuss with his ears tentatively. "Mr. Györgyey, dear colleague and the socialist hero of French fish soufflé and Russian meat salads, would you regale us with your story?"

"I'm a French spy and a member of the university conspiracy...."

Before I could go into details the door opened. and Jancsi Kisházi stepped in, accompanied by a sergeant. It was lights out. There was a head count, and then every one of us quickly found a place for his mat, getting ready for the first night in the cooks' quarter.

Around us three hundred prisoners went to sleep hoping that, starting the next day, excellent cooks would be feeding them culinary delights. Well, perhaps not exactly starting the next day, because – as I was hoping and telling myself – it might take a week or two before the pots and pans were delivered. Might even take a month... Who knows, by then, we might even get someone who could actually cook!

DREIFUS HAD A MAIDEN NAME: LAJOS RUSCSAK –
OR THE CRUTCHES OF A POLICE COLONEL

One of the most authentic grotesques I encountered in my prison career was Dreifus the camp commandant of Buda-South. Missing one leg, he strutted around on a pair of crutches (hence the nickname), meting out physical punishment on helpless inmates with the deft use of his existing facilities; thus, his position and nasty disposition gave his handicap a sinister aspect.

Everything I know about the background of this freakishly fearsome figure I owe to the vast research work done by Dr. Zsögöd. He was one of my fellow inmates at the time, but earlier he had been a clever attorney and, according to legend, the most successful defender of those who were interned during the post-war period in Hungary. He was immortalized in a little ditty, popular with everyone in the Buda-South camp, whether a client or not:

"If you're put inside by the Ministry
Doctor Zsögöd will spring you free."

What the folksong neglected to mention was the fact that, once inside, an inmate could only go further inside by a decree of the Ministry of Internal Affairs which gave an automatic six-month extension to all internment orders. But as the class-struggle intensified and the brilliant lawyer himself met his downfall, new stanzas were added to what was slowly becoming an epic:

"Doctor Zögöd got the sad decree,
And who is there to spring him free?"

Great epic tales are marked by layers of history: this little fragment originates from the time of Dr. Zsögöd's own internment.

I don't know exactly how it happened, how it came to be that neither Dr. Zsögöd's debonair whiskers nor his expertise, nor his connections could save him… But miners sometimes can get buried under dirt, doctors infected with measles, and lawyers arrested by the long arm of the People's Democracy. When I met Dr. Zsögöd he was already putting in his third stint in the camp. He had not lost his optimism, only regretted the loss of his hair which had been mercilessly shorn off every time he was admitted.

I did not belong to his circle of friends, but I had a chance to listen to some of his lectures on the camp's commander-in-chief. Each scholar has his field of specialty; Burckhardt concentrated on the Renaissance, Ignac Goldziher on Islam, and Zsögöd on the internment camp.

"Dreifus had a maiden name, Lajos Ruscsák," explained the eloquent jurist. "In civilian life he was a grave digger, but he had a lucrative sideline as the jailbird correspondent for a newspaper, Népszava, the daily paper of the Social Democrats. Every time there was a libel suit against the paper he was put forward as the author of the disputed article. The short two- or three-month sentences quickly added up to years in jail, and for his pains he was awarded a position in the Buda-South internment camp.

"The Dreifus nickname has nothing to do with Zola's famous defendant or with Devil's Island. What happened – according to reliable sources – our commander got drunk one day and lay down on the streetcar tracks which resulted in the loss of one leg and the gain of two crutches. These later became an integral part of his body. By now he's learned to run on them so fast that the crutches become a blur; they look like a wooden fence from a distance, with him riding over it. Another trick of his is to lean on the crutches and swing himself horizontally some six feet towards you to deliver a kick in your pants. Hence the nickname Dreifus, which means three-legged in German."

“Some of us know that much German,” remarked Rátonyi tartly. He owed his renown to the fact that he had been married once to Annie Suli, the famous American singer. She had two other ex-husbands in the camp. I envied all three of them for their memories.

“Take it easy,” said Zsögöd. “No need to take offence. Interestingly, Dreifus likes to refer to the accident in other terms. ’I am a victim of oppression and the war,’ he keeps saying. He never mentions the role of alcohol in his misfortune. But he has managed to overcome his handicap with remarkable skill and single-minded devotion. If you get denounced and dragged in front of him, he props himself up on one leg and a crutch while using the other crutch to beat the shit out of you. He’s quite talented. He could’ve become an acrobat,” added Zsögöd, lost in thought for a minute or two before going on with his lecture: “And then he sticks you into solitary for thirty nine days where the grub is scarce and fags non-existent. Forty days would require approval from the Ministry. Generally, it’s not a good sign to run into him. For example, every time he sees me he gives me a thrashing. On Sundays he’s always out there, hopping around, sometimes he even locks up the visiting relatives if he doesn’t like the way they look.”

“Does he have the right to do that?” We were horrified.

“As a lawyer, I especially disapprove of that,” Zsögöd raised his sententious voice. “He doesn’t do it very often, but he has other tricks he can get away with, like spraying the shivering parents, wives and sweethearts from a hose in the dead of winter.”

“There are some who are not intimidated by him,” Bill Bullenstein interrupted. “You remember Anci? A pretty 17 year-old high school girl, who came to visit her brother. He happened to be in solitary on account of some trumped-up escape plans. So Anci was not able to see him and went to Dreifus to inquire. ’What’s your brother’s name?’ ’Lászlo Papp.’ ’He’s a rotten Fascist, he’s in solitary, and he’s gonna rot there,’ Dreifus howled. ‘Stop howling at me. Everybody knows what a wild beast you are.’ For a minute there was deadly silence, people around them were convinced he was going to kill this young chick who dared to talk back to him. Dreifus snorted a little and then mumbled something about her being a brave girl to tell the truth to his face. And then he ordered the sergeant to let the girl visit her goddam Fascist brother whenever she felt like it. After that Anci Papp had unlimited visiting rights."

I had been incarcerated for about a month when I first ran into Dreifus. His inspection tours usually lasted less than three minutes. He roared through like a tornado leaving wreckage in his wake. As it happened, we were being herded out for our daily walk, and just when we reached the bottom of the stairs the door popped open. Suddenly everybody was running like crazy away from the scene, in any direction they could. I happened to be standing in a corner, and from my vantage point was able to take a good look at this strong, broad-shouldered figure who vaulted himself forward on a pair of crutches. His rugged, weather-beaten face could have been carved by a dull axe. "Good morning men," he yelled out and in the next second he delivered a kick into the pants of an old Nazi that sent the pants and its occupant flying up to the landing. Eyes glazed over with fear, I watched him set his crutches on the first step and stiffen his body like a pillar. "Imre Szabó, you rotten Fascist dog, if I ever catch sight of you again I'll have you thrown into solitary. Carry on, men..." he took his leave and rode on, well-satisfied with the job he'd done. The whole thing was over in thirty seconds, but this brief and bizarre scene was enough to convince me that there was no one in the camp who could stand up to him.

As it turned out there was such a man: Ferenc Ludányi. He had put in some time in the jails of the old Horthy regime for vagrancy. After the '45 Liberation, he spent the first few years in the Buda-South internment camp where he developed an interest in politics. We learned all this from Bill Bullenstein who acted as scribe for the illiterate Ludányi when the latter wanted to send a letter to his sweetheart, Erzsi Görög. The recurrent theme of these love notes sounded something like this: “Erzsi, don’t you dare play *fidi* with anyone else. I’m no ordinary bum, I’m a political prisoner now.” (I should remind the reader here that playing *fidi* was a sort of sign language whereby the members of the segregated opposite sexes managed to communicate with each other at a distance. The lady in question was a prominent figure in the female regiment. Love notes, as any other written letters between prisoners, were strictly illegal.). The *political* designation caught Zsögöd’s attention, because it was never backed up by an extension notice to Ludányi’s name. He filed a petition on behalf of the prisoner, and his client was immediately released. Later it was discovered that Ferenc Ludányi was a victim of mistaken identity; he had served four years in place of a right-wing journalist by the same surname but a different given name, Tibor.

Ludányi was still a full-fledged member of the camp at the time he took a stand against Dreifus. Some of his critical remarks concerning the camp and People’s Democracy in general had been reported by stoolies. The big chief was his usual brusque self when Ludányi was hauled before him, but didn’t start the interview with the usual beating, because the two of them had spent some time together in the jails of the previous regime.

“Feri, you lousy bum, who the hell d’you think you are? You never had it so good in the Fascist jails.” The chief was trying the gentle, good cop approach.

“Lajos, you’ve gone gaga,” answered the prisoner with injured dignity. “Those jails had much better grub, more visiting hours, regular beds... They were luxury hotels compared to this garbage heap. And the solitary was hardly ever used. Of course it’s better for you now, because you’re the big cheese. The problem with you, Lajos, is that you’re a goddamn liar.”

The colonel flew into rage. “If you don’t shut up, Ludányi, I’ll have you thrown into solitary. Thirty nine days.”

“I’ll have to escape then, Lajos. As soon as they lock me up.”

Off he went to solitary. That very night he lowered himself from the tower on his blanket and disappeared into the night. Detective Pálfi, who was sent to pick him up, found him in his old apartment. He was busy preparing breakfast. "I'm looking for Ferenc Ludányi", said the detective. "My brother Feri is not at home at the moment", answered the prisoner while breaking an egg over the sizzling bacon. "He should be back any minute now. He came home last night. From a long stay in the country."

"In the country, indeed," Pálfi was laughing.

The omelet was cooked and consumed. Ludányi took his leave of the detective, assuring him that his brother was expected back any minute now.

He was caught again a few months later but never again locked up in solitary.

There was another way of dealing with Dreifus. Izidor Mermelstein's psychological approach was radically different from Ludányi's. Our paths crossed often. He was already an inmate of Buda-South on my arrival there, but he was released soon afterwards. A year later he was brought in to Kistarcsa Prison as a newly arrested culprit, but when the rest of us were transferred to Recsk, he was again let go. Again I watched him released from the prison mine of Várpalota, but when I was finally given my freedom, Izidor Mermelstein said good-bye to me as the inmate of the Csolnok prison mine.

So what caused the conflict between the young Izidor Mermelstein and the even younger People's Democracy? Izidor didn't believe in borders. He was dealing in wholesale illegal emigration, getting large groups across the border to the West. This sixteen-year-old kid smuggled hundreds of Romanian Jews to Austria. Later the minefields and barbed wire restricted his business to smaller parties.

Mermelstein was brought before Dreifus with the charge of trying to send a note. A thrashing with the crutch, followed by solitary confinement, would have been the order of the day, but the young man seized the initiative. Leaning over the desk, his eyes fogged up by tears like those of a calf being led to slaughter, he looked at the colonel. "I am a poor orphan boy, and I look up to you, sir, as my father."

According to Izidor, the colonel's eyes, too, immediately glazed over, and that was the beginning of a loving father-and-son relationship. From that time on Izidor was prince of the camp.

Buda-South was staffed with regular policemen (as opposed to the newly formed State Security Force AVH, an independent force directly under the head of state). Most of them were all right, but some of them took perverse pleasure in making life miserable for us. We had a way of dealing with those. We'd present Izidor with a box of illegal chocolates; his job was to walk up and down in front of the policeman until he made some remark, and at that point Dreifus's adopted son talked back to him. The set-up guard would grab him and drag him to Dreifus. But before he had a chance to make his report Izidor blurted out, his eyes filled with tears: "This guard was cussing out my father." That ended the policeman's career in the camp and he was immediately transferred out.

But I don't want to make a hero out of Lajos Ruscsák. It was just that he had a duality to his character, which was soon discovered and exploited by even those untutored in psychology. For example, on his birthday a chorus of thirty interned appeared in front of his house and belted out a popular song:

The frost is on the fields today,
the old outlaw is turning gray...

At the end of the serenade the window opened and Dreifus addressed the crowd in a voice choked with emotion.

"Thank you, men, thank you very much. My very favorite song. I don't deserve it. I'm an evil man, yet you honored me with that song. The missus will give you each a shot of brandy. Maybe two." And then his raspy voice skidded into falsetto. "But if someone takes three he's gonna end up in solitary. And rot there for good."

The missus was a very nice person. If an interned ever got near her kitchen, she would offer him something to eat. Her eyes radiated sympathy. The genuineness of the feeling was supported by the words she was overheard speaking to her husband on quiet summer nights: "Listen Lajos, they'll string you up someday. You keep these law-abiding people locked up, and you beat them, too, what do you think will happen to you someday?"

"You've been talking to those nuns again."

"It doesn't matter where it comes from. The point is you'll hang someday. I only hope your floozy will too. Right next to you like Mussolini's."

Unfortunately, I never had a chance to see the above-mentioned female. She was called Berta the Red, presumably referring to the color of her hair rather than to her politics. Pali Alexa was the interned who knew her best, because he was the commander's driver. While the Ruscsák couple's marital disputes could be heard only by the immediate neighbors, the altercations between the colonel and his driver took on legendary proportions, mostly due to the volume they were able to muster.

Pali Alexa was a good-looking peasant lad. According to his detractors – who generally found his education lacking – the cow-dung would have had to be dynamited off his bare feet. Sounds like a picturesque but rather derogatory way to describe plain country folk, and I take no responsibility for it. And I don't really know the truth, for I had only a nodding relationship with him, and we never engaged in any deep philosophical discussions. His nocturnal exchanges with the colonel were definitely not conducted in highfalutin literary language, nothing approximating the style of Proust, but rather something closer to the traditions of hard-boiled detective fiction.

Pali used to drive Dreifus to and from his trysts. Sometimes the boss was so inebriated when they got back home late at night he could not stand up on either the crutches or the one leg.

“You stinker, you drunken pig,” the driver started the taunting, “How the hell are you going to get into bed?”

“My dear Pali, my best and only buddy, you will carry me upstairs.”

This conversation, while true to the original in content, is presented here in a lower register. The actual exchange between Dreifus and Pali would evoke the specters of moral degeneration even in the hearts of the toughest neo-realists.

“Let your mother’s this-and-that *(=unmentionable anatomical part*) lug you upstairs! I won’t touch you with a finger, you rascal! You let me wait in the street with one glass of wine while you were getting plastered....”

“Time flies, my dear Pali. But enough of this fooling, carry me up or else I’ll have you thrown into solitary, you....”

“What d’you want to do to me? Who’s going to lug you to and from your chick?”

The wrangling ended with the management having its way, and Dreifus was finally deposited in his bed.

Our commander liked plain folks like Pali. He couldn’t stand intellectual types, especially when he felt they were trying to pull one over him. He often showed up at the reception building to look over the newcomers. He asked them their names and occupation. A ministry official couldn’t get away with saying he was a mechanic, because Dreifus would immediately check his hands. If they were smooth, lacking a real working man’s calluses, he would immediately unmask the impostor: “You’ve didn’t worked a day in your life, you rotten Fascist! Off to solitary with you!” This test led to an illustrious career for a renowned attorney. When he was picked out in the line he showed hands that were covered with warts. Dreifus mistook these symptoms of a disease for calluses which had been acquired by honest labor. The jurist was made the swineherd for the commander’s pigs. His important position allowed him to make frequent trips into the City and even to continue his practice on a modest scale.

During the Christmas of 1948 a strange character visited us in our stable-like surroundings. We were all pretty sloppy, but this unshaven older gentleman was dressed skid-row style. He had a shoebox tucked under one arm. Inside it he had a miniature crèche complete with shepherds and the other figures shaped out of bread dough. The display had no artistic merit, but the old gentleman's words could wring your heart, in spite of his voice of a huckster at a village fair: "This Christmas is not our Christmas... Our loved ones are shivering at home around a single candle... We shall celebrate when we finally get out of here....etc...etc..." After the show the artist took up a collection, (small pieces of bread, jam and tobacco) and moved on to the next barracks.

There were some among us in the camp who rose up to defend the ideological purity of our fledgling people's democracy. In less than an hour the performer of the Christmas show was in solitary; the incident was explained to us by Dreifus over the public address system.

"Listen everyone," he said, "all right, it's Christmas. I come from a devout Catholic family, and the exalted holiday of love is indeed sacred to me. But this no-good Miklósi belongs in the deepest, darkest dungeon. You know what I told him? This is not your Christmas? To solitary with you, you lousy Fascist! You can celebrate there as much you like!"

For consolation, he sketched out the salutary conditions of the camp: "Listen you guys, you don't know how good you have it here. Recently an international committee came to visit the camp. Generally, these people are hostile to us, but before they left this is what they said to me: 'Colonel sir, hats off to you. Buda-South is without a doubt the most advanced and most humane penal institution in all of Central Europe, maybe the whole world.' So you'd better make the best of it, life doesn't stop at the gate. Why, we can even perform marriage ceremonies here. Stop hankering for the life outside, I even get letters from Vienna. Some of the released interned who defected to the West are begging to be allowed back in here. For them it's too late now, but those who make the most of opportunities here will have it real good. Those who try to escape will be caught and will rot in solitary. Good night and

Merry Christmas."

Our curiosity aroused by these words, we sought out our lawyer, Zsögöd.

"Take it easy boys," said the legal-eagle. "What our commander preached falls somewhat short of the truth. Or rather, it misses the truth all together. There was indeed an UNRAH or Red Cross committee inspecting here some two years ago, but I happened to be out. Dreifus evacuated the guards' barracks, the two buildings facing the gate. He picked out the fattest prisoners and had them lie down on the guards' beds. The committee went around admiring the blankets, the radios, and the meals delivered from the police kitchen. Dreifus explained the scarcity of the prisoners to the committee by saying the rest were away working in Budapest. The fat ones lying around were either sick or unwilling to work. This Swedish committee marveled at the bathroom and then left. Only three hundred yards away thousands of people were jammed together on the bare floors of a bombed out barrack without glass in the windows, but of course the committee missed all that."

"How could they not see the real Buda-South?"

"Because they were dumb, as dumb as only smart educated people can be," said Ernő Vágo sadly, but Zsögöd continued:

"The marriage ceremony did take place. Gyuszi's fiancée was allowed in to visit and they were wedded in a short ceremony. But that was it. The happy bridegroom is still here and I expect he'll stay for another few years yet. You can figure out the letters by yourself. There was a joker who managed to escape and sent a postcard from Vienna to Dreifus, calling him a sadistic beast. He also expressed a desire to come back here and hang the commander in the middle of the yard."

Later I learned how to interpret Dreifus's speeches. Unfortunately they have not been preserved for future historians; his dramatic expostulations have been lost forever.

The international committee figured in almost every one of his orations, and so did a certain Colonel Nándor Pápa, an interned Dreifus had taken special care of, coddled, given a good job to, and yet the wretched villain turned against his benefactor; he received snacks from his wife through the fence. “He never had it so good, not even in his mother’s belly, but the bastard didn’t know it, and now he’s rotting in solitary.”

At the beginning of 1949, the camp was moved to the village of Kistarcsa. The local chapter of the Communist Party organized a demonstration in front of the gate. “Let us in, let us teach these Fascist pigs a lesson, let us beat the hell out of them,” they were yelling. The guards grabbed their rifles in consternation.

Soon, Dreifus was on the scene. Waving a crutch in the air he quieted down the vociferous little group, and then he addressed the progressive elements of the village:

“Hello, folks, I hear you want to crack a few fascist heads. That’s fine with me. But if in five minutes I still see any of you here I’m going to open the gates. And then, when these two thousand Fascists get through with you, we can clean up the mess with one dust pan.”

In seconds, the whole area was deserted. Too bad the inspectors from the Guiness Book of Records were not around, otherwise the event could have been immortalized in its pages as the shortest political demonstration in world history.

We were not aware of it then, but the move to Kistarcsa marked the beginning of the end for Dreifus’s reign. His downfall, like that of the Roman Empire, is open to dispute. According to some opinions he fell out of favor, because his thefts were out proportion with his position, albeit not with his lively personality. But I don’t agree. True enough, he certainly helped himself to free labor provided by the interned population and had a truckload of coat hangers recovered from the bombed out portions of Buda-South delivered to his house. But we are talking about trifles, and the Dreifus residence compared to that of Comrade Rákosi, our Wise Leader, was more like comparing a slum to one of the mad castles of Ludwig II of Bavaria. No, stealing was only a subterfuge. My feeling is that our commander was somehow associated with Lászlo Rajk, and that was the reason for the decline of his fortune.

In the beginning at Kistarcsa, too, he made his usual inspection tours among the interned toiling in the yard, ordered to dig those eternal ditches. On such occasions there were only two alternatives. You either beat a hasty retreat, in which case the commander would fly on contentedly over the discarded spades and shovels, or else you started to work like hell if you had the courage to face this potentate. These stout-hearted fellows of the latter group started to push the dirt around as if in fast forward. Only an idiot would have expected them to keep up the pace for longer than two minutes, but Dreifus was satisfied. He would ask the crazed ditch digger's name, as he personally knew hundreds of the interned, and he would make special concessions for the bold fellow, such as extra packages from home or extra visits from relatives.

Once I saw him stop by at Uncle Kohn's workshop. The old man was polishing a huge marble plaque; the original inscription "Lászlo Rajk Police Academy" was slowly disappearing under the expert work of the chisel. "Sic transit gloria mundi" would have been an appropriate quotation for the occasion, but Dreifus did not resort to it. He just stood there in sorrow for a while and then remarked: "Hey, Uncle Kohn, you'd rather be burying Russian soldiers, wouldn't you?" The interned nodded thoughtfully.

This remark did not mean that the commander had fallen out of love with the great and mighty Soviet Union. It was merely a reference to the reason for Kohn's incarceration, his overzealous execution of his duty as a gravedigger. He was getting 500 *pengő* for each Soviet soldier's burial. Unfortunately, there had been no significant battle near his village, and the prospects were rather limited; however, the old man was very ingenious. For a while he was burying individual body parts in separate graves, but later he accorded the final rites and last respects to pieces of uniforms. When the distrustful authorities exhumed some of the Soviet heroes they found nothing but a cap, and they arrested Kohn. In captivity he switched from the service of death to the service of new life;

he devoted his time and skills to the renewal of politically obsolete marble plaques.

"Who knows, someday I may have to scratch this name off too," said Kohn and added with prophetic sense: "Someday, the name Rajk may be inscribed on it again."

Dreifus nodded sadly and then hopped on. He thrashed a few more prisoners, but only out of habit; his heart was no longer in it.

He had one more birthday to celebrate just before his public life came to an end. His unsuspecting loyal followers arranged a concert for him. The chorus was singing the usual, *"The frost is on the fields today...",* but even more off key than usual. I worried that the critical appraisal might send the hapless performers to the solitary. In the middle of the song *("...nowadays nothing else is mine, but my pipe and my glass of wine...")* a rather agitated policeman called Dreifus to the phone in staff headquarters. There was no logical explanation for it, but suddenly I had a feeling a historic moment had arrived.

It took a while before the commander returned. His steps were slow and hesitant as he wended his way among the small band of well-wishers, who stood around like the mute trees of a winter forest. The mood of celebration had drained from both the cowed celebrants and the celebrated. The latter hobbled away, head hung low, his gaze unaware of the silenced singers. He was a broken man, just a cripple on crutches.

We later learned the call had come from a very high place. He was informed of his dismissal. He was not implicated in the Rajk case, didn't get executed, didn't even get arrested. Didn't even appear in court – he had become a non-person. Years later I heard he had been seen lying at night on a snow bank in a street of Budapest, with his broken crutches next him. Apparently, some of the former interned, once entrusted to his care but now newly released, had paid their respects to him. The roughed-up cripple couldn't move, but the curses poured out of him as loudly as ever.

For four years Lajos (Dreifus) Ruscsák single-handedly

reigned over his own little kingdom in the middle of a small country. He ruled over life and death; he was feared by thousands and genuinely liked by few, but he left his mark on every one of his subjects and subordinates. He was not a singular phenomenon in Central Europe; there were plenty more people in leading positions who were even more unhinged, given to drunkenness and cruelty than this ex-gravedigger.

Ruscsák's significance lay in his singular personality. Perhaps he was the last of the oligarchs, the last of the petty potentates whose self-indulgence served the dictatorship of the proletariat so well for a time, but shortly afterwards cruelty and sadism were put to more systematic use. The newly created AVO-men who took over from the Ruscsaks of the chaotic early days of the People's Democracy rarely relented; they could not be appealed to, could not be amused with a perfect squelch or a witty remark. The delirium of unrehearsed, spontaneous slaps and kicks and whacks was passing – and an era characterized by the scientific use of unemotional but carefully designed tortures began. Calculated sadism and terror were the two cornerstones of the Communist Utopia, imposed on us by the Soviet liberators and their local sycophants.

THE LEGEND OF ÖDÖN SWECHAT

The truly great figures of history usually have to die first before they are recognized by their contemporaries. The ignorant masses only look up at statues with gratitude and praise; those still alive have to earn all recognition by the sweat of their brow. It is in defiance of that ossified old tradition that in this chapter I attempt to erect a monument to a truly great man of our own times, wherever he may be pursuing his historic mission now.

Pallas Athena popped out of her father's head complete with miniskirt, copper inlay, and sandals. Ödön Swechat was similarly born fully formed as a middle-aged interned in Buda-South Internment Camp at the beginning of 1949. Before we go into his story though, a little description of the old Károly Barracks is in order. The buildings were – like much of the City – partially in ruins. The windows were boarded up, and two thousand interned peered out through the cracks into the barren yard. The place consisted of five buildings, each housing a "regiment", and two smaller ones, one of them serving as an admission center for newcomers and the other as a bathhouse where the inmates could have taken a shower once a week if hot water had been available.

The relevance of the geography of Buda-South internment camp to Ödön Swechat's story may not be immediately apparent, but the physical layout definitely had a bearing on his birth.

The admissions building had an inmate clerk, and the bathhouse was staffed by inmates. These two places were the focal points of all news and rumors. During our daily outdoor walk we dropped off all news items to the bathhouse staff, and they passed them on to the other regiments during their exercise period. Each internment case was supposedly reviewed by the Ministry of Internal Affairs (Department of Law-Enforcement having power over the entire police force, national and local) every six months. When these cases came up for review before a supposedly impartial court the Ministry sent a list of those involved so as to find out if those individuals were still being held in the camp. The Communist power had not had a chance to fully organize itself, and the leaders wanted to make sure they were not letting out people who had actually been sitting in Viennese cafes for months.

This strictly confidential list was delivered every Tuesday to the admissions office clerk. The names on the list quickly leaked out and were soon shouted from behind the windows during that day's exercise period: "Rátonyi's on the list! So is Fülöp!" Those who had come in at the same time as Rátonyi or Fülöp would get their hopes up: maybe on the following week they, too, would be on the list. The crimes and/or notorious cases associated with the names were also on the list and made public. If the would-be defector Faragó was released then every other unsuccessful defector would feel eligible.

Bill Bullenstein was on the staff of the bathhouse at that time. This modest young man acquired his sobriquet through his skill in spinning stories of the Wild West. He was a veteran camp resident, widely known through his job, and ideally situated for the dissemination of news among his fellow criminals.

Poor Bill had never made it on the list. Being a newcomer, on the other hand, I had a long wait ahead of me before I could expect to hear my name shouted from the rooftops. Despondency over our shared situation gave birth to Ödön Swechat. On a bracing spring day, having delivered messages to every Tom, Dick and Harry, we made up the name and started yelling it as a greeting to each other: "Ödön Swechat's on the list!"

"Who is this Ödön Swechat?" the interned were curious. Bill in the bathhouse and I in the fifth regiment enlightened the uninitiated. Ödön was a long-time interned. He was not very talkative and spent the whole day sitting on his gear. He had fallen from high places but still retained considerable influence in the Ministry of Internal Affairs, perhaps even in higher reaches of government.

We didn't have to work long and hard on shaping this shadowy figure. Soon it became common knowledge that Swechat's case was a very serious one. "When Swechat is released, we're all going to go free!" so went the saying.

Before the Buda-South camp was moved out to Kistarcsa Ödön Swechat's name figured on the list twice within six months which was unheard-of in the history of the establishment. The inmate clerk stubbornly denied ever having seen the name, but that only added to the mystique, if not the credibility, of the character.

We arrived in Kistarcsa in the summer. The place was in a turmoil; jammed into inadequate facilities we slept on top of each other, sometimes lacking water, sometimes electricity. One minute we were told to work in the non-existent garden, the next we were expected to manufacture toys, dig latrines in the yard and peel potatoes. In a chaotic, restless crowd there are always a few smart Alecs who have the affrontery to pull their pranks on the most respected individuals. That explains how Ödön Swechat's name appeared on widely different lists of volunteers, such as lathe operators or engineers. Dr. Swechat was nominated as a reserve nurses' aid, and reputedly his name was the first on an apocryphal list of those assigned to work in Budapest.

On account of such rude jokes, this very sober and somber gentleman, who spent all day sitting silently on the edge of his bed, was the target of incessant searches. Temporary supervisors and messengers were constantly running through the rooms, hollering, "Swechat, into the office, on the double!!!!"

On these occasions a more seasoned prisoner would always come forward to inform the rash intruder: "Ödön Swechat cannot be summoned just like that! He's not going anywhere, neither on the double nor at his leisure! Get it through your thick head he still has more connections in higher places than the camp commander ever will."

A chastened inmate on day duty would ask hesitantly: "Moscow?" The experienced prisoner would lift a finger to his lips in denial, while intimating assent with an imperceptible nod.

The next day a new camp commander was put in charge. There was no doubt left as to the mysterious powers at work behind the scenes. Some rumors had it that Swechat saved the life of Mátyas Rákosi in the 20's. It may be noted that that particular incident did not serve to swell the popularity of this secretive gentleman.

Ödön Swechat's portrait is a mosaic consisting of innumerable incidents and rumors and other people involved in his mysterious existence. Let's take Daniel for example. His appearance was that of a typical Dostoyevsky character with his sad ox eyes and walrus mustache. He started his public life as a Fascist party secretary in the small town of Jászkaszalaba. After the front had swept through his area our clever Daniel metamorphosed into the Communist party secretary. Basically though he was not a malicious person and failed to send anybody to jail, with the result that he himself was incarcerated in Kistarcsa for dereliction of duty.

In the summer of 1949, Protestant Sunday services were instituted. Unfortunately though, the hymnals brought in by the minister soon disappeared among the faithful. Those who attended these religious meetings solely for the purpose of catching a glimpse of the nearby female regiment did not join in the singing and, therefore, were above suspicion.

Daniel, having firmly shed his earlier political convictions, transmuted himself into the most confirmed member of the congregation. He even undertook the recovery of the lost hymnals from overzealous thieves.

As mentioned earlier, the camp was not free of frivolous individuals who sought amusement in silly pranks. Some such jokers passed the confidential information to Daniel that Ödön Swechat had been seen to retire to his quarters with a stack of five hymnals, but the exact number varied with the informant.

Daniel started a thorough search for Swechat. But the quarry, too, seemed to be on the move. He was said to have moved from Room #64 to #12 a week earlier and then two days later to #26, but then just the day before he was transferred to the third regiment from the fourth, but that piece of intelligence turned out to be a mistake, because he was actually assigned to Room #9 in the fifth regiment. I, too, was a resident of that particular room, and thus I was an eyewitness to the scene when the bald-headed, walrus mustachioed prisoner deacon (or presbyter?) of baleful countenance tore into the room, all out of breath. Righteous indignation endowed this otherwise mild-mannered man with a resonant voice: "Where is Ödön Swechat?"

And now we come to Boldizsár Fodor, another character in the drama that was about to unfold. He was a man of many virtues, but piety, at least at that time, was not one of them. Boldi (his nickname) could not be called puritan by any stretch of the imagination. He was interested in nothing else but the female sex, with the emphasis on the second word, and with such intensity that "Epicurean hedonist" would not begin to describe him. "Sybaritic" might approximate his moral convictions. Of course, in the camp he had zero opportunities to indulge in his favorite pastime. The only way he could treat his body to even a minor sin was to take an hour's nap after lunch. His dreams seemed to be even more vividly erotic in the afternoon than at night. He was dating his sexiest girlfriends between the hours of two and three.

Such were the circumstances when Daniel's voice thundered through the room

"Ödön Swechat has been stealing the Protestant hymn-books. I am here to reclaim them from him. Where is he?"

Without a word, everyone in the room pointed to Boldi Fodor. He was fast asleep in the upper bunk, with a lecherous smile curling his lips. Daniel walked up to him, stepped up on the lower bunk, looked over the sleeping figure with distaste, and then grabbing him by the toes to shake him awake. Fodor was startled.

Needless to say, no one in his right mind would ever disturb Fodor while he was asleep. If an unexpected amnesty had set everyone free, our prison mate would have found himself alone in the empty camp on awakening. Not even such an extreme situation would ever have induced us to wake him up.

When Fodor lifted his head off the pillow he was still in the nether world between dream and reality, apparently concentrating on his big toe as if an explanation of the disturbance could come from there. But it was Daniel who enlightened him.

"I want you to hand over the psalm books of the Protestant congregation at once! You call yourself a political prisoner, when you steal prayer books and hymnals? And probably not for the purpose singing from them, one would be enough for that, but to..."

That was the moment when the sight of the big toe, the bald head, the walrus mustache and the accusation of stealing psalm books irretrievably lifted Fodor's mind beyond the brink of consciousness.

A shiver went through all of us when the storm broke out and all hell let loose. Daniel immediately fell off the lower bunk where he was still standing. Unfortunately, not even the loose language of our post-sexual-revolution age obsessed with freedom of expression and filthy speech is anywhere close to adequate for reproducing what Boldizsár Fodor had to say when he was so rudely awakened from his sweet dreams. When it comes to four-letter words, not even good old Anglo-Saxon English can compete with Hungarian in scope and variety in describing carnal activity, whether it be human or animal, natural or unnatural. And all this in spite of all the new developments in contemporary literature and cinema. In short, Boldi unequivocally refuted the charges of psalm-book theft in a poetic torrent of obscenities (never once repeating himself!) that would burn up the paper if I tried to preserve it for posterity.

After this incident Daniel never again tried to find Swechat, but a lot of other interned, especially newcomers, kept pounding the pavement between the buildings in search of him. These were the halcyon days of the camp when visiting was still allowed, and a prisoner could receive a ten-pound package from home. Ödön Swechat was often called to the visiting room, but no one ever saw him. Even packages were delivered for him. Sometimes when the prisoner-in-charge-for-a-day got tired of lugging the Swechat packages around, Gyula Michnai, a close friend of Swechat, gave permission for them to be opened. Usually rocks and/or torn rags came to light.

"Silly joke", Michnai would observe with acerbity, "stupid pranks perpetrated by small-minded people whose level remains below the soles of Swechat's shoes."

But things were changing rapidly. In the summer of 1950 the AVH (State Security Force, a new armed unit directly under the head of state; it was not part of the police force like the earlier AVO, State Security Unit, but the name AVO retained its currency in popular usage) took over the camp. At two in the morning, every guard tower was surrounded by submachine-gun-toting AVO-men, ready with the password. The watches were carefully synchronized and the takeover was effected simultaneously at every point. A whole brigade of AVO-men was assigned to the "siege". The hapless policemen had no intention of defending the internment camp of Kistarcsa, but the AVO officers were beaming with smiles of victory. "Coup-d'etat!" "Invasion!"; Hitler had his e break-through at the Belgian fortification and his blitzkrieg; Stalin had the lightning invasion of the Baltic states; everyone in history, whether a winner or a loser, had his day of victory ... Fate granted only the takeover of this little internment camp to the heroes of the AVO Headquarter at 60 Andrássy ut, but they made the most of it.

One would have expected Swechat to weather such critical times in silence. But hardly half-an-hour had passed after the invasion and Bill Bullenstein whispered it to some of his confidants that Ödön Swechat had predicted the events to the hour. Stool pigeons passed the rumor on to the AVO-men who regarded it as a serious breach of security that an interned should know about the secret invasion plans. The only problem was the informers were not able to name the regiment Swechat belonged to. The AVO-men, who in their valiant attack on the camp also took possession of the offices, immediately started a wild search through the files, and they were shocked to come up empty-handed; however, there were others in the camp with the given name of Ödön, and for good measure, these unlucky namesakes were all rounded up and herded into the staff building where they were intensively interrogated for hours. Reports were sketchy, but one detail sounded all too plausible; several of the Ödöns confessed to being the real Ödön Swechat.

Soon, in the same summer, a large portion of the camp residents were dragged off to Recsk. Swechat continued to command great respect there, too. He repeatedly refuted the rumors of amnesty that kept cropping up, and later developments proved him right. The cognescenti denied his presence in Recsk, claiming he stayed behind in Kistarcsa. Those who were not transferred maintained that his patrons in high places managed to send Swechat to Recsk, where he obtained early release.

After Stalin's death new conjectures had it that the Swechat faction took control in the Kremlin. Beria's execution only served to confirm this interpretation; everything was falling into place. Several of the inmates were eyewitnesses to Swechat's departure from the camp in a big black limousine. The guards snapped to attention at the gate, and it was only a matter of days before this rehabilitated statesman would take his place in the government.

I did not want to see the reputation of such a great man tarnished by a moral lapse. As a matter of fact, he had told me personally just a day earlier that he would refuse to head up the Internal Ministry as long as there was even a single political prisoner still languishing in captivity.

When the interment camps were disbanded, many of the prisoners were actually put on trial and convicted. These unfortunate ones believed Swechat had been set free. Those who were released told a sad tale about Swechat who had got a fifteen-year prison term, saying: "As long as there is one political prisoner in the country, it will be Ödön Swechat!"

And then came October 1956. Uprising, euphoria, mass exodus, celebrations, resettlement, and then everyday life. Slowly the refugee gets established, becomes a citizen, but then the shocking realization dawns on him: the world around him is again in disarray. A wave of ugly news is coming from Vietnam, Cuba, Venezuela, the Middle-East, the universities. Wherever he looks he sees conflicts tearing up the order of the Western World that used to be taken for granted. Could the day come when it will be necessary to flee again?

I was in the grip of such dark thoughts when I happened to come across a directory entitled "Hungarians in America" On page 393 the name Dr. Ödön Swechat caught my eye. Needless to say the entry intrigued me.

Swechat, Ödön L(ambert), Ph.D., Ichtyologist; born Oct. 23, 1906, Kenderes, Hungary;s. of Ödön and Eszter (Farkas) S.; single.- Education: Univ. of Budapest, Ph.D. 1930. - Career: Asst. Prof., Aleppo, Syria, 1931-33; Prof. Univ. of Addis Ababa, Ethiopia, 1933-38; Univ. of Mexico, 1938-45; Univ. of Auckland, New Zealand, 1945-48; Islamic Univ. Medina, Saudi Arabia, 1948-61; Univ. of Tunis, 1961-65; American Univ. of Beirut, Lebanon, 1965-66. Address: EG Plaza San Martin, Caracas, Venezuela.

The author of this entry is still tight-lipped, he modestly omits the stint in prison, yet every word is emblazoned with special meaning. Syria, Abyssinia, Mexico... In New Zealand a new Asian Alliance is forged, Castro is casting his tentacles toward Venezuela, but Swechat is on the scene. The Marines land in Lebanon and Swechat is already in place...

So let us praise the living for once. The Hungarian refugee is given a chance to build his house, to write his memoirs, to heal and to teach, because there is an unsung hero out in the world tirelessly crisscrossing the Globe, unknown to the news media and unrecognized by any title or prize. He is a man of few words, almost somber, but his reach is long. Even though we can never come face-to-face with him, it's enough for us to know he is on the job. Diplomats tremble and generals become little children at rumors of his involvement. There is a truly major figure, a mature man among us, an influential fish biologist, who can save civilization by tossing out a few well-chosen words at the right place at the right time.

Who knows? Maybe Bill Bullenstein and I created a benevolent Frankenstein monster, who gained independent existence once released from our fertile imagination; or, at the least, we have in Ödön Swechat the most notorious fictitious hero – the most original grotesque – ever to grace the pages of a work of non-fiction. And I take this opportunity to reaffirm the veracity of every incident recorded in this book. I have too much to say even without resorting to fiction.

THE PRELATE SUPERIOR

The internment camp of Buda South was not the crucible of Communism, the greatest social experiment of the Twentieth Century, and perhaps of all time, but the ash heap of history where the remnants of the old social order were dumped, all according to the iron laws of history – to utilize in one sentence at least three clichés of the ideology that fueled the massive social transformations of the time.

Added to the proverbial ash heap were the freakish results of botched social experiments, the casualties of the intensified class struggle, ordinary small-time crooks whose petty crimes were reinterpreted in the light of sinister international plots (thus detracting from the status of spies in general), and other flotsam and jetsam that had come to the surface of the crucible that encompassed the whole country, indeed the whole Socialist Camp, as the Soviet Empire liked to style itself.

At that historic juncture the state was still very far from withering away and in the ash heap of Buda South its iron fist had brought together quite a motley crowd. I have already presented here some of the more colorful characters, some very human, some quite grotesque, some imaginary, but now I would like to remember an unforgettable gentleman who definitely belonged to a rapidly vanishing age that Lenin (or was it Trotsky?) was so eager to consign to that famous ash heap of history. I am referring to István Justh, a prelate from the county of Veszprém, who stood out in the motley crowd of Buda South not only physically, but mentally and spiritually as well. He was a worthy descendent of two historically important families. Zsigmond Justh, an uncle of his, had written a diary of his years spent in Paris, which was the favorite book of my teenage years. He seemed to have been a character straight out of a nineteenth century French novel. He had planned to transplant the effervescent Parisian intellectual life style to Budapest, but history intervened. The prelate's mother was a countess, the direct descendent of Count von Batthyány, the martyred prime minister of the 1848 war of independence. I had grown up in an apartment house right next door to a monument to the hero of the struggle against foreign Hapsburg rule, and felt immediate spiritual kinship to my illustrious fellow prisoner.

I beg the forbearance of the reader, but in the rest of the story I will refer to this most reverend ecclesiastic person by his nickname, Uncle Panci, because that was the name he was known by and he would insist on it. I should know, because his name and the proper way of address became a subject of dispute between me and my boss, Zoltán (Zoli) Thuránszky, the head of the prison barbershop where I worked as an apprentice. I was still a novice in the camp when Uncle Zoli, as my boss was known, approached me with a question of protocol. Maybe he felt that I, as a student of the humanities, was qualified to arbitrate, or else I had already made contact with all the intellectual luminaries in the camp.

"How do you think I should address the prelate superior?" Uncle Zoli asked me one morning before we opened the shop. "You know, that tall gentleman who comes in every morning and uses my straight razor to shave himself."

At that time the camp was still operating under the supervision of the regular police force, not the AVO, and so normal prison rules were applied to the extent of some infractions being overlooked and exceptions to the rules made. There was a rule against an average prisoner ever wielding a straight razor in his hands, but Uncle Zoli, at his own risk, allowed our aristocratic customer to shave himself in front of a small round mirror in the back.

I did not count myself among the prelate's intimates, I knew him mostly by his reputation, but I was quite prepared to pass on to my boss what I knew.

"Most people just call him Uncle Panci." I said.

Thuránszky's red moustache was quivering.

"Nothing but rabble! A bunch of school dropouts, hooligans, what do they know?" He muttered to himself. "You can't address a prelate superior as Uncle So and So. How would you speak to the Pope? Good morning, Uncle Pius?"

"Uncle Zoli, listen to me," I tried to mediate the dispute, even though diplomatic receptions were not really part of my lifestyle as a young man and an involuntary resident of a penal institution, and I could not speak from experience on questions of protocol, but I could appeal to his common sense. "You can always address a Catholic priest as reverend. So why not let it be most reverend?"

"I've got it!" Zoli jumped up. "Aren't the interned in the camp organized along military lines, like army units? So I can address him as Officer Prelate Superior."

I don't know what the Vatican thought of this solution to the problem, but Uncle Panci put up with it, only objecting feebly to the "superior" part. Actually, he had served in the Army during WW I, reaching the rank of lieutenant in the cavalry. It was after the war that he entered the priesthood, bringing a bright mind to bear on church affairs.

A little later, when I became the personal recipient of his wisdom, I could understand and appreciate his stature among his peers. This versatile man was also very good with his hands, especially when it came to dealing cards. His favorite game was bridge. It was in that connection that I really got to know him. He conferred on me the rare distinction of being selected as one of his bridge partners. Very few qualified.

But he was willing to sit down to play even against people whose game he did not approve of. For example, there was Kálmán. Panci revealed to me the fact that Kálmán always managed to deal himself an ace by placing one at the bottom of the pack.

"He should not be allowed to play bridge among gentlemen!" I was shocked. "This is not the Wild West! This is an honorable society of political prisoners. Such a character doesn't belong here among us!"

"Take it easy," Uncle Panci answered slowly while taking a deep, soulful puff on his hand-rolled cigarette through a long holder. "The only reason I let you in on this little secret is that you seem to be a broadminded, unbigoted young man. Let's be realistic. And practical. Kálmán plays quite well, almost at my level, and I look at the extra ace once every fourth hand as the handicap that levels the playing field between us. Don't take it to heart, but neither you nor Kálmán have the faintest idea how to bid and how to play out your hand."

He paused for a few seconds to say a sad farewell to the barely glowing remains of his cigarette before delivering his final judgment:

"You two do not count cards."

"So that's why you rarely pick Kálmán for a partner?"

"Yes. And that's why when I do, my religious conviction and sport philosophy forces me to let us lose a hand now and then."

This was the kind of man Uncle Panci was. His sense of humor was exceeded only by his sense of fair play. We never tired of listening to his stories about the good old days back in happy peacetime, about political figures and famous personalities in funny situations, about his travels abroad that in our predicament seemed to us to have involved the use of magic carpets as a means of transportation. It was a great loss to us when he was suddenly transferred out of the camp to an undisclosed location, even greater than the loss of the makeshift playing cards that were soon torn out of our hands by the authorities. Things were getting tough, hard times came upon us all very soon.

I never ran into Uncle Panci again during my eight-year-stay in various camps as the guest of the AVO, and, as such, I was protected from any news from the outside world reaching me. Thus it was much later and through published reports that I learned about our prelate's subsequent pilgrimage through the system. He went on from Buda South to a distinguished career as a spy. So what else? the reader might very well ask, jaded by the proliferation of that otherwise elusive profession in this narrative. But there were important differences between him and the rest of us, the run-of-the-mill everyday spies. He was not initiated in secret in a dingy interrogation room, but in the full glare of publicity, at one of the famous show trials of the time. And the other thing that set him apart was the actual physical evidence used against him. The prosecution, in a departure from the practice of Stalinist jurisprudence, did not spurn the use of hard evidence to back up its case.

The progressive new legal system, adopted from the Soviet Union as part of the blueprint of socialism, generally relied on the confessions of defendants giving ample evidence against themselves and their partners in crime. Material evidence was used to bolster the case against the enemies of the people only if it fell in the lap of the prosecutors.

Before I go any further I must mention here another fortuitous application of material evidence, because it demonstrates the deft handling of such details by the tireless officers of the court in the newly evolving legal apparatus. That particular case was a side show to the last of the great show trials, the famous Rajk case. Lumped together with that case were those of several secret agents working for Tito, the leader of the breakaway country of Yugoslavia, who was excommunicated by Stalin from the Socialist Camp as a traitor and the chained dog of the Imperialist West.

The defendant in that case was Otto Horváth whose guilty involvement in the plot against Hungary was clearly shown by his past association with Yugoslav guerilla fighters during WW II. He quite willingly confessed to having been the liaison between Tito's followers and the Hungarian underground resistance groups fighting the common enemy, the Nazi occupiers. In order to facilitate his commute between the two countries, the clever Yugoslav comrades rigged up a fake Gestapo identification card, actually a little booklet, for Horvath, thus enabling him to survive the war and celebrate the victory over Nazism.

The fake I.D. card soon became an historic document and as such it was put on display in a gleaming glass cabinet in the Museum of Class Struggle as an evidence of the ingenuity and persistence of the heroic working class fighting against Nazi oppression.

When Horvath fell out of favor with the Stalin-controlled

regime with the charge of espionage around his neck, however, a sharp-eyed AVO investigator on the case not only discovered the fake Gestapo card but also a new use for it; he recycled it as the real thing. The prosecutors did not hesitate to place this damning bit of evidence on the scales of justice. Otto Horváth was duly convicted and hanged as an imperialist agent and a Gestapo officer, based on the incontrovertible evidence of his I.D. card with his picture on it!

But the story of the card did not end there. A decade or so later Horváth was rehabilitated, and the useful little item was recycled again when it was restored to its place in the gleaming glass cabinet in the Museum of Class Struggle as evidence of the historic struggle of peace-loving people of the world for a better future, all for the edification of generations to come. I am sure it would have made the executed Horváth feel good to see his exploits memorialized.

And now back to our prelate, Uncle Panci, and his unique contribution to the rare collection of material evidence in the history of Socialist justice. In his trial he shared the bench with executives of the local branch of the Standard Oil Company. The first step in the glorious march toward socialism involved the nationalization of industry. This was accomplished easily enough by the stroke of a pen, except when it came to foreign-owned facilities. In that case a legal maneuver was necessary; it had to be proved in court that the company operated in a manner inimical to the interests of the Socialist state and its working people. But the courts were ready for the challenge. The local executives of the Company and their local cohorts were charged with espionage and sabotage, etc, etc, the usual trappings of a show trial. Heavy sentences were handed down, including hangings, but Mr. Vogeler and Mr. Sanders, as foreign nationals, were allowed after a year to escape back to their miserable capitalist homelands in exchange for a one million-dollar ransom. Panci got ten years.

The evidence against him was irrefutable. Edgar Sanders regarded him as a friend and often visited him in his country parish rectory. On many of these occasions he made minor donations to the parish that was in dire straits at the time.

On direct examination, István Justh admitted to having received sums ranging from 200 to 3000 Forints, amounts that were certainly far below what any self-respecting secret agent needed to maintain his profession's glamorous life style, and they were partly meant to defray the costs of the visit, food, and lodging.

In order to raise money, the rectory rented rooms to visitors, to a whole procession of them passing through, most of them spending a night before moving on. And indeed, some of them moved on to Vienna instead of Budapest. The prelate was probably aware of these travel plans and he "neglected to report them"; therefore, in addition to espionage, he was also guilty of abetting defectors.

And now we come to the famous material evidence, the unique feature of the case against our friend. At this point I must observe though, that Uncle Panci, all his exceptional qualities notwithstanding, was far from perfect. In fact, we might as well admit it: as a spy, he was a total failure. No real pro in his situation would have left such an incriminating piece of evidence lying around in the rectory as the Visitors' Book, signed by everyone who had ever set foot in the place.

His only excuse for such negligence was the fact that he simply did not know yet that he was a spy, not until his arrest. (Like most of us real-life spies of that time.) Thus he was not aware of the legendary nature of the Material Evidence, which he had so carelessly made available to every visitor.

So after a thorough investigation, the eagle eyes of the AVO unearthed this damning document on a little table in the entrance foyer of the rectory. Panci's fate was doomed, his nefarious, treasonous, socially dangerous activities revealed to the world. That book was the smoking gun the prosecution used against everyone in it.

I have an article about the trial in my hands, and as I look at Panci's picture in it – his clear, intelligent eyes looking out over the court room, his fingers folded in his lap – I wish we could get together just once more for a little chat, just for a spy-to-spy chat like we used to have, dissecting the foibles of this tragi-comical world we live in. I see that he was born in 1897, so he's not likely to be with us now, but I hope he lived long enough to say his masses, listen to some good music, and play plenty of bridge with better players than yours truly.

KISTARCSA

ONE DAY IN THE LIFE OF ALADÁR IN KISTARCSA

The mild sunshine of great-spirited Hungarian May flooded the redbrick buildings of Kistarcsa; the dusty space between the fourth and fifth regiment was teaming with hordes of interned prisoners.

"My second year in captivity," mused Aladár as he climbed the steps. Sitting on make-shift stools along the wall the members of the kitchen detail were shucking beans. On the concrete balustrade an elderly clergyman was perched with a tough-looking soldier, visibly engaged in a theological debate.

"Aladár, tell me, who are those two sitting up there?" Pista Kovács inquired.

It made Aladár feel good that he was now in a position to advise newcomers, especially someone even younger than himself, someone who could benefit from the experiences of a seasoned prisoner. And Aladár was rapidly maturing in the graduate school of prison life.

"The Church is represented by Reverend Winkler from a parish near Budapest."

"And how about that Mussolini next to him?"

"It gladdens my heart that the public schools do not neglect their duty to teach history. That character indeed reminds one of Il Duce, but his bearing is not very military."

"I didn't learn my history in public schools," Pista protested.

"No offence intended. The generalissimo is called Prince Bob, a lieutenant from the quarter master's corps. His gaiters and shoulder straps are misleading. He's not really a warlord, the resemblance between him and the great dictators of our times is purely superficial. In his earlier reincarnation our lieutenant was a tobacconist, peddling cigars to the patrons of better cafes."

"How do we know this? Did someone actually recognize

him? Or is this just another gossip?"

"Prince Bob used to go on inspection tours through the buildings. He liked to show up unexpectedly and enjoyed hearing "Attention!" being roared out; used to go galloping through the corridors in his proudly shining boots, swishing a riding crop. He got a great kick out of striding among the interned, who were petrified at the sight of him, sometimes he even pulled a white glove test on the windowsills."

"So, what's the punch line? You're obviously leading up to one."

"It's a true story, my young friend. As you can see Prince Bob was not malicious, he was quite harmless, he just enjoyed basking in the respect due to the power of position. Then on a nice sunny day he stepped into room No. 10. Everyone in the room snapped to attention, the call for it being even more stentorian then ever. The ensuing silence was only underscored by the martial squeaking of the gaiters and perhaps the buzz of an impertinent fly."

"Enough of the suspense already," said Kovács. "And make up your mind, boots or gaiters?"

"In the back of the room was a newcomer, a *tsuvaks*. It seems before the war he used to buy cigars from our lieutenant and even reward him with generous tips. Prince Bob stepped in front of this former client of his in the full glory of his power. One moment and the military might of the imaginary side arm and fancy uniform collapsed; Prince Bob respectfully tipped his head, removed his cap and greeted the newcomer thus: "At your service, sir, Mr. Friedlander!" But then he caught himself, straightened up, red as a beet, and, according to some, ran out of the room with tears in his eyes. Since then the lieutenant has discontinued his inspection tours."

"A deeply touching story. And who is that distinguished looking gentlemen with a book in his hand?"

"I don't know," Aladár said tartly. He didn't like to be forced by a newcomer to admit he didn't know everybody. He suggested they ask Boldi and Norbi. In spite of their important position in the camp that unquestionably outranked Aladár's as an apprentice barber, these two plumbers were quite modest and kind to their fellow inmates. They liked to kid around like anyone else, but they would draw the line when it came to their work. They would walk around among their fellow prisoners like brain surgeons in the lay population, carrying the great responsibility of their position with beaming faces.

"The old fart," began Norbi, "is from Argentina. Mr. Barna was a leading figure among the Hungarian Communists in Buenos Aires and the owner of a well-known bookstore. He returned home in order to spend his mature years in his liberated homeland, warmed by the balmy sunshine of people's democracy."

"Norbi," Boldi Fodor interrupted, "this is no place for ridicule. While it's true this camp and other prisons are filling up with left-wing political émigrés of the 30's who flocked home after the war to rejoin their comrades and now instead find themselves behind bars, Mr. Barna presents a different case. Yes, he was a Communist, and instead of being rewarded with a high position he got himself interned, but," and here Boldi cheerfully raised his voice and the pipe wrench he was holding, "Mr. Barna is now the librarian in the Fourth Regiment. In effect, he is working in his profession, in accordance with the promises of our people's government."

"Aladár," Jancsi Kisházi, the interned commandant of the third regiment, was yelling, "how would you like to take a kettle of soup over to the female regiment?"

"Sure," Aladár was all enthusiasm. He felt cheated by the camp and destiny when it came to the question of women. He could never forgive his friends' shameless misconduct in neglecting to let him in on the greatest opportunity of the century. What had happened was that the much-feared internal prison that housed the solitary had suddenly become the most popular spot in the camp. Experienced inmates, well-honed in the art of survival, were getting caught one after another for silly things like trying to send illegal messages. Some of them were caught cavorting in the yard after lights-out in plain sight of the guards, and if they escaped the keen eye of the law they walked up to them to wish them good evening. Soon there was a great influx into the dungeons of the jail.

As it turned out, the lock on the men's solitary was broken. The women's cell could be unlocked without a key from the outside; the bacchanal went on for weeks. But eventually, as usual, there was a sourpuss who probably ended up without a partner and ratted on his fellows. A lot of inmates ended up paying for the fun with long stints in the later well-secured solitary; nevertheless, Aladár felt hurt at having been left out of it.

"Did you guys think I was going to report you out of prudishness?" he asked Pista, the cavalry officer.

"Don't be silly, Aladár! Just think, there are two thousand interned here, if we had alerted them all... There's no room for more than ten or twelve at most in the solitary. I didn't even tell about it to the guys I'd come in with. Your turn would not have come before 1980, three decades from now."

There was no telling whether the interned commandant, Kisházi had been in on the affair, it really didn't matter now. Following the order – or request – Aladár grabbed one handle of the kettle while Kovacs grabbed the other, but then the commandant suddenly waved them aside.

"Don't move!"

A stocky man was rounding the corner of the building and heading toward them. He cast a malignant eye at the group. Kisházi intercepted him with a smart salute and then kept walking with him.

"Who the heck is this?" Kovács was curious.

"Detective Zgyerka," Aladár replied with disgust. "A nasty sadist, if there ever was one. A few weeks ago it looked like we might be rid of him."

"How come?"

"It happened in the 'play regiment.' In one room he slapped around a few inmates."

"What for?"

"He likes to whack people. When it was over, one of the interned sat down on his bunk to think. He was a newcomer, and that's why he got into the third regiment assigned to toy manufacture. That was his trade. At least that was what he claimed."

"Do they make anything decent there? Any toys that can be sold outside?"

"The best toys in the world. They would fetch millions in America."

"Says who?"

"The members of the third regiment. I wouldn't know about things like that, I can barely play a game of monopoly. Just shut up and listen! This fellow who was sitting on the edge of his bunk, deep in thought, got up after a while saying: "This particular slap felt familiar." or something like "Somebody slapped me just like this once before." In any case, he probably doesn't remember exactly what he said, but he's quite sure that Zgyerka slapped him around once before, six years ago in the Jewish forced-labor unit."

"Did he do something about it?"

"Sure! He reported his observation to the other detective, and Zgyerka was taken away in handcuffs."

"But what's he doing here now?"

"The next day he came back without the handcuffs and resumed beating prisoners. Can't even say he changed his technique, he just keeps on slapping people in the face."

"And is this what you're so worked up about?"

"To tell the truth..."

"You're mired in misconception, my friend, deceived by the vestiges of petite bourgeois mentality. Do you really believe having a fascist background works against you? Or else, someone who rescued Jews is somehow entitled now to special favors? Are you crazy? Listen buddy, this is not what it's all about! This has nothing to do with humanitarianism or fighting Fascism or other liberal aberrations! This is an alliance of the slappers against the slapped. If you're not a sadist yourself then the sadists will sooner or later get you."

"Wait a minute, Kisházi's coming back. Did he stop us to divert Zgyerka's attention?"

“That wretched Zgyerka’s gone, you two can proceed.” Kisházi instructed us.

Aladár and Kovács were accompanied by the envious glances of their fellow inmates as they carried the kettle into the women’s regiment. This wasn’t the first time that Aladár had entered the forbidden area populated by the quasi-angelic creatures. As a chef at Buda-South he often delivered black coffee to the ladies. This chicory concoction was the means by which he got to meet Gizella Lutz who spent the last few weeks of the war as the happy bride of the fascist leader of Hungary, Ferenc Szállasi. Why this middle-aged school-marm was in the internment camp was anybody’s guess; probably the long years of confinement were the price she had to pay for her short honeymoon.

So Aladár and Kovács lugged the heavy kettle to the other side of the fence where their steps went into slow motion. The courtyard was populated by women. Actual, live women, just sitting around. One of them was reading, the others crocheting and chatting. Among them Aladár recognized Ági, Tamás Perczel’s winking partner, Mrs. Telkes, Mária Ürge, and Marion’s mother who had taken up residence here only a few weeks earlier together with her daughter. He was in love up to his ears with Marion and was dying to speak to her. But it was another female figure that the tender sunshine brought into sharp focus, a figure that was marching toward them like a grenadier. And she could trumpet her words:

“Set down that kettle! Right here and now!”

Miss Red, the sergeant, was fat, freckled and blessed with flaming red hair. Her concepts of biology were quite unique, not at all in conformity with the prevailing theories of the time. As she explained it, she could see a thousand female genitalia reflected in the two men’s eyes, in the same place where barrels of semen were also stored. She categorically proclaimed that a mere glance from the two male prisoners was capable of seriously impregnating every member of the female regiment.

Miss Red did not typify the female guards. Irene, the chief

sergeant, was quite a pretty brunette with a dreamy expression and surprisingly pleasant manners. The guard nicknamed T-34 (after the model number of the famous tank) resembled Miss Red in size, but her curves later came to haunt the dreams of many a male prisoner. It's hard to say now whether corporal T-34 attracted so much attention because of or in spite of her voluminous figure, but Aladár was subjected to numerous lectures on the female guard's thighs by Bálint. "She's a flesh-and-blood Venus," he declared. And he must have known, because in civil life he worked as a masseur whose job it was to relieve spasms in real live limbs. Listening to this, Aladár decided to change his profession to that of a masseur.

"Stop shuffling your feet – stay where you are," Miss Red thundered. "Set down that damn thing and get out of here!"

The disappointed Aladár went back to have his lunch in the fifth regiment, Room No 9. There was nothing wrong with his appetite, but the grub had no resemblance to the feasts he had enjoyed at Buda-South. In this new place he waxed nostalgic about the bean soup and the food packages from home that had been allowed back there. Indeed, where were those chunks of ham and cheese, the very manifestations of a love affair?

And then it was back to his usual place of work, the barbershop.

"Today we shave the first two floors," Thuránszky, the chief barber, announced, brushing the crumbs off his mustache. "Now boys, what's the first thing to keep in mind?"

"Plenty of water on the mug. Keep the stubble wet and the blade will cut right through," gave the correct answer Ernő the Smart.

Aladár was one of the apprentice barbers, beside Ernő the Smart and Imre the Nimble. Imre's friends and enemies both agreed on his monumental laziness, and about Ernő... Aladár had given up scrutinizing the origin of nicknames.

It was with great enthusiasm that Thuránszky whetted the razor blade. He tested it by cutting in half one strand of hair held up in the air, and then stood there thoughtfully staring at Ernő's neck.

Aladár was usually given the task of lathering, rarely allowed to wield the razor. János Batho and Kálmán Hinfner were among the few customers who were willing to offer their necks to Aladár's inexperienced razor. The mild-mannered Mr. Batho even commented on the student-barber's progress and the dexterity of his wrist action. Mr. Hinfner rarely commented, just smiled with an occasional hiss. Both gentlemen had moved to Kistarcsa from the Ministry of Agriculture. Uncle Kálmán's reticence was understandable. Industrial spies are not given to loose talk, they wordlessly transport their invaluable secrets in alligator-skin attaché cases. It was just such a master stroke when Mr. Hinfner sold the secret formula of Gezatol (a local generic brand of DDT) to a Swiss intelligence agency, causing an upheaval in the world economy.

"A good insect-killer is worth a lot more than a poorly developed atomic bomb." Aladár was slowly assuming the role of an experienced and diplomatic barber who is expected to entertain his client with small talk about the weather and other topical subjects, "And its value may run into the millions, even in pound sterling, or Swiss franc," he added with emphasis.

Unfortunately, Uncle Kálmán did not take the bite, perhaps the blade scraping his throat had something to do with his reluctance. The psychological moment soon passed, and the client departed with a modest and silent smile.

But Mr. Batho's skin was much thicker, he did not engage in espionage, only in conspiracy against the government.

"Poor old Kálmán," he expostulated. "What sheer nonsense! The Hungarian Gezarol is a watered-down, cheap imitation of DDT. How could anyone sell it in the West? It'd be like selling the secret of yelling from one side of a narrow street to the other, and selling it to Bell, the inventor of the telephone."

Slowly, Aladár got to the end of the row of bearded faces. He sat down to relax with a cigarette and do some reading, and then decided to visit the fourth regiment.

"It's time for me to get acquainted with Uncle Barna," he said to himself.

Aladár had a sister living in Argentina and he hoped to join her there. Perhaps Barna, who had been a librarian and ardent Communist there, could provide some information, especially regarding the night life of Buenos Aires.

But as it turned out he had been directed to the wrong room. He found István Horthy de Nagybánya standing in the door proclaiming in a stentorian tone that the chill was eating itself into his bones. His real name was Géza Muzslai, a short, paunchy man who resembled the tall and lean and now long-deceased Vice Regent *(the son of Regent Miklós Horth and a fighter pilot whose plane crashed during WW II)* about as much as Peter Lorre resembled Gary Cooper.

His loud imprecations soon attracted a youngish looking policeman.

"What's your trouble?" the rookie asked.

"I'm cold."

"You'll get used to it. And spring is here."

"You guys, too, will have to get used to it next winter when they dump you here together with your party secretary."

This kind of talk was definitely against the unwritten rules of Kistarcsa. Aladár deeply regretted having strayed into this room.

"What's that you say? You want to be shut away?" The policeman was fuming.

The self-made Vice Regent was unperturbed. He stood with the same calm determination he must have displayed at the end of the war in Kenderes, in the Regent's mansion, when he issued his orders regarding the disposition of the furniture. The moving men even followed his instructions for a while, but then some of them started to ask questions. Muzslai explained that during the war he was flying another plane and not the one sabotaged by the Germans. Instead of investigating this exciting incident of Hungarian history, the law enforcement officers of Kenderes sent its hero to an internment camp.

"As the Vice Regent, I have the right to demand heat," he bellowed now. "The parliament made a provision on behalf of the Hungarian people..."

Standing behind the “Vice Regent” was a roommate who rubbed his forehead significantly and glared at the policeman, indicating the mental condition of the younger Horthy. Apparently the rookie policeman didn’t feel like starting his career at Kistarcsa by arguing with a madman, and gestured at them in disgust to move on. But just then he bumped his head into a wooden box on an upper bunk. This piece of furniture was decorated with various signs and sayings, such as “the last tram has left” and “keep off the lawn”. Aladár decided to stick around. He suddenly realized something that had so far eluded the erstwhile young officer of the people’s democracy: the inmates of this room were no ordinary interned, and the person behind the box was Jacob, the apostle. The gaunt prophet of Biblical appearance had flaming red hair and a heavy fur coat which attracted little attention and emitted less smell in the winter than in the middle of summer when he refused to take it off even in the worst heat wave. It wasn’t clear just what religion he represented, except that he was its apostle.

“What the hell is this?” bellowed the policeman.” Who gave leave to store this box on the bunk?”

Jacob rose slowly, holding up a bony finger of admonition.

“This crate belongs to the Master.”

“What master?” asked the confused guard.

“The Master who lives above us.”

“There’s no one above us. This is the fifth floor...”

Then the light went on in the guard’s mind. With a hoarse moan he picked up the box and smashed it to the floor. The redheaded giant admonished him in resounding cadences:

“Our Master will punish you for this. The Lord forgives the sinner and even the unbeliever but does not tolerate His box to be touched. The vengeance of the Lord...”

The policeman strolled on. The next victim he descended on was Dr. Katona who was deep in slumber with a black fedora covering his face.

“What do you mean by sleeping before lights out?” The inexperienced arm of the law demanded to know, lifting the hat off Katona’s round face.

Dr. Katona was no physician. Not even a doctor of law, but he may have been a law-school dropout. His life revolved around cats, and according to his own admission, he himself was a cat. This condition prevented him from passing the finals in medical school. According to others though it was the vigorous investigation of his case that had left pathological changes in his brain.

The doctor sat up. Making soft, round movements with his paws (with claws retracted), he looked the guard in the eye.

"You're not the chief cat, meow, meow, and I know the chief cat, but you're not the chief cat."

The policeman stood still like a pillar of salt. He glared at Katona with frozen eyes. A dangerously playful smile appeared on the round face in front of him.

"Meow, meow," Katona went on purring, "I need that hat. I gather my cat thoughts under it, meow, meow. They will help me get out of here, but you're not the chief cat..."

The policeman stopped listening. Turning on his heels, he shamelessly beat a hasty retreat. Aladár couldn't help it; he burst into a loud roar of laughter together with the other, less exalted, inmates of the room. Katona cold not understand the sudden outburst of merriment and retreated under his hat with modest meows. Jacob started repairing the box while Horthy-Muzslai kept muttering about the parliament, how the whole nation had pledged loyalty to him through the National Assembly.

"What has come of that pledge?" he asked pathetically. "It still gets cold at night. And that impudent, mutinous soldier... he should have obeyed me. What do you think? Should I demote him?" he asked Aladár.

"István, I say, give him another chance," said Aladár and trudged back to his own assigned room.

Sadness slowly descended on him after the echoes of the roaring laughter had died down in his mind. Not every madman had his madness beaten into him by the AVO, some of them were already mad in civilian life.

"And to bring in those, isn't that even more inhumane?

What for? Or is it possible...?" Standing in front of the barbershop mirror he started to examine his face. "Am I one of them? And if so, have I always been like that? Or is this what happens to people after a while… after the torture, the fear of torture, the humiliating hunger…Or is this the only way out?"

Aladár shuddered at the thought. After everything has been taken away from you, you're left with your mind… and soul… that's all you have, so you must hang on to them.

Dusk set in, and then night fell... All was quiet, and then, well before daybreak, there was a distant rumble of trucks and motor cars. And then quiet again....

The iron fist of Hungarian People's Democracy struck a decisive blow against the enemy again that night. Motorized units of the AVH were bringing new spies and conspirators into the Kistarcsa internment camp, demonstrating again the efficiency and determination of that much-feared organization that was later to rule over life and death in the prison camps.

DELOUSING

Is there such a thing as an innocent prank? The question is important to someone like me who is addicted – or was in my more ebullient formative years– to pulling them just so as to give a new spin to boring, everyday reality and watch the faces around me. Watch the initial bewilderment grow into confusion before crystallizing into recognition which then melts down into a good laugh. Ideally, the final stage develops slowly into a life-long bond between the prankster and the victim who have shared a rare moment in which illusion triumphed over reality. And it's this dénouement that makes all the difference.

Contrary to popular belief, it is not only malice and/or callous disregard for other people's feelings that is required to pull off a perfect prank. It also takes shrewd knowledge of human nature, foresight, skill, opportunity, and the inability to put up with the boredom of everyday life. But, as we know, man proposes and God disposes, and the most perfectly laid pranks can have unforeseen consequences, especially if the innocent prank and its consequences are separated by prison bars. On the one side, I would have been seen as a carefree student, a man about town whose worst crime in freedom was wasting more of his precious time than he could afford to lose; on the other side I was deemed a hard-core criminal, reminiscing wistfully about my lost youth and innocence. And about a prank that came back to haunt me in a totally unexpected light.

The cast of characters included Maki, the victim of the prank (Maki is derived from monkey, a sobriquet often lovingly bestowed on friends who bear an uncanny resemblance to our forebears), Tibor, my partner in crime and co-author of the prank (one never thinks of these things alone, without the synergistic effect of a like-minded pal egging one on...), and, inevitably, myself. Act I also called for an off-stage character, who was the other target of this silly business, a quite respectable lady who, I am happy to say, survived not only Act I but also Act II totally unscathed, except for the loss of her job. Economic dislocations and adjustments, however, were inevitable side effects of the glorious march of socialism into a happier future.

The rest of us were not quite so lucky, for we all reconvened for the Act II dénouement behind bars with a supporting cast of thousands – mostly prisoners, prison guards and AVO officers.

But I am getting ahead of myself again; let's get back to Scene 1, Act I. Location: the offices of Actio Catholica, Youth Division, in downtown Budapest (Franciscan Square) where Maki had an important position dealing with university students. My good friend Tibor and I were associated with that organization in a more minor capacity and did not rate a desk of our own, we always used Maki's modest desk and chair to rest if our business was taking us to that part of town. In fact, it was a rather congenial bunch of fellows, and we ended up spending quite a bit of time sitting around and shooting the breeze. Strategic secrets or questions of national security rarely if ever came up for discussion. Contrary to the allegations of the AVO, there wasn't much of a conspiracy going on; however, we did come into the possession of some confidential information. The most significant such tit-bit involved the strained relationship between Maki and his administrative assistant, a rumor engendered by various factors, none of them involving sex. Far from it; the secretary was a rather straight-laced lady of conservative tastes who took a dim view of my friend's very urbane, sophisticated ways.

In other words, the situation in Maki's office presented fertile ground for little jokes and witty innuendoes that, given a little push, could grow into a full-blown prank. And that push came in the form of a little leather-bound appointment calendar which stared us in the face from Maki's desk. In the absence of its rightful owner, Tibor and I were taking a respite there from the toils of the day, smoking cigarettes and chewing roasted pumpkin seeds. It must have been the latter stimulant that finally aroused our curiosity about the elegant, gilt-edged, giftquality pocket diary and made us riffle through its pages – contrary to all the rules of gentlemanly conduct. The only excuse I can offer is that, being perfect gentlemen, I'm sure we would have shut it immediately if we had seen any notes in it, but we didn't. We were getting into the second half of 1948, but the pages were all pristine, clear, unused, unoccupied, almost crying out for a little human presence, a friendly touch, a few random thoughts or events to be noted...

The nutrients in the pumpkin seeds and the stimulants in the smoke must have made for a potent combination, for it didn't take long for us to come up with a few entries as the footprints of a romance to warm up the cold and lonely pages.We had the odd couple first meet in St. Géllert Park in February, and, as evidence of his unquenchable passion, we had Maki kiss his secretary by the end of that same month, take her out to dinner in March, and on a glorious early April day conquer her resistance. To balance out Maki's impetuosity we also gave him credit for solid character by having him accompany her to the gynecologist before the end of the month.

But as far as Tibor and I were concerned, that little whiff of happy domesticity concluded the affair, and we had nothing to put down for May. We had to think of something, but what? We looked at each other, and suddenly the entry "Delousing!" demanded to be entered into the notebook. And then we may have scribbled some other, more innocuous entries for the rest of the year, probably planned events, work-related appointments, etc., just to lend an air of authenticity to the juicy parts.

The time-bomb was all set inside the innocent-looking little calendar we left on Maki's desk. All we had to do was wait for the explosion. So we waited in gleeful anticipation for a few days, but slowly the days added up to a week, or two, still nothing happened. Maki didn't say a word about the calendar. He didn't complain, didn't go around looking for the culprit; he acted like nothing had happened. Tibor and I began to get a little nervous. After all, there were quite a few priests posted at Actio Catholica; what if the little notebook belonged to one of them? But it's not in the nature of young people to fret about things for too long, and the whole thing was soon out of our minds... and was not brought back home again until... until the whole cast was re-united again in Act II.

The location was the internment camp where all of us arrested under the same charges ("business") were sitting around, each of us relating his experiences, so that we could figure out just exactly what sort of conspiracy we were accused of, and – in our new language – how we could beat the rap.

We were up against unfavorable odds and formidable foes.

"How low can you get?" Maki was talking about the AVO-men. "Can you imagine that? Not only did these brutes open my private diary but they even scribbled some stupid entries in it!"

My heart stopped. But no matter how hard I wished it, the ground under me refused to open and swallow me up.

"On the third day of my interrogation, I noticed they had brought in some little item that they acted very cagey about, half hiding it, like some important piece of evidence, a smoking gun or a bloody knife. After a while, sure enough, Colonel Cologne *(footnote: many of these officers were drenched in cologne to hide the smell of sweat; after all, beating is hard work)* suddenly whips it out from his pocket and shoves it in my face. 'And what the hell is this?' he asks with great sarcasm. It turns out it's this pocket diary I used to have. So what? I laughed to myself; I never bother with reminders. Either I remember what I'm supposed to do, or else I forget it, in which case I also forget about the reminder. So what's the point? In our enlightened age forgetfulness is seen as a psychological problem..."

"Monkey," I urged him gently, "stick to the facts and forget psychology for a moment."

"So, knowing that I had written nothing in it, I admitted to owning that diary, and assured the officer there was nothing in it. Before I finished talking, wham, he slaps me in the face."

I could almost feel it on my own face, but urged him again

to go on.

"This bum then proceeded to open it. Some kind of surreptitious trysts were recorded in it. And you'll never guess with whom. These brutes scribbled kisses all over the pages, and other distasteful mess... But what really got me was an entry for May 26th; Delousing! These people really had to be out of their minds! I didn't hesitate to let them know what I thought of them, even though I was black and blue all over. If they wanted to fake evidence against me they should have at least checked my handwriting first and tried to think of something more relevant than the frivolous gibberish they were showing me... Why didn't they write something political, something about weapon shipments and submarines?... But they jumped on me again: 'Don't you go telling us how to do our work, you're the one who wrote all this stuff, you dirty Fascist rat. Delousing is probably a code. You really think we're so stupid that we expect the imperialists to write down everything for us, just to make the courts' work easy for them? Who do you think we are, you louse? We know all about counterespionage!' But I stuck to my guns, because I knew I had not written a word in that wretched little diary, and yet, they beat the hell out of me again. All on top of having rudely invaded my privacy. How can you deal with this kind of brutality? This kind of sewer mentality?"

"Listen, Maki," I said quietly, "every coin has two sides to it. In some rare cases maybe even three."

"Hey? What the hell are you trying to tell me?" he asked me, confused.

"Let Tibor explain it to you. He knows a lot more about it, it's actually his business..." and with that I beat a hasty retreat from our little gathering and went to the chef's headquarters.

The extra beating Maki had suffered on account of the diary still stings my face whenever I think about it. As it turned out this particular prank jumped tracks in the intermission and in Act II the comedy became a tragedy. The curtain came down without ovation or applause.

MERSITS, THE ASTRONOMER

By now the reader has quite rightly concluded that the malady of identity crisis is endemic to the lifestyle forced upon secret agents by the nature of their profession. The need for secrecy, the continuous revelation of layer upon layer of conspiracies, the insatiable appetite of the authorities for more and more exotic details of one's already convoluted adventures, and especially the separation from one's accustomed surroundings that has supposedly provided a comfortable cover, all combine to loosen one's grip on one's identity until one finds oneself at sea, rudderless and anchorless in what we used to call reality.

I have presented quite a few examples of this malady so far, but now I would like to recount one more, the unique case of Mersits which was particularly severe but not dangerous.

There is nothing peculiar about reticence concerning one's profession even in prison, but Mr. Mersits didn't seem to have any reason for hiding his. This respectable-looking paunchy gentleman, with silvery hair that was less frost and more of a solid snow cover, introduced himself on first entering the room simply as Mersits, but on further questioning let it slip that he was an astronomer.

Later, however, he declined with disarming modesty to go into further details, preferring to sit on his bunk, singing popular ballads and accompanying himself on a guitar.

He didn't seem to realize the important role the natural sciences played in the intellectual life of this penal institution. Many of the prisoners were eager to make use of the weeks, months, years of incarceration they had earned by their subversive activities. They wanted to learn. And since books were a rare commodity in the prison, they had to learn from their prison mates. After all, one cannot walk out of prison without a thorough knowledge of the Seven Wonders of the World (the eighth is in dispute!). The names of the Muses is also essential for life on the outside, and Latin ("ante apud ad adversum") is indispensable to subversive elements, while espionage cannot be carried out successfully without an accurate list of the Kings of Hungary, at least the first dynasty. The crucial role of languages is impossible to overemphasize. And again, spies were the best and most diligent students of English, French, and German. A spy who could speak the language of the country he spied for enjoyed a lot more respect than one who couldn't say so much as "au revoir." Even esoteric skills attracted avid students. Béla Kerekes was constantly besieged for the secret of being able to speak backwards. He and a railroad-worker friend of his managed to carry on animated discussions without any of us understanding a word of it (= ti fo drow).

Of course, the natural sciences occupied a place of honor among all subjects; physics, chemistry, mathematics, were in great demand. Although Sztáray and Nyeste were knowledgeable on most subjects, the arrival of a professional astronomer aroused uncommon interest. (At that time Faludy was still on the loose but was already being chased by the ever-vigilant state security forces. They were on his tracks and about to strike.)

I must admit here that I was a dissolute young man with no aspirations in the field of history. I felt no particular urge to learn the correct order and dates of all the French Louis's or how they called Moses' mother-in-law. On the other hand, I had limitless curiosity about the bars of Marseille, the attractions of Hamburg, and Italian restaurants and casinos. To balance things out though, I kept a tab on the bookstores of London, too.

In spite of my eagerness, however, I learned not a thing from Mersits, neither the secrets of the night sky nor the nightclubs of Barcelona. Cassiopea and Sagittarius remained dark spots in my still developing mind. But this strange astronomer's influence still left a mark on me; he enriched my store of experiences with popular songs that are bound to outlive many a quasar. Such was his favorite ballad, the one starting with the lines:

In police lockup she died
on a rainy autumn night

Playing the guitar, Mersits delivered the lines in a scratchy but emotional voice:

The police arrested her,
Love's undying prisoner.

Even Caruso could not have rolled his ratcheting r's with more conviction when it came to the part:

She's now but a police rrreporrrt!

But it doesn't end there. The molly's boyfriend breaks into a flower shop so as to get some flowers for her grave. He, too, gets caught, but the arresting police captain is so touched by the story of the star-crossed lovers that he goes out and buys flowers to take to the cemetery in place of the incarcerated outlaw.

The song elicited my great respect for the eminent scientist who had been torn away from the splendid isolation of his ivory tower. I was very impressed by the way this sophisticated intellect, who was more accustomed to more abstract cerebration about remote subjects, was able to identify so fully with the simple life of common prisoners. I even enjoyed listening to such ditties as

I'm fresh out of jail, my good sir,
my blood is still a prisoner

and rather resented some smart alec coming along asking finicky questions like How far is Pluto from Jupiter?

Seemingly unperturbed by the interruption, Mersits stopped his guitar picking for a few moments to consider the question before delivering his answer:

"Far, very far."

And then he went on with the song with the same devotion to tone and words:

We was buddies in the gang,
everyone they didn't hang,
a classy hipster everyone.

More complex problems put to him received the same thoughtful, yet readily accessible explanation.

"How much bigger is the volume of Jupiter than that of Earth?"

"Much, much bigger." Was the succinct and concise answer.

Some of the inmates started to complain that the information obtained from Mersits (How big is the Milky Way galaxy? Enormously big…, etc.) would be of little benefit to their higher education after being released.

Perhaps the full truth will only be revealed by a definitive history of Hungarian astronomy – and I am not referring here to the volume of various planets. Sometime later, I heard rumors about another researcher of the universe being admitted to the camp. When the disappointed inmates asked him why another astronomer and why not a zoologist or a phyto-physiologist was brought in by the AVO, his answer was simple: the people's fist had no concern for the needs of the inmates. And in any case, who was that resident astronomer? "Mersits", was the unanimous answer. The newcomer thought about the name for a minute and then, having been given a physical description of his colleague, declared that Mersits was no astronomer but the doorkeeper at the Astronomical Obscrvatory.

Which one of them was right? I am only telling the truth as I know it. And the truth is that I learned a lot from that modest old gentleman. A picture of him sitting on the edge of his bunk remains forever etched in my mind, and so does his bittersweet voice, romanticizing the bleak, everyday reality of prison life.

After the first whack you'll spit it out,
whatever you stole, without a doubt.

Now I am convinced that identity crisis was not a malady caused by incarceration but the cure for it; maybe a healthy response to the unreal reality around us.

SKORKA

Skorka, the shoemaker, distinguished himself with one little anecdote that he never tired of telling us and we never tired of listening to, maybe because it was about something we all dreamed of all the time: escape from this human madness, from the military discipline, from rules and regulations and ideologies. And, in his story Skorka, this simple country-bumpkin, had worked up the courage to put that dream into practice and say good-bye to our uncivilized 20th-century civilization.

This message, of course, was never postulated by Skorka, a man of few words who preferred to hammer away at leather scraps all day long, but by us the educated listeners who were tantalized by the story not only because it was couched in unusual political terms, but also because it was delivered in such a heavy country accent that we had to consult among ourselves before we could agree on the actual words. And yet I wish I could reproduce his way of talking; it came out of him with such great conviction and simplicity that it should have been made the standard language of the land.

The time and place of his story involved the Eastern Front in the final years of WWII.

"I didn't enjoy being a soldier," revealed Skorka, "that was not my line of work. And the war looked hopeless. As good as lost. So why should Skorka lay down his life?"

Most of us agreed with his sentiments, and cheered him on.

"One night I got my gear together, what little I had, and crawled out of the trench. No one saw me and I saw no one, it was so dark, but I started walking in a forward dircction. I figured I was bound to run into the Russian lines where I could surrender. Lay down my arms, instead of my life. Not that I had any arms with me to lay down."

"Under those conditions that would have been acceptable for an enlisted man," at that point in the story some smart-alec ex-officer might observe with suitable acerbity, "but for us officers, it was different. We had sworn loyalty to the flag as officers and gentlemen...”

“Even if they had sworn me in eighty-six times,” continued Skorka with unswerving conviction, “I would not have stayed there. No sir! So there I was, crawling forward in the dark, creeping slowly straight ahead, trying to keep away from the left where a German regiment was spread out, and keeping away from the right where our troops were, that’s how I was making my way forward....”

Most of us already knew the story word for word, but still we listened to it in reverent, if not rapturous silence, as one can listen to La Traviata without ever tiring of it.

“It looked like I was somewhere right in the middle between the lines, the Russians were about five hundred meters off, so were the Germans and the Hungarian troops that I’d left behind. It looked like I was gonna be giving myself up to some tovarish in another five minutes, when suddenly they started shooting!”

“Who? The Russians?”

“All of them! I was getting it from every side! The Russians, the Germans, the Hungarians, too, they were all shooting at Skorka. And with artillery! So I tell myself, you poor Skorka, there you are, still in the middle of it all, still fighting, with everyone against you. And I think to myself, here is Skorka, fighting the whole Union! That poor little old Skorka against the whole Union!”

The audience broke into a good laugh. Skorka’s thin, Chaplin-like face was full of smiles, he was basking in his success. This simple modern-day Svejk never did explain just what he meant by the Union, but he didn’t have to. We all knew what it felt like to have the whole world united against us. We didn’t have to ask about the end of the story.

But he was much less inclined to relate another story of his, and he gave it a unique Skorka ending whenever it was dragged out of him.

It started with a Wassermann test done on all the inmates, which – to our surprise – came back positive for four of our roommates, including Skorka!

"No, no, no!" protested the devoted shoemaker. "I'm innocent. It must be a form of cancer bug that's spreading it among us."

"Now, wait a minute, Skorka," thundered Thuránszky, a barber with a handlebar mustache. He had worked as a barber in the central police lockup, the catchall place where all of underworld had passed through, and where he had acquired quite an expertise in venereal diseases. The fact that he remained negative gave him extra credibility.

"Tell me Skorka, did you repair shoes in the police lockup?"

"Yes, I did, just a few, and only for two short little weeks."

Skorka's dark hair was showing a few silver streaks, but his mustache was still jet black. He was probably dying it with shoe polish, but after the Wassermann test I was afraid to go near him and sniff around his face to confirm my suspicion.

"Did you do work for prostitutes in exchange for cigarettes?" The barber continued the interrogation.

"We're all human, no better, no worse," was the answer. On Skorka's face the usual good humor was now dampened by humility.

"And how did they repay you when they were out of cigarettes?" Asked the veteran research worker of police lockups.

"Yes sir, how right you are!" Skorka raised his voice for a confession "How smart this Mr. Thuránszky is! Yes, some of these naughty girls must have spat on their broken high heels before they asked me to reattach them to their shoes."

With that Skorka retreated to his corner and resumed his incessant hammering. There was nothing more to be heard on the subject from him. He was not to be disturbed until we were ready to hear him tell the story of his battle against the Union.

* * * *

Up to this point, even though we were locked away from it, we still felt we belonged to a real world out there somewhere, a country we were part of, a civilization that was waiting for us return to it some day. We had no idea that we were about to be totally cut off from all that, from family and friends, and enter the world of the living dead. The Soviet gulag of forced labor camps was just a stuff of legends, propagated by returning POW's, and we had no idea what was looming on the horizon for us, we had no idea that we had Recsk waiting for us.

RECSK
GYÖRGY FALUDY'S CANNED GOODS

With all its privations, discomforts and humiliations, my imprisonment so far seemed like time spent at a resort in retrospect when I got to Recsk. In the forced labor camp we were not merely interned, excised from the population like an infected body part, but also under an undeclared death sentence, to be carried out by torture, hard labor, starvation and exposure to the elements. It was a slow but deliberate form of execution invented and perfected in the Soviet gulag system, and it would have liquidated its victims just as effectively, had it not been mercifully cut short by Stalin's death.

Starvation does not only prey on the stomach but on the mind as well. Even the most refined, highly intelligent mind can concentrate only on food with the exclusion of everything else when food is not on the horizon. I thought of György ("Gyurka") Faludy as perhaps the most civilized person among us, but he was not quite immune to this law of nature. He was already then one of the leading poets of the country. As an ardent supporter of progressive causes and an active anti-Fascist he had spent the war years fighting Nazism as a soldier of the US Army, and he had been rewarded with immediate US citizenship, but as a loyal and patriotic Hungarian he had returned to his homeland to do his part in building socialism. Needless to say, his exposure to the West had also contaminated him in the eyes of the bullies who were in charge of the class struggle and they sent him to Recsk to build Utopia.

Actually, the only thing we built there was a stone quarry, but first we had to clear out the forest covering the stones. All that work was done by hand tools alone and hard labor, probably the same way as the slaves had produced the building blocks of the Roman Empire.

Sunday was not a day of rest but somehow the drive

always let up a little bit, because only half of the guards were on duty to drive us on, and we could take a break now and then with impunity.

On that particular Sunday afternoon I was working with Faludy in the pleasant sunshine. His blister-covered body was hardly moving; he seemed to be composing a poem in his mind while barely scratching the ground with his shovel.

"Tell me," I turned to him, "if the Allies ever come marching in here, could you, as former member of the American armed forces, intercede on our behalf? I'm worried that the potential Anglo-American liberators may not know who is who around here."

Gyurka stopped to rest, slumped over his shovel. Suddenly his eyes lit up, contradicting the sorry state of his mortal shell.

"The best thing that could happen to us," he answered wistfully "would be if the First Army got here first. That was the unit where I served, and I know all the staff sergeants there. They're the ones who can make a difference. Commanders come and go, but the staff remains the same."

"That's right, the quartermasters are the ones that matter," Ödön, a fellow prisoner butted in. "They're the ones in charge of the grub. If you know them you could get us real American canned goods. Cases and cases of them!"

"Cocoa, chocolate, sausages, big chunks of patent ham!" Dini, another fellow toiling next to us, let out a big sigh.

What on earth is patent ham? I asked myself, but did not want to stop the reverie of my mates. Prague ham yes, Prosciutto di Parma, yes, but patent....

"The quartermaster of the First Army was a good friend of mine," Faludy mused, his eyes still lit up with vision of endless provisions. "His name was Jim something, it started with an N, N something, but unfortunately the name escapes me now. I used to write love letters for his assistant to a woman by the name of Corky in Hoboken, New Jersey. If I recall correctly he still owes me two thousand cigarettes for that job. And as far as grub is concerned, don't you worry, my boys. You'd be sick from all the rich food you could get from them. And cigarettes, too, by the dozens."

Tears gathered in Ödön's eyes.

"Oh, my God, how I'd love to be sick from rich food, rather then fainting from hunger all the time," he blabbered. "You know what I like about Faludy? He has good sense. He may be a great poet, he can come up the most beautiful lines, such as "with the dripping dew of your blood" and "for sixty six days I've seen no sky", but at the same time he has good common sense. He's as practical as an engineer. He wants the First Army, because then we're sure to be fed without delay. And that makes good sense! He doesn't fool around, he doesn't ask for the Eleventh Army or the Marines, no matter how much better reputation they may have. Jim what's-his-name in the First Army would feed us with no questions asked. So this was the perfect unit for the job. Except, if... suppose..." and here his eyes were clouded by fear, "what if this Jim is no longer alive or he's been arrested and interned?"

"Quit worrying already," I tried to calm him down. "American sergeants don't get arrested just like that, and if he's dead, his second in command will be on the job. Gyurka doesn't take chances. He puts his bet on a sure thing. But tell me, have you ever heard of patent ham"?

"Patent? Maybe Dénes meant pretzels. Ham with pretzels, maybe that's what he had in mind."

Ham with pretzels. I let my gaze scan my surroundings. The landscape around me lay in peaceful repose. There was not an AVO man or a stool pigeon in sight. We were free, for the time being, to converse about armies and canned goods. Our skeletal bodies could hardly hold up our rags, our eyes worriedly watched Faludy's staggering steps, his spreading blisters, but our minds were busy imagining the inexhaustible supply of canned goods the American First Army was sure to travel with.

TREESTONE

In the latter part of our sojourn, the vacation paradise of Recsk was blessed with the services of an outstanding AVO squad leader.

"This creep's so dumb he can hardly talk," observed a fellow vacationer, Novak, who himself was never in danger of being invited to join the immortal intellects of the French Academy. "He can't even say tree stump; he calls it a tree stone."

I usually refrain from passing judgment on any issue without first giving it serious thought. In my opinion it makes little difference whether one calls a stump a tree stone or a tree stone a stump. High-minded people of good taste did not make this issue a subject of debate in the year of 1952 at Recsk. As for myself, I was only longing for a chance to go for a walk in he shade of the forest without being burdened with the job of cutting down the trees, sawing them into smaller pieces, and lugging the logs; I was longing for a time when I could let roots and stumps lie in peace in the not-so-sweet soil of our homeland.

Squad leader Treestone (his contribution to the vocabulary of the camp stuck to him and became his name, since he never bothered to introduce himself) had the appearance of a square toilet-bowl brush. Before joining the AVO he had worked as a swineherd, not so much by choice, according to his detractors, but as the only profession open to a retarded orphan, who had been born accidentally in a brothel. I did no research on him, his civilian name is still unknown to me, and I merely report these rumors without further commentary of my own, except that Treestone's frequent outbursts and loud and lengthy public statements lacked any form of grammar, any mark of originality; in short, his vulgar language betrayed serious shortcomings in his schooling.

As an example, let me quote here from one of his diatribes:

"You people say to yourselves now: let that motherfucker

squad leader go and fuck his whore mother! But," and here there was a dramatic pause, "just to show you, I am NOT gonna fuck her! There's no shortage of brains here!"

And, saying this, he pointed not at his armpit or his belly, but at his forehead, thus earning credit for his knowledge of anatomy.

He was a very conscientious and strict supervisor, and the people under his care could not easily take a break by pretending to go to the latrine. The first prisoner in the morning returning from answering the call of nature was thoroughly investigated by Treestone. The squad leader ran into the latrine and carefully examined the last droppings on top of the mound. If he deemed the evidence too dry, he vigorously bawled out the feckless fascist spy or conspirator.

The worst thing about him was that he never tired of his job, never lost his voice or the willingness to use it. He was not one of the topnotch sadists, but what he lacked in physical performance he made up in vocal production. He would never shut up: he kept hollering his gibberish, cussing and cursing in an unending flow. I should know, because on one occasion he singled me out for his undivided attention, for a period of time that just seemed timeless at the time.

Truth be told, I must remark here, that Treestone was not the only guard who turned into a wild beast watching me work. The reason for that reaction totally eludes me to this day, for I know I was always doing my best, wielding the pickax or shovel with equal enthusiasm whenever I sensed the approach of an AVO-man. But, as in most cases, in spite of my best efforts, this time too I managed to bring the wild beast out of the squad leader.

According to their user's manual, prisoners are not allowed to respond to the guards' exhortations no matter how vociferous or unjust they might get. Treestone usually showered his victim with three and a half minutes of vituperation and then moved on to entertain someone else. But on this particular occasion I could stand it no more than two minutes before I felt the irresistible urge to turn around and take a good look at the source of verbal abuse, this mythical creature who was capable of producing such an overflowing sewer of uninspired obscenities. Just turning around was a serious enough form of insubordination to incur substantial physical punishment, but instead, I received another ten minutes of his tirade. Maybe a few whacks, the usual, would have been easier to take.

Turning back to my work, trying to look as diligent and servile as possible, did not help fend off the tons of raw hatred piled on my back.

I never did figure out a way of dealing with Treestone, and, perhaps, that was why it filled me with personal satisfaction – if not a feeling of revenge – to witness an incident in which one of my colleagues managed to put this overbearing squad leader in his place.

The hero of that story is Miska Csikász, a middle-aged peasant interned as a kulak, but I can't imagine that good-humored, level-headed man of the soil having ever harmed anyone. It was a pleasant spring day, and perhaps affected by the mild breeze, Miska was hammering on the rocks with somewhat less conviction than Treestone would have liked to see. Needless to say, our leader held very high standards with regards to work pace.

"Put your back into that job, you dirty, no-good Fascist swine! Hit that fucken rock and hit it harder! Harder, I say, you shit-swilling swine!"

And so on, and so on. Posterity will lose very little if I leave out the rest of Treestone's rather unimaginative and repetitive oration and skip to the end of it:

"And, anyway, what got you here? What was your crime?"

By that time, Miska had increased the tempo of his hammering and answered without looking up, like someone too involved in his work.

"One night somebody beat up the local Party secretary, and I was among those they rounded up."

"You Fascist dirt! You beat up a respected and important Party secretary? You lousy vermin! Rotten swine shit! What was you occupation outside?"

The unexpected turn in the conversation cast a sudden shadow over Miska's otherwise expressionless face. He slowly raised his sad brown eyes and let them rest on his interrogator's face for a few seconds before answering:

"Sir, I was a swineherd, sir."

Treestone turned on his heels and rushed off without another word. Paying no attention to the other prisoners, he ran past the blue piles of crushed andesite at a gallop, beyond the quarry. He could not have gone very far to investigate the prisoner's statement, because he reappeared at a steady pace a few minutes later. Every eye was on his sweaty face when he stopped in front of the now busily hammering Miska.

"Fuck that bastard. You did the right thing!" Our leader yelled at the top of his lungs, his cheeks burning red. "You were right, fuck it!"

He was visibly shaken when he moved on to other parts, out of sight. Then, Miska Csikász, taking his time, sat down carefully on a small pile and lit a cigarette.

THE RUDOLF KNOEPFFEL ANNIVERSARY

Our civilization thrives on its great depths in time, on our awareness of history. One important way of keeping history alive is by the observing the anniversaries of decisive moments in the past and the birthdays of great cultural figures who have contributed to the grand edifice of our civilization thus enriching our lives.

At times when a civilized man is deprived of all means of maintaining his ties with his soul-nourishing civilization he must improvise. He must assert his human dignity by cultivating the customs of his civilization on his own, he must find ways of replenishing his waning inner resources by interrupting his perpetual search for a bite of grub to take time out for his spiritual needs.

It was something like this kind of evaluation of our situation that prompted my roommates on a dreary fall day to brighten up our drab, humdrum existence at Recsk by organizing an observance of Rudolf Knoepffel's birthday, that is, its 250th anniversary. That epoch-making artisan deserved to be remembered by a grateful posterity, and we deserved the elevating feeling of re-joining Western Civilization, at least in spirit, for an evening.

In Camp Recsk we had no access to books, periodical, newspapers, nor any other form of printed matter. Someone working around the latrine reserved for the AVO personnel sometimes retrieved torn-up pieces of the Party daily (we, the interned, had to do with dry leaves, etc, in our less luxurious facility), but these important documents were in circulation only in fragmented form, and they retained their smell even after repeated rinses. In the three years of its existence the mountain resort of Recsk successfully kept itself free of any books, except for one assigned to the camp's workshop. That singular volume contained a discourse on the manufacture and repair of shoes, in a rather dry, didactic style. It's hard to imagine any of our fellow interned reading that book and actually learning the secrets of shoemaking. Considering the condition of the boots at Recsk I very much doubt any of them ever read it.

Unfortunately, I never laid eyes on that critical tome. There was, however, a frustrated journalist among us by the name of György Egri, whose craving for the printed word drove him to desperation and the eventual devouring of that craftsman's manual. I am sure he would have preferred to get hold of a collected volume of Shakespeare or a Bible, but there was no other choice. I don't know if he ever made use of the information thus gleamed, whether he ever made as much as a pair of slippers, but as he was feasting his eyes on the printed lines he came upon the following footnote on page 36:

"Rudolf Knoepffel, the inventor of the three-nail technique for the making of the upper, was born on Oct. 20, 1652 in Würtenberg. His method is still in use; modern shoe industry owes a debt of gratitude to this...."

Egri decided right then and there that Oct. 20 should not be allowed to pass without our paying tribute to this historic figure of the shoe industry, no matter how miserable our circumstances. He planned to broaden participation by not bothering to go into specifics as to the exact nature of the celebrant's accomplishments.

I had not been included in the commemorative committee, and so I was totally unaware of the above preliminaries and unprepared for the big event. On my return to my home barracks in the evening I was surprised to see it decorated, probably for the first time in its history. Naturally, in the absence of neon lights and other fancy stuff, the walls were decked out with pieces of paper from cement sacks, but the result looked impressive. The members of the organizing committee (Egri, Faludy, Gábori, Garamvölgyi) were waiting at the door, each with the importance of his mission etched into his face.

"What's up?" we asked, surprised.

"Did you forget? Today's the birthday!"

"Whose birthday?"

And there followed a long list of guesses. As I recall, Churchill, St. Francis of Assisi, Einstein and Napoleon were all mentioned as possibilities, but none of us could find the right answer. Finally, Egri, assuming an official pose appropriate to the occasion, informed us in a little solemn speech that on that day three hundred years ago the one and only Rudolf Knoepffel was born.

The emotion-filled atmosphere was underscored by respectfully murmured comments. We were all lost for words, but the silence didn't last long. A brash inquiry from a late arrival, Kovácsi, was followed by a heart-felt statement that summed up the reaction of most of us in the room.

"Egri, you are the voice of our conscience! Thank you for bringing this to our attention. We shall be honored and overjoyed to join you in commemorating this important occasion."

"We've regressed into animals!" Sobs came up from Fat Molnár who certainly didn't live up to his nickname at Recsk, if he ever had. "This place kills off the last vestiges of spiritual and intellectual life in all of us. I've become an animal!" He kept repeating, "And I might as well confess... Koepffel has not been in my thoughts lately and that's why his birthday had completely skipped my mind."

"Knoepffel, you ass," Gábori corrected Molnár with loving concern, for the latter indeed had started looking like an animal; a donkey on its last legs.

Then another one of our roommates stepped closer to Egri and whispered to him in a tremulous voice:

"I'd forgotten! I should have known, of course, but I'd just plain forgotten. Please, forgive me!" And he shook Egri's hand with a long face.

"Gentlemen!" Faludy raised his voice. "Let's get started with the program. The hounds of the Santa Hermandad (the old Spanish vigilante police of Inquisition fame) will be here very soon to take a roll-call and we have to finish by then. For starters, I would like to give you a picture of the world Rudolf Knoepffel lived in, the Würtenberg of the seventeenth century, and the historical events leading up to the world we are living in now. Even after three hundred years we can still feel Rudolf Knoepffel's presence, he's still with us in our thoughts and on our feet..."

"Yes, he is!" roared the crowd around him.

An hour later, Egri stepped up on a cot and recited a poem "For the past two weeks my thought have flown to Rudolf Knoepfell", Faludy's variation on a poem by Attila József, a harmonious mixture of words from these two great figures of Hungarian literature. Unfortunately, it's no longer extant, because no one thought to memorize it in the absence of any writing tools the way we did other poems written by Faludy in the camp. So much the poorer we are for this omission.

After the official part of the program, conversation continued on the subject until we had to fall into formation for the evening roll call. At that time the mood of celebration subsided; the hounds of the AVO could not to be expected to appreciate the cultural significance of the event. But the next day the news spread throughout the entire camp, and other buildings held their own belated celebrations.

All in all, the hearts of hundreds of interned were filled with a warm feeling. Almost everyone claimed to love and know all about Rudolf Knoepfel and to have had his life greatly influenced by this unique personality. In rags and starved as we were, we embraced the memory of that important shoemaker, even in the midst of hard forced labor. When Egri had discreetly let on as to the occupation of our hero, the enthusiasm for him did not abate. We all recognized the important and crucial role the crafts played in the development of our civilization.

My role in this affair was limited to that of a skeptical bystander. I didn't fall for the gag for a minute. My first response was to inquire – sotto voce – who that Knoepffel was. The name, of course, rang familiar. After all, I had come from a cultivated middle-class family, but I did not wish to pretend to be a jack-of-all-trades, I was still young and eager to augment my knowledge of the world around me. And I was sure that Rudolf Knoepffel would someday play an important part in my intellectual development. There's no doubt that this important German shoemaker certainly stands out in my memory.

It never occurred to anyone else besides Egri to peruse the single book available to us; thus I came to realize only recently the magnitude of Egri's contribution to the event when I started to do some research for my own memoirs. The name Rudolf Knoepffel completely eluded me; I found no trace of it in Würtenberg, in the whole of Europe, nor on any continent. The touching ceremony we enacted in the barracks owed its origin entirely to Egri's creative genius. It was he who gave birth to both the great shoemaker and the idea of celebrating him. Like the lonely monks of Ireland in the Dark Ages before him, Egri single-handedly saved Western Civilization for us on that memorable evening at Recsk.

In parenthesis I might mention one of Egri's more recent achievements; "Menora," a Hungarian-language weekly newspaper he puts out here in Connecticut. It has become my favorite source of information, and I consider myself privileged to be able to read it, even before I reach for Newsweek. The main feature of this small tabloid is his editorial commentary that far surpasses the bigger national news magazines in quality and its ability to navigate the treacherous waters between the cliffs of liberal and conservative extremes. His love of the printed word is matched by his love of truth.

THE CASE OF THE DEADLY HEPATITIS

So far, no one can accuse me of indulging in purple prose, that's not my style. I like to stick to the facts. But the facts of this episode lead me directly to a vivid description of colors, purple being the most important of them. Facts are facts, and colors are facts, not just the invention of a poet who has nothing else to write about. Not being a poet, I write only about facts.

But not to worry. The subject of this episode is not a sunset in a romantic location, and the object whose purple color I will strive to describe as accurately as I can is not the sky but my urine, at least the way it appeared for a while in the decidedly unromantic hideaway of Recsk. And in addition to purple, the color yellow also played an important role, especially as it covered my eyes and the bend in my arm. These two colors herald the appearance of hepatitis, a deadly disease that at one time invaded the camp in its infectious form.

Needless to say, I began to keep a wary eye over my arm. In the absence of mirrors, I could only see my eyes from the inside, but I had no problem monitoring the changing hue of my urine. The advantages of acquiring this disease were extremely tempting; at least six weeks in the nice and warm hospital barracks (where twenty others were already vacationing with this excuse), no morning roll call, no marching out to work, no stone crushing… Perhaps even the casual beatings would be suspended. A possible mild case of this blessed hepatitis was looking to me like a lifesaver!

"Hepatitis is a terrific thing!" explained Graf, a fellow hopeful patient, with his usual gruffncss. "It will not make you impotent; it only destroys your liver, but so what?"

"Man has two livers and one kidney," Ludmilla, another self-appointed medical expert, informed me, but this was the only occasion when I heard him venture into a serious scientific subject, otherwise he knew his limitations. "No problem!"

I don't wish to show off my knowledge of anatomy but even back then I knew Ludmilla (the origin of this unorthodox nickname escapes me now) had got his facts mixed up. The facts were the other way around, one liver and two kidneys. And these facts made it hard for me to decide what to wish for. Life is not a chess game where you only have to think ten steps ahead. I had no wish to die, but the rigorous work schedule made me think wistfully of a little respite.

Being prey to such indecision, I could hardly believe my eyes when one morning my pee was coming out in a perfectly purple stream. And everywhere I looked my skin was covered with a dull yellow glow. Of course, I had no way of checking out my eyes.

Medical treatment at Recsk was not quite in accordance with the Hippocratic Oath and what it implied. A prisoner could report sick and ask for relief from work, but if the hospital barracks was full, not even serious death by drowning was sufficient cause to get him off work detail. The Official procedure required the patient to explain his complaints at the door and to receive one of the following remarks of encouragement:

1. It's swollen, yes, but not red! Back to work!
2. It's red, yes, but not swollen! Back to work!
3. It's red and swollen, but there's no fever! Back to work!

This kind diagnosis had the advantage of being susceptible to infinite number of permutations, e.g.:

4. There is fever, but no swelling... and so on.

That was why the purple color of my pee, worthy of a Byzantine Emperor's cape, suddenly filled my life with sunshine. Not one part of my body had to be red or swollen or feverish, the purple color of my urine was the only passport I needed to my vacation refuge.

I immediately reported to sickbay. I was only too glad to

show off my passport by peeing into a tin can, as it was demanded of me, of course, before being allowed inside.

"Get your stuff, and into the hospital with you!" was the verdict from Dr. Ács, also known as Dr. Mengele by the camp population.

Before he could change his mind I rushed back to my barracks to get ready for the vacation of my dreams. It didn't take me very long to pack, and soon my happiness was complete when I was peacefully lying stretched out on one of the straw mattresses of the hospital.

This R&R was heaven sent, and I was enjoying it so much, that it began to worry me. Six full weeks in Paradise? Would it really last that long?

"Don't be so stupid! It takes six full weeks for a case of hepatitis to run its course." István Dénes, a more or less permanent resident of the establishment, was quick to assure me. That meant a lot to me, because he was an intelligent young man, probably the most advanced medical authority I knew among my fellow inmates.

He became my constant companion and solace during my one and only vacation during my eight years in captivity, I must remember him here in a few words.

His "business" had its roots in a casual meeting he had had with a British college student at the World Youth Conference of Budapest in 1949. God only knows what this otherwise quite decent and normal young Hungarian was doing at that big Communist propaganda festival, designed to impress the world with the peace-loving intentions of the Peace Camp within the Soviet empire and to hide places like Buda-South, Kistarcsa, etc. (Recsk was instituted the following year, but must have been in the planning stages in the Ministry of Internal Affairs). Probably it was just idle curiosity that had brought István to this charade where, instead of fraternizing with delegates from the friendly Socialist countries, he then made the mistake of stopping to converse with someone from the West. Perhaps, he simply wanted to practice his English.

Admittedly, we don't know very much about the student

from Great Britain, but let's be generous and grant him the benefit of doubt. He was clearly innocent of any malicious motives and subsequent developments. He was simply one of those misguided souls who had come under the spell of Communism and accepted the propaganda barrage from the East at face value. After all, what could be more important after a devastating war than peace? And what festival could have better intentions then the one organized in the name of world peace? And what better way to make a sweeping new change then letting the youths of every country come together and map out a better future? Fired up by such ideas, the British student sought out some of the locals so as to bring the message of peace from the progressive elements in his country and to establish a dialogue with members of the Peace Camp who were working for true peace like himself, as opposed to the dark forces of imperialism still ruling the West.

István was not too interested in the political discussion, but he gratefully accepted the offer of a real Players cigarette. By the time the two young men parted the package was nearly empty, and the visitor generously left it with our grateful local boy.

That fatal pack of cigarettes! Nearly empty, yet so full of possibilities! It was to play an important role in István's life for years to come. What had seemed to the visitor like a gesture of friendship was soon uncovered by the local guardians of Socialist peace as an act of espionage. István was arrested and commanded to reveal the secret instructions he had received from that imperialist agent.

As for the British student, I feel free to speculate that he returned to London or Manchester, where he could happily report back to his friends of the success of his mission, and where he was feted for his courage in getting the word out to the Socialist Camp about the progressive forces in the West who were waging a valiant struggle for peace against their evil leaders in the imperialist government, etc. etc.

"The communists are people just like us," he probably assured his more open-minded English listeners by that endearing little slogan of the "enlightened" Left. "I even gave one of them a pack of cigarettes and he thanked me for it warmly. We really hit it off and parted in complete agreement about the need to fight for world peace, especially in the West."

Those progressive cigarettes from the Western sympathizers cost poor István Dénes dearly. Since he had no secrets to reveal, he was beaten by the AVO-men so severely, that he eventually developed Jackson syndrome, a form of epilepsy generated by injury to the brain. His condition seemed permanent; every day he would go into a fit lasting several hours. It was a horrifying sight to watch him in a spasm, rolling on the floor and drooling with foam; he seemed to be on the verge of death.

Between fits, however, he was a very pleasant young man to talk to, especially on medical topics, because by that time he had had a couple of years to educate himself on the subject.

"Hepatitis is a very serious infection and not easy to shake off. And not without mortal danger; a lot of people have died of it."

István's well-intended words cheered me up no end, and it was with happy anticipation that I prepared myself to suffer through a long, serious illness. It was not a difficult chore, and I had a lot of help with it. Every evening, after roll call, my friends came to visit me, surreptitiously, of course. They looked at me with envious glances.

For the first three days, I managed to suppress my nagging apprehensions about an untimely recovery. "Carpe diem," I told myself, enjoying the well-earned idleness. But my happiness was not to last long undisturbed. At the end of the third day some troubling signs appeared that could not be ignored. No matter how carefully I examined my arm under the elbow, I could not help but observe significant fading in the yellow discoloration. The spot was hardly a deeper yellow than the cigar-smoking porter's tongue.

I could hardly wait for Maki, my friend and "business" partner, to come and allay my fears. I highly valued his opinion, and it made me feel good to see him laugh.

"Hepatitis, six weeks!" He announced with finality. "Sometimes even more..."

"But my color... it's not quite as yellow as it was..."

"You are as yellow as a sunflower. Not as round, but just as golden yellow."

"Maki, I'm worried, my urine is not as dark... I'm afraid I'm fading...rapidly..."

"This may vary according to the time of day when the urine goes through the kidneys. In the morning it's thicker, but in the dark you can't really see it, so in the afternoon it looks different. Metabolism thickens during the day." He meant well, but he was a fellow student of philosophy and not physiology.

During the his evening visit Dr. Ács-Mengele betrayed an expression that not even the most experienced doctors can hide; his face was stamped by the unmistakable sign of doom; the silent decision to abandon treatment was written all over it. After a cursory look he moved on to the next patient. My apprehensions had proven well-founded. As I was to find out very soon, this illness, much like everything else in adult life, is oversold propaganda, not a serious problem.

I felt no sign of illness. I was rapidly regaining my strength, inexorably drifting toward full health. Maki tried to keep my spirit up for a few more days. But he could not hide his distress. He looked like a distant relative visiting someone else, someone about to give up the ghost, and he had only run into me by accident.

"Don't be such a fool! Six weeks. You look absolutely terrible. The truth is I'm worried about you! You know you could even die of this?"

And he rushed off. But his words of encouragement didn't sound convincing. I could detect no conviction in his tone of voice, only pity...

Two days later I was discharged and ordered back to work. Back to crushing stones in the quarry. Stones that were meant to crush the crushers, both mentally and physically.

CRAPKO MANUREVITS, THE WRITER

Faludy was not the only writer among us, only the best known. The others were yet to make a name for themselves, and so I am sure Crapko Manurevich will not mind if I remember him here by the prison name that had become attached to him, most likely by his detractors.

Courting popularity was not a habit of his, but apart from a certain aloofness natural to towering intellects, I couldn't see what anyone could have had against this very serious gentleman. His once tall, heavyset figure had turned rather gaunt on the camp diet. It seemed very effective in his case, except that loosing weight had not been the purpose of his stay with us.

He was one of the few among us who could bear physical and verbal assaults without taking notice, without letting them damage his dignity. He did not judge people by their worldly achievements; he was totally unimpressed by my high status as De Gaulle's personal spy. My ticket into his intellectual realm was the fact that I had been a student of the humanities until my studies had been so rudely interrupted. I don't recall now whether it was an undoubtedly memorable comment of mine on Mauriac, Knut Hamsun or Apollinaire that broke the ice between us, but for a while he often favored me with his company, seeking me out during the evening hauling exercises involving stones or logs.

Let me digress for a moment from literature, and say a few words about economics. The internationally recognized expert planners of Socialism in the camp (The Whip, The Quarry Ogre, The Monster Master, etc) hit upon an ingenious discovery: there was an unutilized resource in the prisoners' returning from the quarry in the evening after work. They were walking back to the barracks empty-handed, without carrying anything! What a waste of energy! What potential for increasing productivity! For my part, I felt that dragging myself alone was an accomplishment worthy of honorable mention, requiring more energy than there was left in my aching limbs, but these eminent theoreticians of Socialist economy managed to heave the maximum load on us.

Weighed down with an enormous stone I was more staggering than strutting on the uneven trail through the woods, and so was Crapko. But that did not seem to affect his mental state; neither the stones nor the ravings of the AVO-men ever penetrated the elevated level of our discussion.

"Modern literature, and I am referring to prose, especially novels..." expounded Crapko, shifting the weight on his shoulders and almost falling flat on his face, "...must come from life, from deeply felt personal experience."

"I am glad that you specified 'modern'. On the other hand, according to Faludy..."

"If you allow me to finish, I insist that literature must reflect the inner life of the writer with the total exclusion of the world around him, except as an incidental factor in his inner life. This is why my new book, the one I've been working on for the past two months, is such a significant departure...."

"I thought you've been lugging stones, that's what you'd been working on...ha-ha-ha..." Laczoffy, a fellow quarry worker, butted in uninvited. He had caught up with us, because he was carrying an unconscionably undersized load, thus shortchanging Socialism. But, of course, he had a big, square head to carry too.

"As I said, my new novel is an exception to the rule, but can afford to depart from the norm. The lead character is a young man, a writer, who marries into a rich peasant family, you might say he marries a kulak daughter. The family is at first very much against the marriage, but love triumphs. But then, later, they want him to start working. Out in the fields with them. The whole family turns on him and start pushing him around."

"That doesn't sound like a very interesting plot. In a novel you need suspense, mystery, adventure!" The layman Laczoffy rudely interrupted again.

Manurevich suddenly stopped, dangerously swaying under

the load.

"Sir, I don't see why you have to meddle in the conversation of two literary men, especially when they ponder stylistic problems."

Hearing that from the great writer I pulled myself up, as if the stone had become lighter on my sagging shoulder.

"Why can't we chat a little when the guards aren't looking?" Thus Laczoffy.

"Because you don't know what you're talking about!" answered Crapko with the melancholy fatalism of a intellectual who was much saddened by the abyss his pen had explored. "Tell me, what kind of work did you do outside?"

"I worked for the railroad."

"Railroad workers do not read!"

"What do you mean? Of course we do. I do."

"What? Books?"

"Yes, books! Sometimes even thick ones. Like "Gone with the Wind". I read it from cover to cover if you must know."

"Did you hear that?" Crapko turned to me, or at least as much as the stone and the trail conditions allowed. "What do you say? A railroad worker and he reads! Books! I'd never heard of anything like that before!"

"Too bad," Laczoffy was complaining. "Railroad workers deserve more credit."

"And what happens to the young writer at the end?" I was impatient to know. I had never been interested in the literary tastes of various professions.

"He holds out against the pressure. But his young bride, who sides with him at first, turns against him, too, siding with her parents, and starts nagging: Why can't you go out to the corn patch at least once a week and do a little hoeing? Or supervise the hired hands once in a while? And things like that. But my hero doesn't give in, because Art comes before everything else..."

At that point, the barracks came into view. But there loomed a giant in front of me who inspired tremendous respect in me and whom I was ready to present to the literary world. Let me introduce Crapko Manurevich, whose new novel has swept away all critics! I felt sure that someday, once he had access to a typewriter or at least pen and paper, he would create a monument to himself in the person of the erstwhile young writer stuck in a kulak family....

But for the time being, he, like all of us, had access only to stones. Silent, cruelly heavy stones, mercilessly cutting into his shoulder bones.

THE BIG LEGAL REVIEW

In the summer of 1952, new construction was started at a furious pace in Recsk. Special interrogation barracks were erected and divided into numerous small cubicles with smartly painted but flimsy partition walls. New young AVO officers arrived with the rumored duty of preparing new files on everyone. Every morning fifty names were called out, and their bearers were promptly swallowed up by the new buildings. For years prior to that no one had talked of our supposed crimes, and thus our apprehension was inevitably aroused....

The excitement had already "exceeded its own peak," as it was recorded by Gyurka Pethő, a notary, in his very personal chronicles of those historic weeks. Contact between those already interrogated and those waiting their turn was strictly forbidden. According to Maki, a usually well-informed source, all the interned were required to sign an ultimatum to the USA, and those who had seen the text were not allowed to talk about it. "The AVO-men are worried that, once informed of the delirious details, we might go on a rampage and create a bloodbath with our sabers". And even the Yanks would be against that!

In retrospect it's easy to see what could.ve troubled Eisenhower's sensitive soul. Dani, the ex-Nazi and ex-Communist inmate with a Dostoyevski mustache theorized that the job of the new officers was to acquaint us with the details of our resettlement in Siberia. "I had hoped to find final rest in the soil of Recsk," said our nation's leading pessimist, "but that dream has now been demolished. I'll be resting under the icy sod of Verkuta."

It is not the aim of this little discourse to analyze the raison d'etre of the big legal review of 1952. To this day the motivation behind it remains unclear. Inmate Egry speculated that the new AVO officers were given a chance to practice their skills on us in the same way as medical students learn to do injections by first practicing it on rabbit ears before plunging the needles into human buttocks. (Of course, nowadays rabbits are getting more expensive than buttocks, and the conclusion should be obvious to anyone possessing such a body part.)

The psychological effect of the renewed interrogations on the prisoners was written all over every face. Take for example István Harmath. A middle-aged, well-meaning machine-shop supervisor and an old-time Social Democrat, he was not an outstanding producer in the quarry. He seemed to take comfort in being just an average inmate. The only thing that could upset his even temper was a question concerning the reasons for his incarceration.

"It's not nice to talk about rope in the house of a hanged man," he explained reluctantly. "Obviously, I am here in Recsk, because in 1950 all the old-time Socialists were rounded up. But the AVO wanted to make a thorough job of it. They needed crimes to go with the arrests. And I could see how they worked in the overcrowded cell where I had been thrown when I was first pulled in. My cellmates came back from interrogation all bloody, barely able to speak. Based on the beatings they had received I was waiting for my turn with trepidation, and when I heard my name called I started shaking. Right at the beginning I told the lieutenant to go ahead and write down whatever he had in mind, I would confess to everything. But the officer would not buy that. 'That's a provocation against the AVO!', he thundered at me. So I pleaded with him: 'Please, officer, I am a skilled mechanic, but I know my limitations. Writing briefs and confessions is not my profession but yours. There's no point in messing up a good case for the prosecution with amateur work.' The AVO-man just sat there staring at me, and I began to fear that the beating was inevitable. But then, nothing happened. Maybe he was just all worn out, or else he had come to agree with me, because after a while he started dictating something about the wicked way I had sabotaged the Economic Recovery Plan. I was so relieved I couldn't concentrate on the text, I just signed it and went back to the cell a happy man. I knew that while this madness possessed the land I would have to rot in jail, but at least I would not be bothered with that nonsense again."

But our skilled mechanic was proven wrong, and his mental equilibrium was completely unhinged by the great legal reviews of 1952. Mr. Harmath was in first group to be hauled into the new barracks. His interview was conducted by a young AVO lieutenant.

"Why are you here, István Harmath?" The AVO-man seemed friendly enough.

"I don't really know, officer!"

"Try a little harder. After all, no innocent person is held here!"

"It's not a question of innocence," protested Harmath. "It's just that I don't actually know which particular crime of mine has landed me here."

On further prodding he related the circumstances of his arrest and interrogation. Needless to say, the lieutenant didn't believe a word of it, so finally Harmath confessed to the sabotage of the Plan as something that stuck in his mind.

"Very good," the AVO man was elated by the progress. "And how did you sabotage the Plan?"

"In every way possible," answered Harmath with deep conviction.

Surprisingly, this rather sketchy description of a major political crime satisfied the interrogator who didn't ask for further details. But the interview wasn't over yet.

"And what else?"

This unexpected question threw our hero into despair. He had to think of something quick, before the beating started. In the camp a statement made against democracy was considered the mildest form of political crime, and that was what Harmath came up with.

"Very good, but what did you actually say?"

Harmath was no dummy, and he did possess a degree of imagination.

"I made derogatory remarks about Rákosi's mother, accusing her of having an immoral profession," was the rather prim reply.

"And what else?"

"That's all, there was nothing else."

"What do you mean, nothing else?"

Harmath was beginning to feel an uncontrollable tremor come over him, but when the officer went on to ask about espionage, the shakes ceased.

"Why, of course, there was espionage!"

"For whom?"

"What do you mean, for whom?"

"Whom did you spy for?"

"Whom would one spy for?"

"I'm the one asking the questions, not you. Whom did you spy for?"

"For the Americans, of course." Harmath knew that the better spies didn't work for Marshal Tito of Yugoslavia.

"Where were you recruited?"

That was a tough question. Harmath had received his education in the public schools of the Horthy era, where the subject of intelligence gathering had been unforgivably neglected. Thus Harmath was stumped for an answer.

"In Salzbug?" The officer prompted.

"I've never been abroad."

"Never?"

"Oh yes, Salzburg, Austria." Geography was one of his subjects in public school.

On further prompting from the kind and helpful officer, Harmath was able to dig up the American colonel (after being talked out of a general) from his remarkably productive memory who had recruited him. Effective espionage is impossible without effective recruitment. But of course that still left the question of contacts to be worked out.

After two very productive hours, the interrogator and the prisoner were ready to part on almost cordial terms, the only thing remained was to fill out the personal data in the fist part of the report on the suspect. Mother's maiden name was next.

"Rózsa Kalmár," said Harmath. The lieutenant started to

write it down but then stopped and riffled through some papers instead.

"Valéria Takács," he corrected the prisoner.

"Fine, let it be Valéria Takács!" said Harmath with resignation.

"But you were not born in 1942!" The officer was upset.

"It's very nice of you, officer, to take me for a young kid, but I was born in 1904."

"Is there another István Harmath in the camp?"

"Yes, there is. A young kid."

The outraged officer jumped to his feet and, screaming bloody murder, shoved the frightened prisoner out the door.

"No problem," said Harmath later in the quarry, shoveling gravel half-heartedly into a cart with only half-filled shovel. "You see, the next time they interrogate me I'll have plenty to talk about. So now when my actual turn comes, I will surprise the interrogator."

In order to avoid any misunderstanding, I must add though that neither István Harmath, nor the nameless AVO officer found the incident humorous.

On the other hand, the great legal review did produce a case that elicited a few faint snickers from those of us who witnessed it. It involved József "Uncle" Horváth, a ironmonger, used to the life of hard work and even harder drinking. He came to Recsk at the age of sixty with a typical case of brain calcification and in an advanced stage of dementia. According to the general opinion of his fellow prisoners, the blood could circulate in Uncle Horvath's badly clogged arteries only when mixed with a daily dose of a gallon of wine and a liberal application of brandy to the gullet, and the sudden withdrawal had caused the total deterioration of his brain function. I don't know whether modern medical science would concur with this diagnosis, but in truth Uncle Horvath's contribution to the intellectual level of the camp was rather minimal.

But most of us liked the old boy, except those whose boots he chose for his nocturnal (No.2) dumping. Gyurka Faludy, who was able to discover some good in everyone, seemed to detect a pattern of fine discernment in this behavior, asserting that at night, even in his dream, Uncle Horvath managed to spare the boots of those who had given him cigarette butts during the day.

Pressured by his friends, the old man made frequent visits to the infirmary. Those wearing the Hippocratic mantle at Recsk told him flatly and often enough that there was nothing they could do for him, but he persisted in his regular visits. If nothing else, his persistence slowly led to an ever-deepening friendship between him and the chief medical officer of the camp. This noble soldier, a chief sergeant, was known to us by the nickname "Gypsy", not only because he was one, but because professional AVO modesty forbade him to reveal his true name to us, as was true of all the staff in the camp.

The gypsy chief sergeant had a dark complexion, a huge red nose, and a trumpeting voice that sounded as if it was coming from a cracked brass kettle. He started each day with a stroll to the infirmary where he always blared at our friend:

"WHAT'STHEGOODNEWSOLDMANHORVÁTH?"

Horváth acknowledged the cordial greeting with a respectful "Good morning, chief sergeant, sir". This exchange must have taken place at least seven hundred times without variation. The chief sergeant was not a malicious man, to my knowledge he never harmed anyone, but it was only with József Horváth that he was capable of true human contact.

To this day I am convinced that Marshal Stalin kept an eye on the legal reviews, and demanded an immediate report on Horvath's interrogation as soon as anything developed. I can just see Stalin and Beria sipping vodka, waiting for the special telephone to ring by their side.

The old man's interrogation started with the recording of personal data, and it went something like this:

"Name?"

"József Horváth"

"Mother's name?"
"Eszter Kocsány."
"Married?"
"Married."
"Wife's maiden name?"
"Eszter Kocsány."
"That's your mother's name. Who is your mother?"
"Eszter Kocsány."
"And who is your wife?"
"Eszter Kocsány."
"Who is your mother?
"Eszter Kocsány."

This was not something Uncle Horváth had dreamt up for the interview; he always insisted that the two most important women in his life shared the same name.

"Father's name?"
"Elemér."
"What was your father?"
"Elemér."
"What was his occupation?"
"He worked on the railroad."
"What did he do?"
"He made babies."
"What was his position? What did he do?"
"He made babies."

We have no information on the state of the interrogator's nerves, all we heard was that he called in a second officer for backup. The final scene of the interview is common knowledge though, for it took place just outside the new barracks. It was close to noon, a nice sunny day, and suddenly from that closely guarded building a stubby old man emerged on thc run. The chief health officer was passing by on his way to the infirmary when he recognized his friend waddling there with two AVO-men on his heels.

"WHAT'STHEGOODNEWSOLDMANHORVÁTH?"

But this time the cordial greeting was not returned in the usual manner.

"Chief, sir, these two young whippersnappers keep bothering me. Please tell them to lay off and leave me in peace."

Here again we run into an information gap; we never found out what took place between the two AVO officers and the chief medical officer. But shortly afterwards the old man was transferred to a prison hospital.

The story of Uncle Horváth's dramatic entrance at that medical facility slowly but surely made its way through the prison grapevine to your humble chronicler. His new hospital room was spick-and-span, having been cleaned by the "house" prisoners under the supervision of the guards. But the first thing our friend did as soon as he had been led in was to walk up to a wall and urinate on it, without a moment's hesitation. The guards just stood there, petrified, until they found their voice and started to howl with rage.

Joseph Horváth turned to face the guards like a Caruso graciously accepting the ovation of his audience after the first aria. And like a Caruso with a great and varied program still ahead of him, he tried to remain calm and thereby calm his audience that otherwise would not be able to cope with the ever-increasing excitement of his performance yet to unfold, and spoke to his escort, the chief medical officer:

"What are they going to do when I start crapping all over the place?" he asked evenly.

Uncle Horváth never returned from the prison hospital, and I have no more information about him or the disposition of the legal review.

It should be remembered though that his lack of co-operation was unique and directly related to his mental condition. The beatings we received at the initial interrogation after arrest had conditioned us to automatically sign any confession that appeared on a desk between us and an AVO officer; maybe the sight of a desk would have been enough to provoke this reaction in us, as in Pavlov's dogs. Add to that the daily beatings at Recsk, it's no wonder I didn't hear of that kind of incentive being applied at the big review.

I have put together this chronicle without the benefit of any research materials or interviews with the people involved. For example, another interned I would like to hear reminisce now with the hindsight of a half of a century is Aladár Negrelli whose claim to fame rested on the uniqueness of the final verdict handed down to him. In most cases this was a page-long document that invariably started with the phrase : "X.Y.Z's internment is justified, because it is reasonable to assume, that…" But in his case this ponderous legal phrase came only at the very end of a very terse document, which is presented here in its entirety:

"Aladár Negrelli accompanied his friends to a saloon." This sounds more like Hemingway, rather than an AVO officer. "As the evening progressed the group got drunk and later started to sing rebel-rousing, Fascist songs. Even though by that time Aladár Negrelli was already fast asleep under the table, it is reasonable to assume that had he been awake, he would have joined the others in singing these songs."

The science of psychology has lost a great research opportunity by not having one of its practitioners present at Negrelli's interrogation to witness the exploration of the interplay between the Ego and the Id. What did the suspect dream about on the floor of the Marble Bride (now a gentrified saloon, favored by drunken German tourists)? But the analysis would have required the skills of a Freud who, by the way, was at that time still regarded as a bourgeois decadent freak by the prevailing Communist ideology.

Some of the other final verdicts stand out in my memory by their simple clarity, for example this one:

"Lajos Kukucs's internment is justified, because it is reasonable to suppose that he was planning to abduct the Hungarian People's Army to the West."

This is good, solid material. An expert jurist could carve a masterpiece out of it, like Michelangelo did out of marble. And the preponderance of evidence! Indeed Kukucs was a restaurateur who rented the Stutz Hotel in Kőszeg, a town well-known for its proximity to the Austrian border. Sometimes army officers also turned up among the patrons. One of them was arrested with a notebook on him, in which the Lajos Kukucs's name was recorded. Most likely the name occurred in the following context: "Stutz Hotel, run by Lajos Kukucs; good blueberry sauce, veal a little dry."

These internment cases could get very complex, but the ones that moved on to an actual trial could expect resolution in such gems of jurisprudence as the following, proudly displayed years later by its subject, Dezső Bencs, in a coal mine:

"The People's Court convicts the defendant to ten years of hard labor for the crime of espionage. The Court finds the defendant's obstinate denial an aggravating factor while taking note of the total lack of evidence as a mitigating circumstance."

This conservative and logical legal decision should satisfy the most critical members of the International Court at the Hague.

Looking back after all these decades I cannot help but wax nostalgic about our interrogating officers. These outstanding legal eagles of the 20th Century tackled a very difficult job indeed when they were faced by the great investigative review of all those complicated cases at Recsk. There were at least six hundred heavy-weight cases of espionage, involving the British Intelligence Service, the American CIA and the Swiss Secret Service; in addition, there were at least three hundred high-level conspirators who nearly succeeded in toppling not only the Hungarian but the Soviet Communist regimes. Plus there were several statesmen from former governments and a number of kulaks. Typical of the latter category may have been a rich peasant, who cut down a mulberry tree in his yard or assassinated his own pig.

Those were exciting times, involving exciting personalities! And I was among them. When I had got over the review of my case and was allowed to get back to work in the forest on the banks of Zerge, surrounded by hills that were changing from the light green of spring into the darker shades of summer with hints of the blood-red mantle of fall to come, while pausing to answer the call of nature, I realized how thankful I should have been for the opportunity to relive my past. One can feel enriched not only by one's virtues but vices, too.

It had been four years earlier that I had signed my first confession at AVO headquarters. The great review gave me a chance to experience déjà vu.

The golden mean has always been my guideline; to be less submissive than Harmath but also less inflexibly obstinate than Horváth. Confirming my original confession, at my review I reaffirmed my position as De Gaulle's leading spy. Great people cannot deny their ambitions; just think of Bismarck hiding his scheme for the unification of Germany! I garnished this first count of my indictment with a little conspiracy, smothered under the sauce of attempts to skip out of the country. This seemed like a full fare, but my reviewing AVO officer was not satiated yet.

"And how about the other espionage?"

"Which one did you have in mind?" That was my clever way of parrying his question, even if it's impolite to answer a question with another question. So I added for good measure: "Not the Vatican... It doesn't belong here..."

Why, of course! Among diplomats and international businessmen certain hints and code words are sufficient for effective communication.

"Well, now that I think about it," the young officer went on, "it begins to look less like espionage than recruitment."

"Recruitment?"

"In 1948, you confessed to having recruited mercenaries for Franco. Here it is: you can read it in the report!"

It was as if he had handed me an action-packed adventure story. Actually, at the time of the Spanish Civil War I was in fifth grade, and later on Franco had no need for foreign mercenaries. According to the record, at the age of eleven, I was able to take the time out from my arduous homework to recruit and send fighters to the Iberian Peninsula. Was that really me? Aladár, meet your other self, I said. Finally, I had a chance to meet myself as a young, zealous mastermind, whose hand reached out over the Pyrenees, leading his men into death in Madrid and to final victory in Barcelona! The only fly in the ointment was the fact that I could never stand that diminutive Spanish dictator, but a warlord cannot be picky in his associations!

None of this was on the record, of course. My flight of fancy was inspired by a very straightforward sentence: "He recruited soldiers for Franco so as to ensure the victory of Fascism."

"Please, officer, sir, the dates don't quite match. It is true, back then, at my first interview, I would have confessed to having had Czar Nicholas for my grandmother, but..."

The AVO officer cracked under the great responsibility; the final version of his report made no mention of my Spanish adventures.

We were convinced that the renewed interrogations would lead to fundamental changes in our lives, either for good or bad. We were bound to be either freed or else sentenced to death. But neither of these eventualities came to pass.

Nothing happened! The interviewing officers departed, Zerge Peak, the mountain range around it and the whole forest dressed themselves in white. Winter was upon us without relief. But then spring sprang and with it the obituary of Iosif Vissarionovich.

In the fall of 1953, when the Recsk camp was being disbanded, I was finally hauled into court for a proper trial. The nameless People's Prosecutor, acting for the infamous Gyula Alapi, lovingly fondled a fat folder in his soft hands. The indictment against me turned out to be based on the full text of my judicial review, but without credit for my decisive role in the Spanish Civil War. However, my trial deserves another chapter...

THE SCALDED APPENDAGE

I would be remiss if I left a totally negative image of the AVO-men, depriving them of all vestiges of humane instincts. Yes, it would be unfair of me to leave out the glimmers of humanity that these men sometimes displayed, almost accidentally, and never in a way that these glimmers could be appealed to or depended on, because they were only glimmers, gratuitous, ephemeral, and totally unpredictable.

A good example of that anomaly occurred in connection with a minor accident involving an unusual injury that required immediate medical attention, at the beginning of our stint at Recsk.

Two rows of barracks were already up, and after the evening roll call they were surrounded by AVO-men. At that hour it was impossible to visit the latrine or the infirmary. A prisoner trying to reach either of those places was heckled, tortured, and harassed until he crapped in his pants or else dropped on the ground from his ailment. And that was when the accident happened.

It was a dark and rainy night, and it felt good to finally get inside the barracks. Mr. B., an older gentleman who was in for the crime of being a Social Democrat, was sitting quietly at his place on the upper bunk, dressed only in the ragged remains of his thin cotton underpants, looking forward to his supper. The usual unidentifiable vegetable stew, actually too thin even to be called a soup, was finally delivered. That night we may have been the first in line to receive it, because it was still unusually hot. Nevertheless, it was quickly snapped up by the hungry crowd, and a friend handed Mr. B. his portion in a mess kit.

In the ensuing confusion, it was impossible to tell exactly how it happened, whether the friend was clumsy or else Mr. B. dropped the hot tin cup, but the hot soup suddenly ended up in Mr. B.'s lap.

A bloodcurdling scream erupted from Mr. B. Apparently, as he explained between screams of pain, his penis had taken the brunt of the spill, and it was scalded beyond endurance. Everybody felt sorry for this otherwise quiet man, who had never given anyone any trouble before. But what could we do? How could we get him medical attention, or at least first aid?

I felt the unique nature of the accident might arouse the curiosity of the AVO-men. With the help of another volunteer we carried Mr. B. outside on a litter we usually used to transport rocks or logs. Of course, the first AVO-man stopped us.

"What do you think you're doing?"

"Inspector, sir, our mate here, his penis got scalded."

"What's that?"

"The hot soup got dumped on his dick...."

"Go right ahead!"

And that was how it went all the way to the infirmary. Everyone who stopped us waved us on immediately. After delivering the victim we headed back. To our surprise the magical transformation still held all the guards in thrall. They inquired about the patient with what almost sounded like sympathy, perhaps even a glimmer of humane feeling.

"How is he? What's gonna happen to him?"

"His dick is good as gone. He'll never get to screw again."

"Never?"

"Never again!"

We returned to the barrack unhindered, unpunished. Mr. B. recovered after a few days of suffering, but indeed he was forced to abstain from sexual intercourse for another three years. But not for medical reasons.

But now I can't help but wonder about the AVO-men's reaction, whether it was a glimmer of humanity that incident had elicited in them or else was it a kind of mystical reverence for the reproductive organ? Or just the high value these men placed on that body part? And did we owe the sudden relaxation of the strict rules to some primitive instinct?

THE PICKAX

My fellow campers at Recsk generally found me easy to get along with. While I may have had my share of detractors I didn't have any outright enemies. Naturally tempers flared sometimes, and the pent-up resentment against the guards and the system was often vented on others who shared the same fate. On one occasion I, too, found it necessary to assert myself in no uncertain terms.

It was just the perfect day for my provocation. I was on a particularly strenuous work assignment, digging up tree stumps around the AVO building after the trees had been cleared away.

I was not an expert stump digger, and neither was Attila Cserjan, who was working with me. We had dug a trench around the stump, and standing in there, we were trying to unearth the roots with the same care archeologist might bestow on the lost treasures of Troy. The progress was slow, the project seemed hopeless, and we would have welcomed any chance to take a break.

The break was forthcoming in the person of fellow inmate Evil Elf. He had earned this nickname not only because of his short stature but also because of his uncouth manners and rather murky past. He had been transferred directly from the People's Army where he claimed to have reached the rank of a colonel, but according to rumors he had been a sergeant in the troop transportation department where his common thievery had been aggrandized into sabotage, entitling him to an open-ended vacation with us politicals in the resort of Recsk.

On this early spring morning Elf was upset, because someone had stolen the nice light-weight pickax which he had been working with for the past few days and which he had been able to secure from the supply room every morning, claiming it as his own.

But a new person was in charge of the storage facility that morning and he issued the Elf an unwieldy, unproductive and heavy instrument. No question, a light-weight pickax was much easier to wield in a convincing manner, especially in the presence of the guards. Naturally, the much-desired instrument in question was undoubtedly the property of the People's Republic, but according to the unwritten laws of the camp Elf did have some right to it.

He was going from stump to stump, accusing everyone of having expropriated his tool. He demanded the right to examine everyone's pickax, grabbing the handle and swinging it; all the while rudely promising an unhappy future to the culprit, before moving on to the next suspect. He was venting his rage on everyone. We all stopped working and started to watch the proceedings, leaning on our on instruments. The guard, a lower-ranking AVO-man pretended not to notice anything, allowing the detective work to take its course.

At first I found the diversion rather amusing, and like everyone else, watched Elf's progress from trench to trench, listening to his voice gain in intensity at every stop.

"This is it! I've found it! You lousy thief, you stole the tool of your sick old inmate! You call yourself a political prisoner?"

And when it turned out that the tool in question was the wrong one, he moved on without a word of apology. This scenario had repeated itself several times before he got to our trench, but before turning his attention to us he delivered another tirade to the group as a whole:

"Thieves, that's what you are! Rotten thieves! You call yourselves men? Anyone who steals deserves to be locked up!"

He didn't jump into our trench, it was much shallower than the others. He could see that Attila was working with a spade and the only possibly suspicious tool was in my hands.

"This is it!" The little old ex-soldier yelled out triumphantly. "You're the one, Györgyey, you're the one who stole it! Hand it over at once, you dirty rat!"

I felt all attention focused on me. Every eye was on the two of us. Somehow I had totally discounted the possibility that he might cast suspicion on me, thus putting me on the spot. Suddenly, I was overcome with uncontrollable rage. There I was, dirty, hungry, dressed in rags, and compelled to toil at a task that did not have the remotest attraction for me; instead of chasing girls, there I was hacking away at that stony soil without any visible sign of success, there I was with a stump that ignored all my efforts.

I stepped out of the trench to answer the charges so that every ear could hear it.

"Listen to me! And remember, once and for all, that we Györgyeys may choose to steal champagne, diamonds or dancing girls, but never a pickax! Never."

HOMO LUDENS:
IN MEMORIAM PAUL JONÁS

Zoltán Nyeste reminisces about his life-long friend Dr. Paul Jonás, the Hungarian-born professor (emeritus) of economics at the University of New Mexico and a leading personality in Hungarian émigré circles, who passed away in May 1998. Their association reached back to the student resistance movement during WW II and continued after liberation when they worked together to see their progressive-liberal ideals come to fruition; however, there was little room for idealists in the Soviet Utopia. Aladár, being just a few years younger – and truly innocent of any political activity – had missed out on their earlier adventures and met them only at Recsk.

"The ranks of my departed are swelling, here and there..." said Kosztolányi in his poem "Dawn-time Delirium." Yet at that time he was only fifty years old according to the poem. I am quite a bit more advanced in age, more of my friends have passed away, and death notices arrive with increasing frequency. In the past few days I have received two of them, concerning two dear old friends; here I would like to remember one of them. Pali (Hungarian nickname for Paul, pronounced Paw-lee) Jonás, known in the Hungarian émigré community of the US as a beloved friend and as eloquent speaker, was my bosom buddy for fifty five years: we went through the student movements of the early forties together, the attempts at democratic reforms after '45, the revolution in '56, and the inexperienced but well-intentioned forays into émigré politics – and in between a total of six Christmases spent in Hitler's jails and in Stalin's forced labor camps. So I have a lot of stories to tell, but now I'd like to focus on one phase of his turbulent life.

His friends who did not know him in his youth admire and respect him for the decades of his academic work, for his two doctorate degrees, for his teaching career at universities. Thus, there is a lot for his chronicler to recount, and if anyone qualifies for the role it must be I who has kept a record of all his accomplishments and awards from the time he was a student leader through his distinguished professorships.

But it is not in his "Sunday best" that his memory lives on with me, and it is not that aspect of his life I wish to remember now. I feel assured that there will be plenty of solemn eulogies and profound pronouncements recited about him at the several memorial services now being planned. I'd like to strike a different tone, offer simpler words from a human perspective and without the pathos owed the dead, or perhaps even resume our usual banter. It is not that I ever found him frivolous or unreliable – and I knew him better that those who used to pass glib judgment on him. Yes, it's true that at dinner some of the soup ended up in his lap, his cigar was apt to burn holes in his shirt and even the table cloth; however, such mishaps can happen to even greater personalities. But the superficial observer could be easily distracted by such trivialities and even more by his penchant for scandalizing solid middle-class sensibilities ("épater le bourgeois") not only in principle but in practice; he enjoyed shocking his unsuspecting companions. This playfulness seemed inherent in his character, but his love of and early immersion in Gallic culture may have contributed to it. Let me quote here one of his many teasingly witty but never malicious remarks: on Sundays in the forced-labor camp of Recsk – according to our guards – we "didn't work, just carried stones and cut down trees," but, true enough, with half of the AVO guards on leave the supervision was somewhat relaxed and we had a chance to sit down on the stumps. We were puzzled why one of our fellow prisoner on one such occasion kept busy until we found out that he was feeding a family of titmouse with worms which had been forced into the daylight from the split logs. The friend of the little birds was immediately rewarded with unanimous accolades with Pali the only one dissenting in a gleeful tone: "Fine, fine, but did you ask the worm what it thought of the idea of being fed to the birds?" His quips may have had shock value but never offended anyone. The butt of another one of his pranks, a fellow prisoner who was enamored of French poetry, especially that of Francis Jammes, did not take offense on learning that the anthology of poems I "edited" – scribbled down on discarded cement bags in secret – contained a poem the "Maiden With Flaxen Hair" by – Pali Jonás. None of us knew an actual poem by the favorite poet so Pali decided to make one up directly in Hungarian while working in the stone quarry. I "published" it in a translation.

Another incident at Recsk: the work-brigade leaders were usually the worst scum picked from our ranks for their willingness and eagerness to do the job, and their rudeness was only exceeded by their stupidity. The dumbest one happened to invent the strangest – and unfortunately short-lived – form of punishment; anyone making a mistake working at the quarry would be confined to the barracks area the following day! Except for a few who were endowed with extraordinary strength and who were promoted as model workers – or those who knew how to cheat – and who could count on extra rations at the end of the month, the average prisoner could not fulfill even half of his assigned quota, and for them this form of "punishment" represented a life-saving day of rest. That's how one early summer day Pali happened to have "sentry duty," i.e., a day of peaceful sunbathing instead of crushing stones. The day before he had been caught throwing a good rock with the bad! To the questions of an AVO guard checking on him Pali admitted without hesitation that he indeed enjoyed this sort of punishment. The AVO man liked his sincerity, and in the next re-organization he appointed Pali to be the leader of Barracks No. 3. In a new barracks there were always some who were unhappy with their assigned spot in the bunk beds, the elderly and the infirm begging for a lower bunk; but not even a barracks leader chummy with the authorities would dare to grant such requests. However, Pali, who quickly tired of complaints, cut the Gordian knot by announcing firmly: "Gentlemen! Why, naturally, everyone takes the bunk he likes." In no other barracks was order established as fast as in his, and Pali was praised by the AVO man. But only three days later he was put in solitary for three weeks when it turned out the prisoner pulled out of bunk No. 63 and taken for a midnight interrogation was not János Kis but Péter Nagy.

He was punished with much more brutal torture for another crime, a capital crime according to AVO concepts: during a routine body search they found a hand's-breadth piece of newspaper on him. In the clink he could have eased his torture which included starvation, beatings, and being hog-tied with a stick under his knees by squealing on his "partners-in-crime." But Pali Jonás, who had a reputation for having a very easy-going, devil-may-care personality, kept quiet. The AVO henchmen never learned from him how that curious piece of newspaper had wound its way to him from my hands after considerable adventures. My part in the story was not particularly risky, all I did was wash it out; a lot more was at stake for a friend who had stolen it from the officers' latrine. The news item may have concerned a debate in the UN general assembly about the question of Hungary's entry; indeed, many among the wise world leaders of actually believed the official statements of the time, according to which our country was dedicated to the observance of human rights.

* * * *

I could cite such episodes – maybe not quite as bitter but also true to his character – from every phase of our friendship: adventures we lived through during the war in connection with our increasingly perilous participation in student movements opposed to the mainstream, under the barbaric persecution imposed first by Hitler and then Stalin, in the jails instituted by both of those dictators, in the exciting period of the "thaw" that immediately followed Stalin's death and our release from prison, in the fever of the revolution, and later when we were spinning dreams in exile in Munich, Strasbourg, Paris, New York – in him I always saw the same humane attitude, the same friend I had got to know at the age of twenty. His readiness to take on serious problems with the utmost seriousness and to engage in witty banter, both at the same time, somehow reminded me of the devil-may-care nobleman of the 19th century for whom "laughing through his tears" had not become a hackneyed cliché. He also had some of the traits of the traditional hero of folk tales whose brains and bravado we admire while laughing at his actual or put-on clumsiness. There was a little ditty which he made his credo and which we too adopted as our own too after hearing it so often quoted in his speeches – following the example of the poet Attila József:

He who wants to play the bagpipe
has to go down into hell,
Only that's where he can learn
how to play the bagpipe well!

And he certainly learned his lesson well. He knew how to marshal the most convincing arguments in support of something he was willing to contradict with the simultaneous winking of his eyes – as for instance at the end of '44 when we were forced to listen to the deranged ravings of a Hungarian Fascist proclaiming the impending German victory, and we were even expected to comment on such nonsense. Having to deal with that situation only gave him a chance to pull off another dangerous prank by playing the buffoon. Much later, perhaps in '55, in a period of Stalinist resurgence, we wanted to end a night at the opera with a leisurely walk and treat ourselves to what was reputed to be the "best lángos in the world" at the West Railway Station. But standing at the end of a long line we really didn't have much hope of getting served that night. Suddenly Pali let out his stentorian voice singing Osmin's revenge aria (from Mozart's "Abduction from the Seraglio") in which the harem guard gloats over the prospect of seeing his enemies hang from the gallows. My wife, who had never had to go borrowing when it came to courage, immediately joined in. In seconds, ninety percent of those ahead of us in line disappeared, but I was somewhat apprehensive about this way of speeding up our lángos *(fried bread dough*).

The three years we were to have on Hungarian soil between Recsk and the '56 revolution went by very fast. Pali's mother fell victim to a dreaded disease at a relatively early age; the funeral took place shortly before the revolution. I spoke at the graveside on behalf of our circle of friends not knowing that soon we would have to say good-by to our homeland as well. I've often wondered ever since if perhaps the tragedy had left a mark on Pali's soul *beyond* the slow-healing wound of the loss itself, a memento of some kind. It's hard to say whether there was indeed a change in him. In the late sixties he took me to a holy shrine in Santa Fe, and before we left he had me taste a bit of blessed dirt reputed for its miraculous powers against all diseases and evil spirits, but with the same mock-serious expression he had had twelve years earlier when he dragged me to a seance in Budapest. He seemed at home in New Mexico, though he didn't rave about the "beauty of the sagebrush" quite as rapturously as his wife Edie who, in spite of her New England background, waxed enthusiastic about this strange desert-like environment when she showed me around. Their son, Benjamin, was still very young at the time of my visit and didn't like talking to a "Pony" – the name he gave every guest who spoke a foreign tongue. This habit had got started with the first one whose name "Toni" he, with a slight modification, kept tacking on to every one of his father's strange friends.

* * * *

Eulogies often conclude with the commonplace consolation that the void left behind by the departed will be filled eventually. Life goes on. I never could accept that. I believe in the depth of my heart that the opposite is true: everyone is irreplaceable. The departure of any one of us will take a certain color out of this world. Someone else will come in his place, maybe someone better or closer to perfection, but not exactly the same. Just as you cannot step into the same river twice.

Beyond these generalities I have even weightier reasons for

regarding my friend – whom I dubbed the playful man in the title – irreplaceable.

Thank God, I have always been, still am and probably will be in the future, blessed with many friends, but of the small circle of friends who in their brash youth pursued together the dream of a freer, happier, more beautiful homeland very few survive back at home. And none in the US now, as I fulfill my sad duty to say farewell to Pali. In that sense I've been left *all alone*. How could I not be aware of this *void left by the departure of Pali Jonás?*

* * * *

Zoltán Nyeste, a retired electrical engineer of New Jersey, much admired for his ability to recite Hungarian poetry from memory for hours, is no longer alone. In 2001, he joined his friends in the world hereafter.

TWO DOCUMENTARY POEMS

by György Faludy

THE SUPERMAN

Today I happened to get a lucky break:
instead of having to work my tail
off in the quarry, I am among peaceful
flowers, on a gardening detail.

And standing here I slowly realize
something I would not have believed before:
to wield a hoe for twelve hours in mild
sunshine can hardly be called a chore.

I'm with the carnations, and Professor
Sárospataki is in a mass
of roses. But above us, on the hilltop,
stand around the camp's high brass:

the camp commandant, the mine master,
and four other officers, all full of nerves,
anxious to give the visiting Soviet
colonel's jeep the welcome it deserves.

He's round-headed and silvery-haired,
heavy-set but fast on his feet.
The driver with a cottage-cheese face
stays and spits from the driver's seat.

The AVO officers can't seem to decide
how and how many times to salute
this superman who's come to grace
the camp with his brass-covered suit,

but the colonel pays little attention
to the reception, barely pokes the rim
of his hat and starts out down the hill.
The nervy AVO-men all run after him.

The Russian greets Sárospataki in
Hungarian, holding out a hand:
"Good morning! I want another nice
bouquet of roses! Yes? You understand?"

Behind him six AVO-men pant,
shuffle and watch in sweat:
what can they do for the visitor?
Only Sárospataki doesn't let

the VIP fase him: foreign conquerors
and rulers are nothing new to our fate.
"Assorted, as usual?" the prof asks.
"Yes, assorted roses, two kilos by weight."

"Assholes!" The camp commander fumes
in fury, ready to reach for his gun.
"Can't you guys ever remember?
Get the kitchen scale! And on the run!"

The professor is quietly cutting
the roses. It would not take a rich
imagination to read his mind
by watching his pencil moustache twitch.

Across the valley the quarry wails,
and the prison smell of lentil soup
arrives on the summer breeze from
the camp canteen. A couple of skeletons troop

in the valley, a litter on their shoulders.
An interned's knees drop into the loam.
The Russian colonel looks around him
with a beaming face. He feels at home.

The kitchen scale is on its way, and fast.
Joseph Stalin! Franklin D. Roosevelt!
It's time I learned how a superman and
the roses of a rosy rose garden smelt.
(Recsk 1951)

AN EVENING AT RECSK

Lights out. Many are asleep. Come, you mates to the straw mat,
come Dosztál, Vér, Nyeste, Berzsenyi, let each do his part,
come Sipos, Györgyey, Egri, B. Rácz, Földváry, Csendes,
Gábori, Garamvölgyi! Come on, it's time to start!

We look like a gaggle of ghosts huddled around a chimney pot.
It's so good to invoke the spirits together like this:
Györgyey can give another installment from Monte Christo,
and Csebe can whistle the air from Thais.

Would you like me to lecture on Plato or Erasmus?
Or Nyeste on Einstein? Or do you expect from me
a lecture on the god of Plotinus? Who can recite
poetry, classical or modern, from memory?

Whatever you like. And don't worry about collapsing,
we'll gain new strength from the use of the brain
every night. The spirit can mobilize the body,
a secret whole Europe had sought so long in vain.

Plato on the program? My wrists and knees are frozen stiff,
my stomach is an empty balloon. But you guys
can make me feel better by the way you watch out for me
more than yourselves. And now it gratifies

me to return the favor. Return the love lavished on me
during the day, drop by drop, every drop you install
inside me. By the evening I am an overflowing tank,
spilling its contents amongst you all.

What would you like to hear from the Symposium?
I have an easy job, because so many hidden springs
burst forth inside a man. The torch of my spirit aflame,
my body a worn-out skin shed by the soul's whisperings.

Could that be me? I’ve discarded the burdens of
the body and turned heavier. How solid, real and dense
the immaterial is! The world is more transcendental
than I ever imagined. Sensual pleasure grows a new sense

vibrating in my head. Any of you cannot get it?
Happiness is to live or die amongst you day by day.
The universe has become both grander and more torturous.
Was it worth searching for? Isn’t this the only way?

(Recsk, 1951)

VÁRPALOTA
THE PEOPLE'S JUROR

The small mining town of Várpalota was the last station of my calvary, but the two-year stint there was preceded by a short stay in the already familiar surroundings of Kistarcsa. Instead of being released directly from Recsk like most of the other interned (who were let go without a trial but with the warning never to talk about the place!), I was among the hardened class enemy who were held back for trial, which, in my case, eventually paved my way to the coal mine as a proper convict, rather than just an interned, and that is why I choose to relate it under the heading Várpalota.

The prisoner population brought together in Kistartcsa in the fall of 1953 differed from the original inhabitants in many ways. You could tell the old inmates by their prison pallor since they had spent the past three years indoors, whereas the graduates of Recsk and other camps looked tanned and weather beaten and had a more self-confident gait. Perhaps their having survived Stalin's gulag against all odds had given them more pride in themselves. A few hundred of us were now eagerly looking forward to see the newly discovered – and much vaunted – principle of socialist legality at work, and see it produce a just and reasonable verdict.

Perhaps it was this new spirit that enabled Gyuri Révai to confront a newly initiated fellow inmate, Captain Thompson, and beat him to a pulp. I doubt if the latter, this fallen hero of the AVO could speak a word of English, but the name lent some verisimilitude to the numerous conspiracies he had uncovered for the AVO before his fall from grace. And he did fall eventually, in spite of his having helped the Strong Arm of the Working Class to display its vigilance and over-fulfill its quota of arrests. This shadowy character, who was otherwise quite a handsome man, managed to stir up quite a bit of ill-feeling against himself in the camp, not so much for his fabricated plots but for the number of executions that resulted from them. In that respect his performance had only been exceeded by that of the notorious Noel Field, whose name (a real one, belonging to a real American) had figured in hundreds of trials, spread out all over the Socialist Camp from Prague to Moscow. This legendary figure deserves a chapter of his own, but not in my book. Unbeknownst to him, his testimony helped convict hundreds of those who had benefited from his rescue work in France during WW II. As a good Communist, he had helped mostly other Communists, and most of his unwitting victims also came from their ranks. So the general population had little to fear from this master spy, who had spent years in solitary confinement in Budapest but upon his release and rehabilitation chose to live out his remaining life in that city. As a good Communist he wanted to avoid being exploited by the bourgeois forces of the West.

In comparison, Captain Thompson's forty executions seem like a rather modest achievement; at least, this is the figure bandied about by oral history. It may just be an unfounded accusation, however, and the number of corpses swinging in the wind may have been closer to thirty-nine. But let's not diminish the success of this faithful AVO-man. After all, forty could just as well be a low estimate and he could have claimed credit for forty-one. At that time I wanted very much to find out if he had been the one to roll up the case of the conspiring night watchmen (see chapter "One Day in the Life of Aladár"), but unfortunately I never had a chance to interview the man nor his nemesis, Révai. In any case, Socialist legality triumphed: some of those conspirators were released without trial after 5 years of imprisonment

I could, however, tell a lot of other good stories from that time in Kistarcsa, but none of them would rival in dramatic intensity the story of my day in court. If I seem a little too self-centered, then let him who is indifferent to his fate throw the first stone.

The day started early, but I had spent most of it waiting in the corridor outside before being led into the makeshift courtroom, presided over by Jonás (*no relation to Paul Jonás, fellow prisoner*), the hanging judge himself, the legendary overseer of justice in many of the infamous show trials of the late 1940's. He was easy to recognize in that small room, uncluttered as it was by unnecessary crowds of spectators. But he was not alone; in his judicial work he was assisted by a panel of two permanent "people's jurors," an innovation of the socialist justice system that had eliminated the need for the public and the press to be present. Family was only notified of the verdict, a great improvement over Recsk when no news of the interned had been ever allowed out, good or bad, dead or alive.

I didn't get Alapi, the big-name prosecutor of political cases of the time; a lower-ranking subordinate monster did his job for him, and did it with equal ferocity. He informed me that I was a corrupt class enemy, whose enormous wealth, industrial empire and extensive estates put him, in the natural course of events, in an antagonistic position *vis-a-vis* the nascent People's Democracy. He expressed admiration for my acumen in choosing espionage as the most effective way of doing the most harm to the Socialist Block. Obviously I could not hope to topple the people's power single-handedly, I certainly had done my best to promote the triumph of the imperialists.

This was the first time I had met my court-appointed lawyer for the defense, but still I would have liked him to point out some discrepancies and inconsistencies in the prosecutor's writ. For example, although my parents once had possessed some modest wealth, I owned none of it. Not that it would have made much difference; the same prosecutor branded a poor working boy, Bandi Kun as class enemy. It would not have helped if all my ancestors had slaved away day and night. My lawyer was a frightened-looking old gentleman, who seemed not to have the faintest idea why I was there and he didn't care either. At least he discerned his role in this charade and he stuck to it; even if he neglected to defend me, he didn't accuse me of anything. In a tremulous tone he managed to say just one thing: "May I request a light sentence."

But before we got to that point, and before my eight-year sentence was announced, a shocking thing had taken place in that rather puritanical courtroom, in that place designed to reflect the victory of justice with its elegant simplicity. I don't know if it ever happened to any other defendant, but I was singled out for recognition. Maybe it was my importance and the gravity of the case against me that made one of the people's jurors speak up.

It happened toward the end of the trial. By that time we had gotten well past the prosecutor's initial remarks about my wealth, etc, and had covered a wide variety of topics. We briefly touched upon the major Western powers, the leaders thereof, with particular attention to General De Gaulle, and all that time the people's jurors, flanking the judge, were fast asleep, as was their wont. They didn't seem to be bothered by the judge's irritable tone of voice, which, true enough, by that time had lost its blood-thirsty growl. His heart wasn't in it. Wear and tear was beginning to show in this otherwise tireless champion of justice. All the interned had to be tried and convicted by the end of October, and this grueling schedule had put a heavy load on his shoulders. Playing hanging judge for innocent people may be fun, but not if it's done by mass production. He didn't really know anything about the defendants, and didn't have a chance to work out a credible indictment; there was no room for his imagination to freely do its creative best. For example, my case was the thirteenth on that nice fall day, and slowly a mask of noble indifference descended over Jonás's face.

That was when a people's juror on the judge's left spoke up:

"I have a question for the defendant!" he said.

Jonás seemed flustered by the unexpected interruption and stuttered, "Why, yes, of course, please, go ahead... please... of course..."

I was no less surprised, especially because so far the trial had been very short on surprises – not that I had expected any, because the Socialist court system was known to operate at 100% efficiency, no cases were ever lost – and my main concern was beginning to focus on my need to urinate. I had been waiting on a bench out in the corridor since eight that morning, now it was getting on to one-thirty in the afternoon, and that need was beginning to assert itself with increasing urgency. I had pleaded with the guard earlier to accommodate this weakness of the flesh, but he gruffly refused to grant me any special favors. I had experienced many varieties of other corporeal methods of persuasion that the Socialist legality had seen fit to mete out, but not letting one pee was totally new to me. And it was effective; it definitely secured my cooperation.

In spite of all this, the impending question aroused my curiosity. What did this representative of simple folk wisdom and honesty had in mind? What new twist to my already elaborate conspiracy scheme was he trying to unearth? What new form of madness was he going to confront me with? But when the question came, it was a letdown. It did not whisk me into a lunatic asylum, but into a home for retarded children, minus the loving care of devoted nurses.

"Tell me one thing, Györgyey," the judge's worthy assistant turned to me, "if you had such a huge estate, why did you want to flee to the West?"

Indeed, planning an unauthorized exit from my homeland had been mentioned in passing in the indictment, but it paled in comparison with my other villainous attempts to topple the Socialist state, and was not even listed among the crimes for which the guilty verdict was being prepared.

Unfortunately, in my acute discomfort, the only thing I could think about at that point was getting the whole thing over with as fast as possible, and declined this chance to sketch out for him Hungary's history in the twentieth century, leading up to the German and then the Russian occupation. I could have talked about the land reform that had broken up all large estates at the end of the war, about the nationalization of industry, and the fact that the new regime sought to usher in Communism by jumping over several historic milestones at a time. But how come a people's permanent juror was unaware of these rapid developments? Where had he been all that time?

“The estate was not actually mine,” I tried to bring him up to date as briefly as possible, “and then in ’45 it was confiscated, broken up into small parcels and given away.”

“Now, there you go... Now you see?” was the triumphant answer, as if it had thrown new light on this complicated case and made it clear for everyone to see.

I didn’t see what there was to see, and neither did anyone else; there were no further comments or questions. My only explanation for the juror’s anachronistic remark was that he had been asleep, and in his dream he was back in the 1930’s.

What else? The trial was over. I got eight years of hard labor and managed to get to the restroom in time. Nature’s call cut my last statement very short: “I didn’t do any espionage, I wouldn’t have known how!”

It could have turned out a lot worse. How about twenty-five years and wet pants? A catastrophe involving the pants would have had serious consequences; I only had one in my wardrobe.

Plus, my last and concise statement did not draw an extra punishment. Not much attention either, but by then the people’s jurors were asleep again and the judge was busy with the paperwork But now, strictly speaking, I can’t say I had a proper show trial, because I deviated from the script with those few modest words of mine. My puny little voice of protest at the end could have turned the whole thing into a real flop, but with a meager audience like that, it didn’t make any difference. Every one present was paid to be there to do a job, and they did it with routine skill. There was no one there to impress. So, there was no show.

KORBULY

It would be unfair for me to characterize the judicial proceedings at Kistarcsa in 1953 by using just one example, namely my own hopeless case. Not everyone came away from his trial disappointed like myself.

Not every trial involved an open-and-shut case like mine. I, by assuming I didn't have a chance, failed to give myself a chance to get off like Korbuly did, as I found out a day later. I don't know if the trick he pulled would have worked for me, but it added one more item to the long list of missed opportunities in my life. And the most galling thing about it was that the fellow was actually guilty. He had served in the German SS, a "business" that commanded no respect from the fellow prisoners, it rated well below smuggling, etc, and was completely outclassed by espionage. I wouldn't have bothered with the fellow at all, but otherwise he was a good-natured young man, totally apolitical. As a teenager and juvenile delinquent, he had got into trouble with the law, and he joined the German SS as a way out, much like others used to take refuge in the French Foreign Legion, behind the protective gates of the recruiting center in Oran, Algeria.

"Dumbest thing I ever did, signing up in the SS," he explained, "it would have been much warmer in the Sahara. Maybe hot as hell, but still better than that bitter cold in the Eastern Front."

Every time I ran into him, I used to tease him about the poor choice he had faced with a little tune popular at the time, but not one of his favorites:

"In the desert so
quietly they go
marching the Foreign Legion,
the hot hell of Sahara
burns up your cadaver,
the dead alone enjoy this region...."

Singing is not something I do to annoy people, it's just another form of release for me, be it ditty or operatic aria, but the reaction is uniformly discouraging, which I usually choose to ignore in my search for unimpeded self-expression in song. My pitch may be off key and my choice of material inappropriate, and having a captive audience around me may have spoiled me somewhat; so some of the harsh criticism I had received in that respect may indeed have been justified. Korbuly was one of the few among my listeners who usually listened to me with an indulgent smile instead of running in the opposite direction.

"I think it's all right for people to sing if they feel like it," Korbuly would say in reply, revealing better taste in music than most people around me; besides, he was in the habit of bumming cigarettes from me. And in his own awkward way he even tried to atone for his unsavory past.

"Politics is way beyond me," he used to say, "I wouldn't want to tell people what to do. And luckily my "business" was never mixed up in politics. I was caught up in battle for ten months, I nearly froze to death, and then suddenly it was all over. I hung around in Germany for a while, and then – what a dumb jerk! – I came home to my Ma."

Instead of Jonás – who had made his fame by trying Grosz, a Catholic bishop, and later me, the famous Gaullist spy – Korbuly got another giant of jurisprudence as his judge; Olti who had presided over the trial of Mindszenty, the head of the Hungarian Catholic Church. Both of these judges were tireless in their pursuit of the enemies of the people, while enriching the judicial system with their wisdom and ethics.

"So what do you say?" The great judge turned to Korbuly mechanically with the routine question. "Do you accept your guilt now?"

"You are the guilty ones!" Korbuly cried out to his judge and the panel of people's jurors.

"What is that?" Judge Olti suddenly woke up.

"Just like I said," the kid's Adam's apple was hopping up and down in his long thin neck. "You people are guilty! I was just a young kid, I didn't know what I was doing. Where were you back then? Why didn't you stop me? Why didn't you lead me to the path of righteousness? I would've listened to you, I was a poor orphan, I didn't have a father, you people already knew the truth, you had read Marx and all that, so why didn't you take me by the hand and show me the way to go?" Korbuly embellished his performance with tears running down his scrawny face. But didn't we all look pitiful after years of starvation and brutal treatment? But apparently we didn't all make the same impression.

Even the professional people's jurors were visibly shaken by this new development. They sat there hunched over, the great responsibility weighing over their shoulders. Some of them even came out of their perpetual slumber. Maybe they were bothered by their conscience, because, most likely, back in 1944 they were more Nazi than Korbuly.

And Olti rendered a judgment worthy of Solomon or even Hammurabi.

"Yes, we are all guilty! All of us! And I sentence Lászlo Korbuly to four and a half years of incarceration."

That was exactly the time Korbuly had already served. It was a joke, considering that these "guilty judges" were handing out stiff sentences to innocent people. With that sentence Judge Olti was able to maintain his high conviction rate and yet indulge his sympathy for that sniveling little Nazi brat.

Korbuly came back to the holding pen with a radiant smile. I knew this was my last chance to sing my Foreign Legion marching song to an appreciative audience and I immediately broke into it:

Upon us is a Berber tribe,
t'is no time to save your hide
now or never, take a stand
and defend Sahara's sand.

"Enough!" Korbuly suddenly turned furious, like I had never seen him before. "Listen, I've had enough of that stupid song, and if you sing it once more, I'll kill you even if I have to spend the rest of my life in jail for it!"

Well, that was the end of a beautiful friendship. Now I don't sing that rousing song even to myself in the shower any more. That was an additional sentence Olti had unknowingly meted out to me. And that was justice Socialist style, cca. 1953.

In retrospect, I might admit that my teasing little performance may have been prompted by the devil in me. I felt shamefully upstaged by that young upstart, who had had the street-smarts to pull off a trick that I, a university student well-versed in the accumulated wisdom of all humanity, couldn't even conceive of under the conditions. Yes, I felt shown off as a prankster who could fool people for the hell of it, but could do nothing to save his own skin.

Still, I think his critical remarks were rather harsh considering the genre. I could accept criticism as an operatic Pinkerton or Cavarodossi, but, at least at that time I thought I could have made a pretty good Legionnaire on the operetta stage.

Unfortunately, the opportunities for a musical career were very limited in prison, but on the other hand survival was a distinct possibility as opposed to the labor camp of Recsk, which would have been the death of many of us if Staling had lived to a ripe old age. His shadow cast a long pall on the Soviet system, but with his passing it was no longer a state of terror, only a corrupt, run-of-the mill dictatorship.

MY AFFAIR WITH PRINCESS MARGARET

The grotesquerie in this incident did not manifest itself in any of the characters involved but in the green-eyed monster of jealousy I found at the end staring me in the face. In fact, the lead role belonged to a much-admired and beloved member of the British royal family, Princess Margaret, also known as ex-Lady Snowdon, the younger sister of the Queen.

It was never my intention to make public my affair with the Princess while the principals were still alive. But this Japanese contraption, a pocket calculator I purchased for $9.99 (and now available on sale at $4.99), tells me that I will be eligible to depart from this world much earlier than Princess Margaret, due to our age difference. By letting the facts speak for themselves on these pages, I only want to make sure they do not become fodder for sensation-hawking tabloids but the common heritage of all historians around the world.

My less-than-sensational affair with the Princess started and ended in the coal mine of Várpalota where I spent two years of the eight-year sentence I received at my trial when Recsk was disbanded in the fall of 1953. The majority of the interned were sent home, but the most dangerous elements – like myself – were tried in court (five years after my arrest) and convicted. The hard labor continued in a coal mine now, but the food ration improved; often there was a puddle of soup left at the bottom of the kettle after a meal. The guards used the leftovers to fatten their pigs and the stool-pigeons, of course, whose career choice was greatly influenced by their visions of that swill.

After work, we even had some "free time" in the camp, but it was filled with nothing but unalloyed boredom underscored by the sound of the loudspeakers set up on telephone poles around the camp. The same song about the proud Kazakh by Dunayevski was blared out at least fifty times a day. Our only cultural outlet was to join in the song with our own version "Please, give me back my watch!" at the top of our lungs.

Negrelli, a fellow I befriended in this new camp, agreed with me that clearly something had to be done. Not about Dunayevski, but about the all-pervasive boredom. We decided to stage an elaborate hoax in the form of a put-on quarrel; a fake-feud, as we called it.

This genre is somewhat akin to what they used to call a "happening" but the current jargon would call it "performance art." Two or three inmates engage in a violent quarrel over a made-up dispute. The feigned anger looks so realistic to the others that they don't realize it's feigned, and they are pleasantly diverted from their own problems for a while. The players have the satisfaction of knowing they were able to fool their (captive) audience.

We were on a short break down in the mine when the idea first came up.

"We have to think of something that's intellectually challenging," Negrelli proposed, "something that's almost impossible to believe."

"Let's spread the rumor that you saved Rákosi's life once, and that's why I turned on you."

"You crazy? You'd have me save Rákosi's life? You want me to be killed?" The coal dust gave my friend's face a truly frightening aspect.

"That would certainly relieve the boredom for a while." I remarked modestly.

"Bull! We need a story with romantic interest! How about this? You were involved with Rákosi's daughter, but you chose prison over the prospect of…"

"Dumb! It's a dumb idea! For one thing he doesn't have a daughter, but if he did, who would ever look at her?"

"True enough. Well, then, how about his wife? That exotic Mongolian woman? Suppose you were arrested for having an affair with her…"

"You're sick to suggest something like that! Can't you think of someone nice? We might as well, if we are dreaming up the whole thing…"

"Okay, let her be the Queen of England… Or perhaps her

younger sister. Yes, that's it! Let her be Princess Margaret!"

We ruminated over this in silence for a few minutes. This certainly seemed like a true challenge, nearly an impossible one. It'd be quite a feat to pull something like this over a bunch of hard-boiled skeptics…

At precisely seven o'clock that evening, Negrelli entered Barrack No 6. Just as he had expected, he found three of the most astute minds huddled together. This triumvirate consisted of Dr. Kálmán Litz, Vanyek, and Jóska Brenda.

Dr. Litz had served in the war as surgeon in an SS unit, but the People's Court had seen fit to convict him of an illegal abortion. His medical expertise was greatly respected; even the civilian employees working with us sought his advice, and he willingly dispensed it for cigarettes. The local pharmacies were happy to fill his prescriptions, because his handwriting was clear, logical, and legible.

Vanyek had been a commercial traveler, a man of the world, who had met all types of people and believed none. His favorite song was not that of the proud Kazakh but the following little ditty:

The moon on summer-night display
For me has nothing new to say.
I will beg for love no more,
I've heard it, seen it all before.

Vanyek only hummed the third line (having conceded that after five-years of abstinence he'd be willing to crawl on his knees for it), but he belted out the fourth one.

Jóska Benda was a devoted teacher and a legendary conspirator.

This little clique enjoyed great reputation and commanded the respect of all in the barracks. No wonder that, even though Negrelli embellished the hither-to-undisclosed royal scandal with his personally observed details of our clandestine sojourn in Biarritz, France, his casual account of my love story with the Princess was greeted with resounding horselaughs. Brenda was slapping his thighs uncontrollably. I timed my appearance carefully at 7:05 p.m. so as to be on the scene before the three wise-men had a chance to solidify their negative reaction. The pregnant silence of the barrack was broken by Vanyek.

"So tell us, how did it go with the princess?" He asked with a contemptuous snarl.

Taking my time to work up a red-hot rage, I slowly turned to Negrelli and roared at him.

"You rotten rat! Tattle-tale old bag! You just couldn't hold your loose tongue! Is this what your word of honor is worth? You, you wretched…" And I bounded toward his cot, but he rolled off toward the other side and took off through the door. With me on his heels.

"I'll kill you, you hyena!" I screamed on my way out.

We ran all the way to the other end of the camp before we stopped to wave to each other with a conspiratorial smile. I returned to the barrack, gasping for air and looking preoccupied. Every eye was on me.

"Well, my friend, what's the truth? Did you have anything to do with the princess?" Vanyek was a shade more courteous this time, couching his inquiry in more neutral terms. No doubt, he was an experienced salesman.

"Listen, you guys, how can you fall for such absolute nonsense," I answered in an emotion-laden, tremulous tone. "How can intelligent, well-educated people like you consider such a thing even for moment, that a no-account, poor college student might ever come into contact with the British royal family! And as for that Negrelli, I'm going to skin that rat, if I ever lay my hands on him. A gossipy old spinster!"

My voice skidded into a staccato scream by the time I finished. And then, with a bitter growl, I retreated to my cot and spread out on it, exhausted and definitely not open to further discussion. My eyes were closed, but my ears registered the affect of my performance with satisfaction.

The triumvirate convened with a few select inmates for a serious debate of the issue. When any one of the conferees considered it necessary to address a question to me, I wearily repeated the same refrain: "I am not going to lower myself to comment on such rubbish… You are too sophisticated for such stupid talk…"

In the next few days, the news spread all over the camp. My obstinate silence and implacable hostility toward Negrelli (as manifested by the clenched fist I raised at him every time he came near me and my repeated but unsuccessful attempts to catch him) slowly bore fruit. Our dramatic conflict reached its climax in a scene in which I chased him around with an ax. The effect was electrifying.

In those days, I was assigned to work with Uncle Feri, an old-time civilian coal miner.

Soon, on one occasion while waiting for the dynamite to do its trick and loosen another big load of coal, the old man pulled out a slivovitz bottle from his haversack and offered it to me with a mysterious grin.

"Well now, let's hear the one about the English Queen and how you almost came to marry her…."

"For one thing, she was not the queen, only her sister, and another, not a word of it is true. You are a wise old man, Uncle Feri…"

"I'm only a coal miner but no dummy. If it comes to something that important, I want to be in on it. You can tell me all about it, I'm not gonna breathe a word to nobody. And you should remember I smuggle your forbidden mail in and out, I let you sip from my flask sometimes…"

That did it. I finally broke down. Swearing the old man to secrecy I related the story of my meeting the princess at a garden party and our subsequent trysts in small cafes… and the nightclub in Biarritz where we snuggled close to each other, smooching in the subdued light… and how, considering the hopelessness of our love, we tasted the tears running down from our eyes into our lips…(this little detail especially appealed to the tough old coalminer)… and how Negrelli, who as a news reporter happened to be passing through town, stumbled onto us but gave his word of honor as a gentleman never to speak about it to anyone…

When after the blast the All Clear signal came, Ucle Feri left me there to shovel the newly loosened coal, but it wasn't long before he was back with Zsiga, the dynamite expert. The latter, also a free employee, had a bandito moustache and I had never heard him speak in any other than abrasively loud voice (and only on matters concerning production), and I was shocked to see him greet me as respectfully as if I had been the British Queen herself, rather than just her lover, or her sister's…etc, etc,…

"We've always been good friends, Györgyey, and it bothers me to be the last one to hear about your love affair. Such a great romance must be shared with friends…"

In the meantime, Negrelli was broadcasting the story in his own way in other shafts. While I preferred the romantic traditions of the older school in my style of spinning out the tale, he resorted to the more naturalistic approach, moving well past Zola and anticipating Henry Miller's masterpieces.

A week later, I had a command performance at the entrance to the shaft. Our shaft supervisor had brought with him the director of the whole mining company. Prior to that, the various members of the management team had (each individually) professed their profound dislike for the regime and disavowed any responsibility for my imprisonment. In fact I had started to worry about all that loose talk that might come to the attention of the AVO with dire consequences for me. Or all of us, for that matter… And I might be hauled back to court with new charges in connection with the British Intelligence Service…

When I finished reciting the story of my star-crossed love affair, the shaft supervisor turned to me:

"What would the Queen say if she knew you were working in a coal mine?"

"We're not talking about the Queen but the Princess," I had to make the correction for the fiftieth time. "Didn't you tell me about some newspaper accounts of a new affair with a Captain Townsend? I'm sure she has long forgotten me."

The erstwhile supervisor stepped in front of me with eyes

blazing and hands clenched into fists. His voice was like a bugle call:

"Can anyone ever forget a love affair like this? No! Never! Never! Never!"

The applause was deafening.

"That's right! You've got it right, Kálmán… You said it! Bravo!"

The supervisor accepted the accolade with a modest nod and stepped aside to make room for the director. The big man had important things to impart to me and pulled me aside for a private conversation. His face was clouded over by dark worries, which I, too, began to share.

"Györgyei, listen to me, let's say… you know, I'm no warmonger… but should it come to that… and the British Army… that is, the British Marines, you know…. that is… you know what I mean… if it should come to that… that is, when they come to liberate you… I… I'd like to…"

I don't know to this day what he wanted me to say, but he found me in a magnanimous spirit. Overcoming my nagging doubts about the feasibility of landing the Marines in a landlocked country, I generously reassured this concerned citizen.

"You have my assurance that neither the mine nor the town will ever be bombed."

He gratefully squeezed my hand and then hurried over to the shaft supervisor:

"Can't you assign this gentleman to a job appropriate to his station in life?"

Actually, as soon as my connection to the British royal family had come to light I was reassigned to a job that could not be called inhumane by any stretch of imagination. My new job was to attend to a pump, where I spent eight hours a day reading and receiving visitors. The only work I was required to perform was to push a button in case the pump stopped pumping. While I was on that job, the pump never failed. I must have been assigned to the most reliable pump of the whole People's Democracy of Hungary. But by then, I was already taking this sinecure for granted, considering my new position vis-a-vis the mine management.

"Comrade Director, as soon as anything better comes up," the supervisor was quick to reply, "we shall reassign the gentleman. We wouldn't want to wear out Mr. Györgyey…"

"Yeah, we must spare his energy for the next time he might cleave onto the princess…" was the comment from a crude and rude inmate of mine. Both the free and the imprisoned workers looked at him with disapproval clear in their eyes. The dynamite man of the second level summarized their feelings:

"You, Grubatz, you are neither a gentleman nor a miner. You don't belong here, in this company…"

Outside, I found Sóvári waiting for me. Being the recipient of two university degrees (one in law and the other in philosophy), he occupied the highest rung in the intellectual ladder of the camp.

"Tell me, my friend, for I sincerely want to know and don't have any first-hand experience on the subject…and the subtle differences elude me…"

"What is it you want to know?" I asked in a rather high-handed and hurried manner, because I had to take advantage of my privileged position as a member of the ruling family in line for the shower. Those first in line were assured of some hot water.

"Tell me, how did it feel to have the great British Empire in your arms?" he blurted out finally.

Of course, I did not dignify his question with an answer, but after my shower I arranged to have a private interview with Negrelli. Sóvári's exalted face troubled my soul with doubts as to the fairness of our game.

"I piss on your soul," Negrelli growled at me morosely. "I have a lot more than doubts about this business with our fake-feud. I want to put a stop to it. It's fine for you to parade around as the emperor…"

"Not the emperor, not even the queen, but her sister, that is the sister's lover…"

"Shut your fat mouth! You know what this game has turned

me into? The gossipy Negrelli! I am the lout who has betrayed the carefully guarded secret of that modest, refined gentleman, Györgyey. I've had up to here with this charade. True enough, my social life has bloomed, cigarettes are plentiful, even a drop of booze is tossed my way now and then, but my reputation has suffered. No one trusts me any more. Things are getting out of hand. How long can I go on inventing new positions for you two love birds? You have any idea how kinky your love games are becoming? The things you did in that bed, right under the royal crest on the headboard..."

Shortly we agreed it was time to drop the curtain.

The very same day, when we were all sitting around at break time down at the bottom of the mine, Negrelli got up to address the small crowd that included Vanyek, Lintz, and at least twenty others.

"Listen fellows, this business about Margaret was nothing but a fake-feud. Not a word of it is true. And now it's time to drop it."

After this terse announcement he turned to me. I got up to speak with the best intentions in the world. But looking at the blackened, dust-covered faces of my mates around me, I felt my heart sink. Something stirred at the bottom of my soul. Did I have the right to take away the greatest love story of the century from these people? So I recited my part like a recorded message:

"We were on a break, just like this, Negrelli and I," my words came tumbling out in a monotone, "when we decided to initiate a truly unbelievable fake-feud. We went over a lot of possibilities and finally settled on this make-believe story about me and Margaret, the British Queen's sister..."

At first worried eyes stared at me in shock from the coal-dust masks. But by the time I got to the end of my hurriedly-delivered monologue the silence hanging over the depths of the earth was shattered by loud laughter.

"The only hitch is that you, Györgyey, you don't know how to tell a lie," Vanyek, the super-salesman, said. "You're trying to pull one over us? You haven't got the talent for that, so don't even try. We know the story is true, and you'll never be able to eradicate its magnificent taste from our memory. And for you, Negrelli, you'll never live down your disgraceful role in this affair. A gossipy gentleman is no gentleman."

Negrelli was lost for words; his eyes reflected a mixture of rage and respect as he glared at me.

"You shameless ham, you!" he snarled and sauntered off.

It was nothing but jealousy, the pure, professional jealousy of an actor jealous of his colleague who gets the better part.

Since that incident, Princess Margaret has been seen in the company of other lucky fellows, even married and then divorced one of them, too, but I sincerely doubt if any of these love affairs were as torrid as the one she shared with me. Of course, I'm not suggesting that the failure of her marriage was due to the long shadow of our romance. The only fact I can swear to is that there is a small mining town in Central Europe where the memory of the greatest love story of the century is still kept alive.

"You wouldn't believe some of the prisoners who used to work here", an old miner is likely to start the tale of the star-crossed lovers with something like this. "Take the fellow, for example, who was the British Queen's lover, but they wouldn't let them get married, and that was why a few years later the whole British Empire fell apart."

This is the kind of speculation I hope to preempt by making public my relationship with Princess Margaret. Looking at the event objectively, though, I must concede that the role I played probably had minimal influence on subsequent developments such as the restructuring of the Commonwealth, Britain's entry into the Common Market or the conflict in Northern Ireland. The question, however, should be decided by professional historians. My job is to make the facts available to them.

All I need now is a good agent to make myself available to the world of theater and cinema. Hollywood! Are you listening? My story, my body, and my proven acting ability are all available for artistic purposes to the highest bidder. Calls will be taken by my wife, one agent at a time, please.

RAINPRECHT

Whenever I think back on my prison adventures, an inadvertent sigh escapes me: Those were the days! And those were the men who made them memorable! Great events shaped by the great upheavals of history call for great personalities, and if they are not forthcoming then the events will shape them. Such were the convulsions of the mid-twentieth century, and such were the men who emerged from them. I have paraded many of them throughout these pages, but there is one more I would like to remember before I put down my pen – or switch off my word processor.

I am thinking of Dr. Antal Rainprecht, a truly great personality who haunts many of the scenes of my captivity in my memory, not necessarily shaping events but certainly shaping my growing and groping young mind. The impression he made was inescapable.

But the force of his personality did not manifest itself in an overbearing attitude. Quite the opposite; he was an extremely humble man whose personality stamped itself on my memory by the fact that he was not just one personality but several, each of them unique in its own way.

It is tempting to associate his multiple-personality syndrome with our occupation, espionage. Call it an occupational disease, but in his case we are not talking of a malady but more like a diversion, an experiment in living, a way of dealing with life by a different approach every day via a different persona that he could assume at will. Or simply his brilliant mind could not be contained in just one personality.

He was one of thc few fellow prisoners who happened to share my fate at almost every one of its miserable stations, from the beginning to the bitter/happy end. That is why this memorial to him appears in the last section of my book, not tied to any one particular place or incident but rather as the summary of my recollections of him, put together unfortunately for a recently presented eulogy.

The year of 1948 was coming to a close when I first met Dr. Antal Rainprecht at Buda South, in the washroom of the fourth regiment. This spacious facility was directly connected to three huge dormitory rooms, all of them inhabited by "Antidemocratic Elements" according to the large cardboard sign posted on the door of each room. A row of washbasins lined one wall, leaving a long strip of space open in the off hours for a curious-looking gentleman to walk up and down. I could not help noticing him. He looked like a cardinal, reading a gilt-edged breviary, in strange contrast to the soft pigskin boots he was wearing. That kind of footwear would not have been out of place in Vaci Street, the deluxe shopping street of Budapest, or even in the most popular mountain resort, but here in the internment camp these beautifully slender and elegant boots looked positively theatrical.

The prelate smiled at me in an absent-minded manner.

"I can see you're new around here," he said graciously. "What brings you here?"

I gave my name and "business". In the exchange that ensued it developed that he had often visited my grandmother in Györgye, the town of my ancestral home. His loving description of the visits immediately made me homesick.

"Cheer up," he tried consoling me. "Those regions, landscapes, towns, grandmothers, they can all go on living inside us. And besides," and here he set aside formality, "please stop addressing me as Most Reverend Father. The time may come for such an appellation some day, but in the meantime I am still struggling to mount the steep steps of my spiritual journey, hopefully in a steady ascent."

And then he read a few lines of Latin from the special-edition volume in his hand. I did not understand the text but felt sure it was appropriate to the occasion and relevant to our conversation.

Most of the time though he had a more elaborate way of introducing himself.

"We Rainprechts are the High Sheriffs of the county of Veszprém, but only subsequent to revolutions!" He was wont to announce when someone inquired about his civilian occupation. And indeed, he was historically correct. His father had been promoted to the top spot of the county administration after the 1918 democratic revolution which replaced the monarchy with a republic, and my fellow inmate followed in his father's footsteps, attaining the same position, after Liberation in 1945. Rainprecht senior had the good sense to resign just before the Communist takeover in 1919, which established a short-lived but bloody Soviet-style regime; however, Rainprecht junior was not as quick to anticipate the changing winds of politics, and he was caught trying to cross the western border without proper documents.

He related all that to me the next day during his usual perambulations in the washroom. I had some difficulty concentrating on his words, so distracted I was by the two upper incisors sticking out over his lip and giving him the caricature appearance of a decadent aristocrat. And there was something else about him, something new that had developed overnight. He was a different person. The book he was holding was definitely secular: what he recited turning to me was definitely not a prayer: "*Ay, that incestuous, that adulterate beast!*"

Luckily, I recognized the quote. It was clear he was not speaking to me but quoting from Hamlet. He rewarded my cultural background with a gracious smile of satisfaction.

"Shakespeare really knew how to curse out someone. I don't think this is the right time and place to prepare a concordance of his adjectives as they may be applied to our noble young guardians who devote the best years of their lives to the difficult task of guarding us. I have in mind a particularly sergeant who kept me locked up with a bunch of other would-be defectors at a border station; he could very well be described as a "*wicked beast*."

Toni – as he had me address him by then – was leaning on a sink as he expostulated.

"When I decided to relocate my office further west of Veszprém, I only packed the most essential items in my rucksack. Among those I counted my published work, a novel entitled "The Philosophy of Love". It added quite a bit of weight, not because of its size but its number. I wanted to rescue all two hundred copies of it. The story is about the lord of a manor who flies a black flag of mourning every time he breaks up with a mistress. There's a big house party with literate conversation revolving around the subject of earthly and heavenly love, the perfection of unrequited love, and the spiritual aspects of sensuality. An excellent work, if I say so myself. But back to the border station: there we were lined up against the wall, facing it. Some were whimpering, some just froze up, but there was no doubt about it, we were all scared out of our wits. The AVO sergeant entered from an office next door. He wasn't pale, but in every other respect he was the perfect Shakespearean personification of evil. Some character like Richard the Third minus the devilishly clever lines; he was just plain evil."

And then Toni, setting aside his aristocratic mannerisms, acted out for me the scene in the border station:

"Which one of you is Antal Rainprecht?" The sergeant bellowed out.

Toni made a proper soldierly about-face and proudly announced:

"I am."

The sergeant's bulky face was turning redder by the minute.

"Did you write this Pilosopy of Love?" he asked, waving Toni's slender little volume. Only one copy, of course.

"Yes, I did," Toni confessed without hesitation. He knew what to expect next. The evil man of battle would get down on his knees and kiss the cuffs of the prisoner's Norwegian ski pants, asking for the privilege of personally escorting the whole group across the border even at the risk of his own life. This simple soldier, who had trouble pronouncing the word philosophy, would be willing to lay down his life for it, for the very idea of it, as it was expounded in Toni's brilliant little treatise. The scenario made famous by Archimedes would be reversed after two thousand years, and philosophy would triumph. *Non tangere circulos mios* would be heard over the din of millennia.

But Toni's momentary dream of glory was quickly dashed. The sergeant started raving with rage:

"This is the worst bullshit I've ever seen! Pilosopy you call it? People just keep talking, yakety-yak and no one's fucking. I've never seen such monumental bullshit!"

Toni thought it wiser not to press the matter by asking the sergeant about his reading habits, even though it would have been illuminating to know the basis of this unfavorable literary criticism. So he survived the incident with a kick in the pants from the sergeant, but deep down he was convinced that future historians of world literature would not leave the incident unrecorded.

This was how Toni related the circumstances of his arrest to me. But there was yet a lot more for me to learn about him, about the different roles he played every day. On Mondays he discoursed on the fine point of theology, mostly in eloquent Latin that would have made the founding fathers of the Church proud. On Tuesdays he stepped over from the spiritual to the secular realm, and on Wednesdays his interest ran dangerously close to the prurient in the risqué stories with which he chose to regale us. On the following day he would return to the elucidation of Church doctrines, with special attention to Saint Augustine. But Shakespeare was never far from his mind, and he could quote the Bard of Albion on any occasion on any day, either in the original or in Hungarian translation.

Toni's colorful personality (whichever he chose to sport at the moment), his encyclopedic knowledge, his sophistication and quick-witted remarks proved to be a great asset to the interned community, both in cruelly difficult times and during long stretches of boredom. But perhaps his greatest contribution was great, old-fashioned courtesy, which always served to remind us of our humanity even under the most inhumane condition. No matter which role he was playing at the moment he always remained a perfect gentleman. Of course, that too could have been only another role; it was not clear how serious he was about his ceremonious manners, but they served well to facilitate interaction among us, and it never occurred to us to question his motives.

For instance, whenever he wanted to join a group for a meal, whether it was at the one common table of the room at Buda South or sitting on the tree stumps at Recsk, it was always by first asking the leave of those already seated there in the mostly courtly manner. Of course, he was invariably welcomed with enthusiasm, and he completed the ceremony by asking his dinner companions:

"Please, don't hesitate to reprimand me if I start chewing with my mouth open."

His courtesy paid off. One night in Kistarcsa the lights were turned off even earlier than usual, before Toni could finish his bedtime routine. There he was, fidgeting in the semidarkness, looking for the small wooden stool on which he liked to bundle up his personal possessions. At the same time Kálmán Himpfner, a respectable old gentleman, an undersecretary from the Department of Agriculture, (guilty of conspiracy to commit industrial espionage), seemed to have the same idea concerning the very same (and the only one of its kind) piece of furniture. Their faces met over the object of their search in the dusk of the camp.

"Is this yours?" Asked the surprised Kálmán, pointing at the stool with a finger that was shaking with visible distress.

"If you need it badly, I will naturally let you have it," answered Toni.

"But what will you do with your stuff?" Himpfner fell for the trap.

"I'll roll it all up and hold it in my hands all night."

Needless to say, the stool remained Toni's exclusive property.

But if the occasion called for it, Toni could also assert himself. Legend has it that in the 1930's he even forced the resignation of the government in power. And he accomplished that without any political clout of his own – if such deficiency is possible when it comes to a Rainprecht. At that time he had a modest position as personal secretary to Leo Goldberger, the textile magnate. It was not in that capacity, however, that a war widow from the county of Veszprém sought out his help but as the son of a former High Sheriff who was bound to have connections in high places. Toni was fond of relating the incident.

"Dr. Rainpecht," she pleaded with Toni, "I am a war widow, I'd like to send my children to school... well, so why is it I can't get a tobacco concession?"

After WW I, the retail sale of all tobacco products became the exclusive domain of war widows by law as a way of helping them make a living.

"Indeed, why not?" Toni was pondering the question *sotto voce*.

"Well, sir, I thought, if you could only talk to the people in charge..."

"My dear lady, unfortunately I don't know anyone in the office involved, I don't even know whose business it is...."

"They handle it in the Ministry of Internal Affairs." The woman informed Toni with hope in her voice.

"There's nothing I can do to help you, I'm truly sorry...."

"But Dr. Rainprecht, we supported your dear father in office. My late husband, who heroically gave his life for the country..."

Toni put an end to her effusions by raising a hand. And with the other he dialed the Ministry.

The ensuing telephone conversation was acted out for us in the way the woman had heard it.

"I would like to speak to the Minister."

Toni was probably connected to the secretarial office.

"I would likc to spcak to the Minister." Pause.

"No, he doesn't yet know what this is all about. Just tell him Dr. Antal Rainprecht wants to talk to him."

"I come from ancient Hungarian nobility, I have a doctorate degree in *juris prudence* and political science, and as a Hungarian citizen I have the right to..."

"Well, if the Minister has no time for me, then the

Government should resign!"

The latter phrase was thundered into the phone, and its effect was unmistakable, even in the retelling.

The war widow from the home county of Veszprem was badly shaken when she took her leave. And Toni spent the rest of the day rather satisfied with himself, safe in the knowledge that he had done everything humanly possible for a constituent.

But he felt even better the next morning when the butler presented him with the newspaper along with his breakfast toast. A banner headline in bold letters announced to the world: Government Crisis!

The news that Dr. Rainprecht had forced the resignation of the Government spread like wild fire throughout the county of Veszprém, causing a meteoric rise in Toni's reputation.

Dr. Rainprecht and the powers-to-be seldom saw eye to eye. Whenever he tried to put his wisdom and experience to use in the service of the public good, small-minded bureaucrats or the representatives of state power frustrated his efforts.

I personally witnessed the classical example of such a situation develop in Recsk at its worst period of cruelty and misery. The scene was worthy of a sculpture piece or a monumental mural, but I have only words to help me immortalize it for posterity.

The incident took place in the second year of our sojourn at the mountain resort of Recsk, by which time we had all become skin and bone. Plus hair. Without the beard we would have looked like walking skeletons, the messengers of death. A neutral observer from the outside would have run away from us in panic and, on second thought, called a hospital, but we had no such visitors. From time to time a group of high-level AVO officials would drop in to look us over, but the reason for their inquiry was not made clear. Were we dying off too fast or not fast enough? They didn't say.

In this case, they surprised us one evening when everyone was already in the barracks, but the AVO colonel in charge of the group picked out Toni for attention, even though by then he looked no different from us. He still had his overhanging incisors, but otherwise his cheeks were hollow, and his features were often stamped by the apathy of the death camp. Only his mind was still the same, still as nimble and uniquely his own.

"What's your name?" The officer of the law roared at him. Actually, it was not unreasonable of him to suppose we were all hard of hearing; how could these human wrecks have functioning senses?

"Dr. Antal Rainprecht."

"And what were you before?" asked the colonel with a jeering grin.

"The High Sheriff of the County of Veszprém."

"So you had the opportunity to do a lot of evil, didn't you?"

Toni raised his chin a little higher.

"*There is nothing either good or bad, but thinking makes it so*, said Shakespeare."

This colonel must have been related to the sergeant of the border patrol. He didn't seem to like Shakespeare either. He, too, started to bellow imprecations of all kinds, quickly losing control over his emotions, which made further fruitful dialogue impossible.

"What the hell do you mean by Shakespeare, you Fascist beast..."

And there followed an avalanche of verbal abuse, but Toni took it all in, standing there in respectful silence, like someone who is usually used to ovation, but who is also able to take criticism.

Later I saw him respond to physical abuse with the same respectful attitude when an AVO-man kicked him off the railroad embankment in a coal mine. He just got back on his feet and put on his cap.

"Thank you for calling my attention to my mistakes and shortcomings, sir." He said without losing his dignity.

After all this praise and appreciation, I think I can now let the truth be known; in spite of all his unique qualities Antal Rainprecht was not perfect. Like everyone else, he had his weak points. He was certainly not a Stahanovite, a shock worker; if anyone still wants to sculpt a monument to heroic

Socialist labor, then he should look for someone else other than Toni for the model. Toni would be out of place even on the fringes of the pedestal to such a sculpture piece. The plain truth is he was not a very good worker! His contribution to the industrial developments and the deliriously expanding economy of the fifties was negligible, as it was so often pointed out to him by so many hardworking AVO supervisors.

It will be impossible for us to forget him. I cannot think back of the mine shaft without seeing his hunched figure in it, or a campfire without him shivering next to it. I can see him stop at Recsk to take in the magnificent colors of the wood, stumbling along between barracks on a trail covered with twigs to avoid the mud, looking deep into the bottom of his empty mess kit or waiting for the water tap to be turned on. Recsk is unimaginable without him. He was a charter member; his memory is welded to the landscape and carved into our hearts.

Multiple-personality syndrome notwithstanding, he stands out as one irrepressible personality who rescued his dignity from the wreckage heaved upon him. Many a time his example propped up the backbone and lifted the spirit in his weakening inmates and fellow spies.

COMING IN FROM THE COLD

My retirement from the field of espionage, from the lonely and precarious existence of being the one and only personal spy to General De Gaulle, was a gradual process, taking place over a period of three years, which culminated in my discharge from the penal system. Actually, as I found out later, my full confession to being a spy at my already described trial turned out to be my last official duty as a spy. After confessing to my treasonous activities on behalf of evil foreign schemes against the Socialist Bloc, I was rarely, if ever, called upon again to play the part of a secret agent, a part I had learned so well and grown secretly fond of. Thus, for the last three years in service the skills and proficiency I had developed with so much pain went underutilized to the point of being neglected.

Perhaps what had led to this change was my new cover, that of a coal miner, which took over my life with the exclusion of all other aspects of the mission. In fact I spent those last three years in semi-retirement, and, as I came to realize, I was already working toward re-entering my humdrum existence in the outside world as an average, innocent citizen. In other words, in plain everyday language, we might say I was already working – in my own way – toward my liberation, even without realizing it at first.

A brief explanation is in order.

There were about 1200 convicts (no longer just interned, but convicted prisoners) working in the coal mines of Várpalota, bringing to the surface a very low-grade coal, more like lignite, as I learned from the ever-present engineers who were also convicts. At that time the quality of our product did not concern me much. It was not my responsibility, but it later turned out to play an important part in my progress to the gates of freedom. So here comes a little science lesson.

The calorie content of this stuff was less than 3000 calories per kilo as compared to 7000 given by anthracite, the best quality coal, but it was deemed good enough – when pulverized – for the nearby new power plant that was to provide electricity to a new bauxite processing plant as well as to the surrounding area which was also the unwitting recipient of sulfur dioxide in the form of acid rain. It is common knowledge that the cheaper the coal the dirtier it burns (sulfur being the most troublesome impurity), but all that was a problem for our Socialist planners who apparently worried about air pollution even less than did a simple miner, such as myself.

What I worried about was making a convincing show of fulfilling my work assignment. And now a lesson in Socialist economics. A whole separate chapter could be written about the way we – and all workers in all phases of industry, etc, were compensated ("allowed to partake in the proceeds of their labor") by the one single employer, the state. In contrast to the rotten capitalist system, the Socialist state instituted a system of compensating workers by the amount of work they produced ("each according to his ability"); in other words, it was piecework as opposed to timework, a system labor unions had fought long and hard in the West to defeat, but now it was touted in our Socialist Paradise as a noble bastion in the Marxist defense of workers' rights. Needless to say, those who were supposed to benefit from it, the workers, regarded it as the highest form of exploitation, but they had very little to say about how their paradise was run for them.

The way the system worked, each job had a certain amount of work quota allotted to it. Job performance was gauged in terms of percentages of the assigned quota (also called norm), and compensation was adjusted accordingly. Those performing similar jobs on 100% level would get paid the same; any variation from that would be reflected in the take-home pay.

But we prisoners were given an added incentive; we were told that for every month with an average of 102% job performance we could get our sentence reduced by one day. In my case, with my eight-year sentence (with credit for time served) I was due to be released in the fall of 1956, but with increased production I could be out months earlier. There was light at the end of the tunnel.

There were serious problems, too. The news failed to arouse in me the desire for higher productivity. For one thing, I had become inured to official promises and deeply distrustful of those in power. For another, I didn't feel motivated to help our Socialist economy roar ahead of that of the US on my back with my Sisyphusian effort. It was totally without any conscious decision on my part that I, nevertheless, got caught up in and greatly benefited from this incentive scheme. The job I was assigned put me in a singular position where I could not lose, because it turned out to be the key to the productivity of the whole shaft and crucial to the economic well-being of all civilian employees and the early release of prisoners.

I was uniquely qualified for the job. Very few others had the judicious combination of defiantly daring laziness and devil-may-care lack of ambition that turned out to be the secret of success in that key position of trolley loader.

And now a lesson in coal mining (as it was practiced in my time): the miners at the work area ("front") shoveled the coal on a long conveyer belt (made of hinged bits of steel rather than rubber), and at the other end a worker (the "loader") shoved a mine trolley under the belt, filled it up, and sent it on its way to the shaft. When the trolley got lifted up the shaft to the surface, the coal was dumped out, weighed, and recorded along with the number of trolleys passing through. Both figures were of great importance, as we shall see. Needless to say, the worker doing the loading was visited routinely by the shaft master, the supervisor, and the guards, all of whom exhorted the loader to load the trolley to the top. Their job was to bellow out regularly: "Top that fucking trolley, don't you hear me!"

My background at Recsk proved unexpectedly helpful in dealing with this stressful situation on the job. First of all, very few of us were sent to Várpalota, and we commanded uncommon amount of respect based on our past suffering. Secondly, being a graduate of Recsk, I had become immunized against verbal abuse. Having been trained by the AVO, I remained deaf to rude and loud commands; my dignity was vulnerable only to rubber truncheons.

As a result, I didn't drive myself unduly on the job. With my usual cool, casual attitude I filled the trolleys about half full and pushed them off on their way to the power plant, making sure I did not break my back while putting on a show of keeping busy.

After a while though, I began to wonder why the loudly remonstrating army of supervisors, civilian and police alike, never actually did anything about my lackadaisical performance. In fact, underneath their perfunctory drubbing, I seemed to detect tacit approval of my way of handling things.

On further observation of the mining operation I slowly came to understand the strange dichotomy that governed the management's attitude. As it turned out, the coal I sent on its way was not just plain old coal but coal liberally enriched with stones, due to the deliberately indiscriminate and speedy work done at the "front". The stones did not add to the calorie content of our product but, due to their high density, they did add disproportionate amount in weight, thus enabling the mine to deliver its quota of coal even while the number of trolleys was lagging behind, at least until I got on the job. Unwittingly, with my back-saving technique of only filling the trolleys half full doubled the number of trolleys reaching the surface; I had hit upon a simple solution that saved the whole section. No wonder there was a silent conspiracy growing up around me, involving labor and management, prisoners and prison guards. Everyone came out a winner. Everyone's pay was tied to the general performance of the mine, and I became everyone's favorite "loader", because I ignored their habitual cussing and cursing. My education at Recsk had finally paid off.

Ironically, my half-filled trolley carts kept the performance rate of the "front" at a constant 190%, which, eventually, shaved 45 days off my sentence, without burdening my back with an extra shovel of coal. On one occasion a reporter for a trade publication even criticized my technique, saying that "...the loader of the second front sends half-filled trolley carts to the surface...", but, of course, my name was omitted from the article. They could not let out the secret of prison labor being employed in the mines, plain old-fashioned slavery being practiced by the Socialist economy.

Since the mine produced a low-grade coal in the first place, nobody seemed to worry about the quality of the coal we delivered, no one in management or the engineering department, that is. So who was I, a lowly slave, to raise the issue? Such a lucky break would not have come my way in Csolnok, the next mine I was transferred to, because it produced anthracite, a very high-calorie coal, whose dilution would have been detected sooner or later.

By that time I had accumulated so much "time off" that even my shaky math showed I was due for release. I even asked some of my prison mates to check my calculations and they confirmed the unbelievable. The day of my liberation was nigh! But finally when it arrived and a list of those to be released was read, the name Györgyey was not on it. I wasn't really surprised, knowing the gravity of my "business"; I had never heard of a French spy, let alone a Gaullist agent, ever being allowed to go free. Giving in to my friends' insistence (to use a cliche usually reserved for introductions to memoirs), however, I finally made up my mind to check things out in the camp office.

The person in charge was Irénke (the Hungarian diminutive nickname for Irene). For a sergeant she was a rather winsome brunette of average height who regarded me with undisguised amusement. She didn't quite greet me with a cheerful "What can I do for you?". That would have been too much to expect of her, but she did smile as she turned to me using the usual vocabulary of the state authority personnel.

"What'd you want?"

"I was due to be released," I explained with confidence but without sounding arrogant.

"Come on," Irénke replied, "you probably figured it wrong."

"No doubt about it," I insisted. "In Várpalota I regularly over-fulfilled my quota! I worked my ass off!"

Irénke must have heard a sexual double entendre in my

assertion and started to giggle, but eventually she managed to get back to the business on hand.

"Well, let's check your file."

My heart sank through the floor. Now she was going to say my file was lost... But then she found it.

"Here it is... Now, let's take a look... Yes, you were due to be released! Will you ever forgive me?"

To this day, I don't know whether it had been her mistake, but I felt certain at the moment that fate had presented me with an opportunity at this juncture. Was she flirting with me? For more than seven years I had been deprived of female company, to put it in polite terms, and for a moment I was tempted to say: "Gladly, but only if you go on a date with me... Perhaps then I can give you a chance to make up for your mistake." But these words luckily remained safely in my mind, on the safe side of my lips, because I believe Irénke would have said yes, judging by the warm glances she sent my way, glances that were ready to boil over.

On second thought, though, I realized that while I had no problem with Irénke's charms and her pleasant manners; she had done me no harm, was never even rude to me, but it did not seem like a good idea for me to start my new life on the outside in the company of a prison guard.

I've had enough of your kind, I thought, still smiling gently at her, implying that perhaps... in the future.... But I ended up asking:

"How long do I have to wait?"

These were my last official words as an unwitting spy, eager to come in from the cold, with apologies to John le Carré. My lackluster career in espionage was over and I was free to go into well-deserved retirement, never to be recalled into active service again.

My hero, General De Gaulle, was yet to reach the pinnacle of his mission in the world as the head of the state he personified, but I followed his activities from a distance only, albeit from a safe distance in the USA. The 1956 Hungarian uprising made it possible for me to ensure my retirement from the agonies of secret service by escaping from the beloved land of my birth, a land then held captive by irrational forces that could, at any time, make a spy even out of an inept and peace-loving person such as I.

There's very little more to say. After the doors of the grotesquerie closed behind me, nothing unusual, nothing exciting happened to me, but there may be some readers who would feel cheated if I didn't say a few words about my first breath of freedom, my blending into the general population and assuming my God-given normal identity.

I had to wait another month to hear my name listed among the lucky ones. Of course, I had no illusions, I knew only too well that I was walking out of a small prison into a much bigger one. But consider the difference! I was put on a train to Budapest with just enough pocket money for a quick drink and pack of cigarettes. (Those were the shameless days of simple pleasures, the still innocent pleasure of smoking!)

Seeing where I boarded the train, no one talked to me, but everyone had an encouraging, conspiratorial smile for me as if celebrating with me. In Budapest, however, the faces were different. They were busy, morose, tired, and preoccupied; wearing just the kind of expression one would expect to see in a crowded streetcar. And I probably looked no different. No one paid any attention to me. I was one face in the crowd. That was when I fully realized I was out in the world, things were back to normal. I was free. So much for my first breath of freedom.

There was exhilaration, too; it didn't come with something I inhaled, but something I saw and heard. Women! Women, women, all over the place, mixed in with the crowd, standing right next to me, young and old, pretty and plain, animated and worn-out, women of all kinds. And hearing their voices completed the picture for me, the high register skating over the general noise of the crowd as if the telephone wires had been talking to me directly, as if birds had suddenly materialized in human shape and invaded the streets! And what shape! Thus freedom meant living in a world of two sexes and having the prospect of exploring the exciting differences between them...

I spoke of Irénke a little earlier, and the disturbingly pleasant thoughts her presence invoked in me, but in that case there was a desk between us, to say nothing of the ideological and spiritual gulf... But here, in the streetcar, on the sidewalks, I shared space with women as an equal, as another human being....

The first person I ran into in our old apartment building was Makra, the old super.

"Are you looking for someone?" he asked.

"Don't you recognize me?"

He looked at me with a shock.

"Frankie boy? My God! Did those beasts finally let you out?"

"Yeah..."

He hugged me, but then apologized for getting so carried away. When I assured him it made me feel good to be welcomed, he summoned his family and the scene was repeated with his wife and two daughters, and later with anyone else who suddenly showed up to join the celebration.

Only my parents were missing, because they had been deported to a small village and had only recently been allowed back to a suburb of Budapest, as they still lacked a residency permit in the capital. I had no such problem, because being in jail I had never had my residency permit taken away and, therefore, I was still a legitimate resident of the city. But a friend soon rounded up a taxi and that very evening I was united with my parents.

Needless to say, eating, drinking and photo sessions livened up the festive atmosphere. The mood of jubilation, however, was not unalloyed by worries about the future. Most people advised me to lie low, play it safe, say nothing about my eight years of incarceration, and act as if I had never left the city.

But I had something to say on the subject, too. In fits and starts I slowly but proudly assured them that I was free, and I was free to talk about all my experiences, they could ask me anything.

“Oh, no! Please, watch yourself, no one is completely free... etc, etc...”

The anxious voices rose up around me, but I did my best to calm them. After all, in contrast to those who had been released directly from Recsk without a trial, I was never required to sign an agreement preventing me from speaking out about my experiences and the places where I had been incarcerated. After all, I had been tried and convicted, and I had served my time, and now I was free. Free to speak. And I did.

The first story I told them was about Sándor Füzessery, the first of many that were to follow later, much later.

Sándor was taken to the AVO office one day at Recsk and told that the People’s Democracy was ready to forgive him, set him free, even help him return to the general population with a job. The only thing he would be asked in return would be a periodic report on the people around him, their conversations, activities, etc. Pista burst out laughing, right in the face of the AVO “administrator”, who just stared at him in disbelief before asking: “What’s so funny?” “What?” Sándor answered. “Funny that you guys are ready to forgive me. First you arrest me for no reason at all, beat the hell out of me, starve me in prisons and labor camps, push me to the brink of death... and then you want to forgive me? You want me to be grateful and report on others... The funniest thing I’ve ever heard.” Sándor Füzessery was thrown out of the office, but no more was said about his reprieve.

One of the guests at this little celebration was a former deportee who warned me quietly that things were changing but not changing that fast, and secrecy agreement or not, I could still be re-arrested at any time. His words sobered me up a little, and I spent the rest of the evening listening to others. There was a lot to catch up on. Being just an average, everyday citizen, a simple man of the street, also required getting used to, and even some practice.

I didn’t start telling my stories again until I was safely out of the Socialist Camp, out of the bigger prison that exploded a few months later in the now-famous 1956 Hungarian

Revolution.

* * * *

But that was something no one could have predicted, not even our little coven of world experts at Recsk. As far as I knew I had to make my plans for the future not in terms of months but years to come, and the prospects were bleak indeed. I soon had to give up any dreams of citywide celebration at my return, if indeed such a thing was ever accorded to any one of the released political prisoners. Nobody had ever heard of me, let alone come out and greet me with jubilation. People were quietly reassuring on hearing of my sufferings in private conversation, and there were a few more parties, too, but nothing like what I had expected and deserved; for example, the respect I had received at Sixty except now with a plus sign: "Did they get Györgyey?"

So how did I adjust to civilian life? Well, I didn't. And civilian society did not adjust to me either; we seemed to remain at odds with each other until I resorted to my usual way of breaking such a stalemate: pulling another prank. What else could I do?

First of all, finishing my university studies was not a realistic alternative; the general opinion at the Department of Art History was that I should be happy to be alive and should not try to rejoin the community of scholars. Iván Boldizsár, a former teacher (and lately a regular contributor to the editorial columns of the official Party newspaper), who had earlier ranked me with Flaubert and Maupassant, could only shake his head with genuine sadness when I approached him in Cafe New York, the favorite hangout of practicing and aspiring writers and journalists.

In the meantime, though, the necessity of getting a job began to press itself on my consciousness with increasing urgency. Friends and family warned me that one way our Socialist system dealt with unemployment was by arresting the unemployed as chronic vagrants. My former prison mates were especially helpful taking me from one job interview to another, but no potential employer or personnel director was able to utilize the varied job experience I had accumulated in the foregoing eight years, even though I had rapidly lowered my sights from some cushy office job to anything remunerative, anything that could be stamped into my internal passport as a place of employment. Finally, it was the little suburban village of Budakeszi, the place that had offered safe haven to my parents in their exile from Budapest proper that now took me to her bosom. I was given gainful employment by the famous Korányi Pulmonary Sanatorium located there; the position made me a member of the grounds crew. Not exactly a very prestigious or well-paid position, and in the social ladder I don't think it counted as a position at all.

My coworkers were a decent sort, not the kind to take advantage of the system or their fellow employees, certainly not social climbers, not like their superiors who looked down upon them. And they were scorned not only by the success-oriented but by society in general. Truth be told, our sanatorium was no Davos, it was far removed from Thomas Mann's Magic Mountain. One of the doctors was supposed to be a famous surgeon, but in my eyes his claim to fame rested on the shoulders (and every other part) of his beautiful wife, a TV announcer, or, as yet, a candidate for the job of an announcer on the soon-to-be-operational first TV station of the nation. This bit of gossip had trickled down through several social strata within the institute to the bottom level where I was safely ignored, my prison record notwithstanding. In a way it was reassuring to me that the idea of a classless society had not taken root in the outside world in my absence. The beautiful TV announcer-candidate did not look right through me like through a ghost on account of her political convictions; the members of the grounds crew, including myself, remained invisible to all except perhaps the kitchen staff, the only other people in sight who seemed to feel inclined to toss a glance in our direction now and then.

No question about it, my status at the hospital was

disturbingly low for someone who had served as De Gaulle's personal spy. In prison, I had been subjected to every form of indignity, but never to the indignity of being treated as a nobody, a non-entity. Back there, I had to be someone important, even if only a small cog in the great machinery of history but at least part of it; otherwise I would not have had all that attention lavished on me even from the highest reaches of the People's government.

The more I thought about it, the more I became determined to turn my low standing to my advantage; I could use it in a little social experiment of my own, an experiment designed to detect the determining factors of one's social standing. Or, at least, answer some related questions, such as what lies behind great reputations? How much mobility is there on the social scale? Or is that whole scale totally illusory? And how about the value system implicit in any social hierarchy? Isn't it basically flawed by false assumptions and pretences?

The methodology of my experiment was taken from the state-run betting system involving Sunday afternoon soccer games. Known as TOTO, it served as an outlet for the work-weary population that had very little to look forward to besides the promised land of Socialism whose construction was sapping their energy and spirit. Maybe my release from prison could not rouse the tired masses to a nationwide celebration, but where I failed TOTO succeeded; all week long it kept the whole country debating the chances of the 24 teams playing 12 games. The general excitement reached fever pitch on Sunday night when the results were announced on the radio and Tuesday when the lucky winners were listed along with their winnings, which could be considerable, depending on the number of correct predictions. At every workplace Monday morning was spent on the evaluation of the games, most bettors cursing their bad luck and the uncooperative soccer players.

The ramshackle hole assigned to the grounds crew at Korányi for a locker room was no different. Coming to work on Monday morning every worker dropped off the receipt portion of his betting slip on a rickety table where the most respected members of the crew were seated, ready to pass judgment. Anyone who got more than half of the scores right was regarded with high esteem and could count on having his opinion elicited in the coming week, not only concerning sports but every other subject, including the weather.

The betting slip had on it the list of the 12 games with three columns next to it; win, lose or tie. That last possibility added an extra permutation to the results which made correct predictions devilishly difficult.

My experiment was, however, ingeniously simple. What if I were to walk in on Monday morning with a betting slip with twelve hits? And what if, to make it more believable (and unselfishly spread the glory!) I draw two of my coworkers into the scheme? It was not unusual for several people to form a pool and fill out their slips in cooperation thus hedging their bets. Or, as it was the case with us, sometimes several bettors of modest means invested in one ticket which was to carry their combined wisdom to victory. Except now, on this particular weekend, my two co-conspirators let me fill out our corporate ticket by myself on Sunday night when the scores were in.

The next morning I walked into work with the usual Monday-morning scowl and casually tossed the receipt portion of my betting ticket on the table for expert evaluation.

"Probably no more than three hits," I mentioned in passing, pure gut reaction. "My partners left it to me, and I really didn't feel like racking my brains out over it… I just marked it more or less by chance."

"Well then, you can't expect much, can you?" said one of the experts, probably the only professional gardener among us (who had lost his commercial garden business to a takeover by the People Democracy), and then he went on to check just how badly I had scored. "This is okay, this one too… and this… and you even got this tie right…"

The sullen faces in the makeshift locker room started to light up, and when the gardener got to the tenth right answer a groan was shaking the ceiling, and, finally, when he had got through all twelve games, and they all checked out right, it was as if the place had caught on fire. The grounds workers all ran out into the yard, yelling and screaming and jumping up and down with excitement. The news flashed through the hospital with lightning speed.

From that moment on all work came to a standstill in the whole place. I can't say if any surgical operations were disrupted, because I don't know if they performed any at that time, but wherever we, the proud members of the grounds crew went, the otherwise inexorable progress of socialism came to a grinding halt. How much did they win? It's too early to tell! How are they going to spend all that money? The air was buzzing with questions and advice. What kind of car should we buy? Where should we build a vacation home? Which seaside resort should we visit? And in which country?... Even I got so carried away that the mention of foreign lands started me dreaming... Italy! But of course, I would never return from there... I had to remind myself that I was a winner only in the small village of Budakeszi, and that my sudden success would soon evaporate with equal suddenness; the latest by noon the next day, Tuesday, my fame would be snatched away from me. But in the meantime even the personnel director (considered a sensitive spot, a "vigilant position", usually filled only by trusted Party members) was shaking our hands, and the beautiful TV announcer was sending a beautifully warm smile in our direction (especially towards me, as I seemed to discern) while the grounds workers were practically carrying me around in a victory parade.

Lunch that day was more like a victory banquette; instead of picking up our bowl at the kitchen window, we had it served to us by the staff, and on leaving the dining hall we received another ovation.

The last hurrah came in the form of the exact figures concerning the loot. It was calculated to be 54 thousand forints for each of the three winners. At that time you could buy a good used car or a smaller house for that much, a serious amount of money, but we took the news with grace and dignity. At least I did. But my partners had not counted on repercussions and on their families being drawn into the brouhaha. The good people Budakeszi soon got wind of the new fame of their village, and the grapevine reached a lucky winner's wife before it could be stopped. In her shock she dropped the dinner tray, losing not only the whole dinner but some of the dishes, too. And that was two miles from the center of excitement.

And on Tuesday, the inevitable disaster struck, when the names of the winners were made public. None of us were listed among them. The whole sanatorium was dumbstruck. The personnel manager gave us the day off so that we could go into Budapest and demand justice. The betting slip was made out in my name, but the other two were warned to take good care of me if anything happened.

"The authorities are capable of anything," the chief chef, a kindly woman, whispered to my ear.

My fellow conspirators and I parted company at the bus terminal where we agreed to meet a few hours later.

"Would've been nicer, had it been for real," one of the yard workers said wistfully. The other only wondered out loud how many of the dishes had been broken. They both left it to me to find the proper resolution to our conundrum.

After spending a pleasant afternoon in the big city I rejoined my partners for the trip back. Some of our fellow employees were still waiting for us. With long faces we reported to them that we – that is I – had made a trivial error in filling out a duplicate copy, but that error was deemed fatal by the bureaucrats in the TOTO office; in short, they invalidated our entry.

"Probably because you guys are not Party members!" Someone remarked with venomous hatred in his voice.

I could nod to that with a clear conscience; indeed that was true, we were not Party members, only members of the grounds crew at an out-of-the-way sanatorium. And with that my little social experiment came to an end and I faded back into the anonymous crowd once again as a nameless yard worker, more readily identifiable by the rake in my hand than by my face.

We may very well ask what conclusions can be drawn from my experiment. This celebrity-mad age of ours now grants everyone his of her fifteen-minutes of fame; on the other hand, we may safely conclude that all earthly glory is transitory. *Sic transit gloria mundi.*

The political undertone of my experiment was, however, quite unexpected. The way it brought to the surface the general population's deep distrust of the system almost frightened me; people had been accused of and convicted for inciting a riot for much lesser commotion than what I had stirred up. In light of later events to follow in just a month or two, I might even say that in my small way I did indeed contribute to destabilization of the regime and the ferment of the revolution. And yet in my mind, I was only trying get by, to cope with unaccustomed civilian life, and perhaps test the limits of freedom that reality always imposes on all of us, whatever the size of the prison we live in.

EPILOGUE 1

FAREWELL TO RECSK

by György Faludy

What is the lesson to be drawn? My old inmates all
keep asking about the secret that sustained us at Recsk.
I can only speak for myself, but let them all come
and testify if I speak the truth!

1.
First, let me thank nature all
around us for its crucial role,
on my eardrums I could feel
the music of the spheres resound,
the mountains and the open sky
softened our prison bars,
because I wore the helmet
of the solar system on my head,
Venus sprinkled her blue sparkles
into my squinting, sleepy eyes,
the sun in winter was an apple,
in summer it bloomed into a rose;
rain came down in arrowheads
or greenish lances at other times,
but the smoke-dark evening shower
poured on us a glass-bead chain;
the Shakespearean forest land!
let's not forget its magic touch,
every tree I could lean against
turned into a chandelier;
my drops of blood, splattered on
freshly crushed black granite stones:
red-dotted ladybug wings
scattered around my feet;
and the giant eagles circling
above the mountaintops! I'd reach
out into the sky to get
hold of their retracted claws;
the Calvados taste of wild apples;
in February the rusty crown
of the still bare-branched beech,

roseate with eager buds;
the caressing wind from the west
laden with the soothing hope
that the West is not too decadent
yet to have forgotten us at last;
the tiny babbling spring that showed
my wretched face in a better light,
for that's what the Nymph of Recsk was,
compassion for the fellow man;
and the roots we decided to
re-classify as creeping nuts
and snapped them up from the shovel
along with the adhering mud;
and the trees! the trees! and their last
soft sighs in between the chop-chop
of the axe and the scream of the saw.
I listened to the falling trees
with peacefully relaxing mind,
You're a step ahead, I said,
but I'm not too far behind.

2.
Before Recsk I'd never paid
attention to my body's role.
Living was my business. But
then my body took control.
My beard began to soften,
my skin though turned quite tough
and numbed its nerve ends wisely
in order to better stave off
the effects of being hog-tied
and beaten on my feet,
so into the bunker of my
hundred pounds I could retreat,
crawling further and further
inside to dull the pain,
and when my back was lashed
by a ten-week autumn rain
I barely took notice
and felt the flow about
as much as the one
in a nearby waterspout.
My stomach with the might of

millstones managed to digest
raw buds, mushrooms, and acrid beads
of juniper and all the rest
of the gourmet delights
good nature's chef creates
for all; whenever I moved
my muscles put on their brakes,
for my body was telling me
I had to save my breath,
sabotage could save my life,
but work would only bring me death;
outwardly I shrank, becoming
coarse and fossilized,
invisible sulfur flames were
burning hot inside:
I captured every sound with
the ears of Dionysius
but sleeping I would turn stone deaf
to everything encircling us;
the eye in the back of my head
was something no one ever saw,
it searched out the space behind me
like a deep-sea lobster claw;
and our sense of smell! when caught
standing around idly in the wood,
taking a break maybe, we could
sniff out our approaching guards,
like frightened deer their hunters,
from at least a hundred yards; –
but what more can I say about
all this? I learned to live
extra- and introverted in one,
sensitive and insensitive;
I learned my multi-parted body
and all its components conspired
in great secrecy in order
to save me before I expired, –
me, I say, because I also learned
as long as I live my fate
belongs to two of us; my body
has a soul too for a mate,
although every inch of me is
a brother, a comrade-in-arms, a friend,
I am not a sum of them, at

the skin my being doesn't end.

3.

We had no pen, no books, to our
depth news and mail were never sunk,
we had to make do with a mess
kit and one half of a bunk,
we lived with stoolies and slave drivers,
they beat us and kicked us till half gone
from starvation and the shivers
with the lime pit looking on,
seven days a week we worked
and without a hope we went to bed, –
our eyes met in silence saying:
you're too among the living dead.
And yet – what was it in most
of us that kept alive the soul?
Back then I only sensed but now I know
the secret of that horrible hell hole.

4.
When you've lost just about everything, there's no joy, no bread,
and tyranny has your hands tied: you still have the power and the right
left to you to use your free will, to choose between good and evil.
This choice is your refuge that preserves your innermost self,
a citadel within you, impregnable to any foe,
for if they knew about it all their sieges would be useless.
Want to know what's good, what's evil? There's no clear answer out here.
Inside though naked we were all of us, the inmates and the guards.
What's evil? For a ladle of grub you squeal on your neighbors,
and your face blackens munching on bean stew.
What's good? Preserve your human dignity and serenity!
Give help, solace, courage! There's so much for you to do!
Be generous and soft-hearted! You'll see how pleasant and
easy it can be! And if not: be noble out of selfishness,
your meaningless existence will suddenly take on meaning.
A good deed is paid for in cash, on the spot. Your mates will
look up at you; the turnkey will turn pale and the stoolie will
fall in love with you. And if no one's there: you'll still feel
the warmth in your rags in winter, and instead of sweat in summer
your chest will bear cool dewdrops. Cheer up, that's how you can

repay the loan your body gives your soul. Now it's your spirit
that moves you, keeps you alive; to be more precise,
the spirit above your spirit. It won't make me great if I puff
myself up like a blimp, thereby diluting my dilute
individuality till it splits, like Arkhishev and Gide
believed at our century's start. Self-worship is of no help.
Don't glory in what nature has already given you,
the beast in a human form; accept it and then pass on, because
your true life begins when you rise above yourself.
But how? It's a complex world. Need a script? I haven't one.
If your schooling lacked in ethics, if your judgment is too shaky,
turn to esthetics, or trust your taste,
or else, look around yourself and ask: who are you?
a newborn chick produced in the depths of an incubator?
the burnt gunk in the kettle left by Rousseau, Marx, and Rosenberg?
Pavlov's dog, drooling at the mouth with saliva?
Skinner's rat that reacts only when poked at?
or a wretched convict with just enough free will left
to protect your honor but not yourself?

This is how we could've mused at Recsk.
I lived through it all but put it all together only in retrospect.
And I couldn't have put together a thing,
had I not been put in jail, where I learned to think
already past the midpoint in my life.

5.
And what is the best part of the lesson?
While erotic desires slowly
abandoned my plundered body,
love remained its steady resident.
Zsuzsa became a weightless cloud of silver as she kept
hovering in front of my eyes even when they slept;
amidst constant toil and torture, in the grips of cruel hunger pains
or blind unconsciousness, love remained to fill my veins,
love, the eternal flame that burns but doesn't scorch,
love beyond mere mating urge, beyond the hormones' work,
beyond sex organs' juice
beyond Boccaccio's smirk,
maybe Dante's dream
and Apollo's muse.

Tell Freud for me he is a jerk.

6.
The suffering. I'd had it coming to me for quite a while.
Had I not surrendered to it, I'd still be an unsated hedonist.
Some were guzzling its cold stream like spring water,
some turned into zombies while others couldn't stop their wails.
Now I am ashamed to say it was easier for me, all my pains
and troubles were numbed when I wove them into poetry.
And if they persisted I rebelled saying What's the use?
Will our years of suffering bring progress to Hungary?

Let us free our minds of Recsk; it's gone. But let the lesson stand:
if we are the better for it, then better is the land.

(*Budapest 1954)*

EPILOGUE 2

TYRANNY IN ONE SENTENCE
(Egy mondat a zsarnokságról) by *Gyula Illyés*

Where there is tyranny
it's tyranny that rules
not only from the gun barrels,
not only in the deep dark pools

of prison cells and
interrogation rooms,
in the midnight wake-up calls,
it's tyranny that looms

not only in the smoke and mirror
of the prosecutor's tale,
in the pliant guilty pleas,
in the word tapped through the jail,

not only in the judge's jaded
verdict: guilty as charged!
it's tyranny that rules in
the military orders barked,

in the "attention!", in the "fire!",
in the drum's dead roll
as the corpse is dragged
into a common hole,

not only in the news
whispered through half-open doors
by lips that fearful twitching
never long ignores,

in the finger raised against the lips
afraid of saying shush,
it's tyranny that rules
not only in the grill-work bush

of facial wrinkles woven
like a prison wall
for a wordless cry of woe,
in the waterfall

of silent tears that flow
from a mute eye socket
missing its eyeball,

it's tyranny that rules
the standing ovations feeding on
the tyrant's smile in frenzied schools;

where there is tyranny
it's tyranny that rules
not only in the clapping hands
as its programmed tools,

in the trumpet, the concert hall,
lilting lies in loud streams
sung by loyal sculptured stones
in galleries, in the color schemes

of all the paintings and already
in the artist's brush;
not only in the midnight car
sliding along without a hush,

in the way it halts
under gateway vaults;

where there is tyranny
its omnipresence is so wide
as your old god never
managed to abide;

it's tyranny that rules
in the day-care centers,
into the father's advice and
the mother's smile it enters,

it palls your child's every word
a stranger may have overheard;

not only in the barbed-wire fence;
in the weighty rows of books
whose slogans rip your soul more surely
than the barbed-wire hooks;

it even rules in the tiny
good-by kiss pecked by the spouse
asking, when can we, dear,
expect you back home in the house;

in the tone of oft-repeated
hurriedly said how-are-you,
in the suddenly much softer
handshake there may be a clue,

in the way your lover's face
suddenly just freezes up,
it's there with you two on your date,
in the park, the coffee cup,

not only in the questioning
but in the confession's whine,
even in love's sweetest words
like an insect in your wine,

for even in your dreams
you cannot be alone,
it lies in the nuptial bed and
in the first sweet longing moan,

for you can only love what
tyranny once possessed;
it's the tyrant, not your love,
pressed against your chest,

it fogs the bowls and glasses,

coats the nostrils and dry tongues,
it's the draft of darkness
racing through the lungs,

with sunshine through the open window
it sends the stench of a dead dog,
invades the house like a gas leak's
unseen but deadly fog,

talking to yourself you answer,
it's up to tyranny to ask,
even in your fantasy
finding freedom is a task,

the Milky Way becomes a vast
no-man's land with search-lights scanned,
the stars are peepholes and behind them
millions of jailers stand,

or the teaming night sky is but
one enormous labor camp;
it's tyranny that speaks in public,
from every church bell and street lamp,

but also from the priest in shrift,
from the holy homily;
the Congress, church or torture rack,
all stage a show for you to see;

you may try blinking but it's still
the same thing looking back at you
and sticks to you like memory,
like a drawn-out flu;

clicking train wheels tell your story,
locked up, locked up, all they say;
this is what you breathe in on a
mountain top or ocean bay;

the smallest noise becomes
a zigzag lightning bolt,
a flash of light ignites a
missing heartbeat's jolt;

even resting you still feel it,
in the shackling boredom's cry,
in the lashing showers,
bars that reach up to the sky,

in the paralyzing snow squall
of your whitewashed cell;
it's tyranny looking at you through
your dog's eyes, you can tell,

because it's there in every goal,
in tomorrow's and the next,
in every move, every thought, every
gesture and your rest;

like the river its own bed
you follow its path and dig it out;
want to sneak a glance beyond?
it's tyranny the mirrors tout,

there's no escaping from its eyes,
you're the prisoner and your guard;
it seeps into your cigarette
and the fabric of your garb

and eats its way into
the marrow of your bone;
crave ideals? it's only
ideology you own,

crave a look? only what it
conjures up is what you see,
a single match stick's flame can
put you in a forest-fire sea,

all you can be sure of
is tyranny's firm stare
watching out for you at work
from posters everywhere;

you cannot taste what life is like,
what bread and meat are for,
what it's like to long and love with
arms stretched open any more,

thus the slave prepares his shackles,
on himself he locks the gates;
it's tyranny his soupspoon feeds,
it's for tyranny he procreates,

where there is tyranny
human links make up the chains;
it's from you folks that it reeks,
tyranny is in your veins;

we stumble like moles in sunshine,
darkness fetters our feet,
we perspire in the office
as if in Sahara's heat;

where it's tyranny that rules
nothing matters, nothing counts,
you chant its praises faithfully
like the water in the founts,

it's tyranny that stands there
waiting by your grave,
telling you just who you were;
your dust is, too, its slave.

Written by Gyula Illyés in 1950-52, at the height of the Stalinist terror in Eastern Europe, this poem was passed from hand to hand in secret until the fall of Communism, but became quite well-known in the West even before then, translated into every major language.

The above somewhat truncated version (see incomplete stanzas) was prepared by the author from memory for quick publication during the few days of freedom provided by the 1956 uprising in Hungary, and this is the version recently published in a definitive volume of Illyés's collected works, instead of a completed version of the 1960's. The editor of that volume (Mátyás Domokos, a leading authority on Illyés and a personal friend of the poet) preferred the version forged in the heat of the Uprising from memory and published in a provincial paper where the author happened to be at the time. This makes it an historical document. He escaped imprisonment but not official harassment, which turned the whole country into a prison camp in those years.

EPILOGUE 3:

A MINI GROTESQUERIE

(An outsider reminisces and fills in some gaps)

Aladár's natural modesty prevented him from burdening the reader with boring biographical details, and I propose to keep to the same policy in writing about my involvement in this project. I was only a teenager in the period covered by the book, roughly 1948 to 1956, old enough to know about the gulag world; luckily, only from the outside. But the terror did not stop at the barbed-wire fences; its ripple effect deformed the whole society. The very word "Kistarcsa" was enough to send shivers down the spine and suddenly paralyze the vocal cords. If we wanted to feel safe, it was best not to mention that word, not even at home, but certainly not in public, not in school or at work.

For example, my best friend's brother was arrested and sent to the coal mines of Várpalota for reading a somewhat patriotic-religious poem to his coworkers in the office. He never knew who had denounced him. Maybe someone who had not even been present and only heard about it secondhand. His crime: sedition. Sentence: five years of hard labor.

One could never be too careful. By 1950 I am sure Aladár would not have taken a chance on talking to that mysterious French visitor. And yet, one could so easily get into trouble. I probably had a close shave when, coming home late one Saturday night from a dance, I was stopped in the street by a man with his coat collar turned up and hat pulled down over his eyes. He asked me to let him into the apartment house. He was on the lam, and his family were forbidden to have a key to the front door, the main entrance. His wife was waiting in the staircase with a finger on her lips.

It was a lucky thing for me the house was not under surveillance that night, as it was a month later when my brother left the building at dawn, late for work, and started to sprint toward the bus stop. There were several AVO men on his track, also at a trot. They caught up with him before the bus got there, but they let him go with a disappointed growl; he was the wrong man. If the people's iron fist had been on the job a month earlier, we would not have ended up joking about that race to the bus stop. I could now be adding my insider's view of the gulag, instead of the view from the terrorized outside world. Naturally, we never discussed either of these incidents with our neighbors, not even with the family involved. It was best not to...

It is not my intention here to try and rival Aladár's stories with my own, but I am convinced the reader will get a better feel for the background of the book from these real-life incidents than from a political analysis, no matter how erudite I could make it sound.

Nothing illustrates the habit of silence more than the following little incident. It was probably in the tenth grade that one of our classmates was out sick. In the absence of telephones the homeroom teacher appointed me and the fellow I shared a desk with to go and check on the missing boy. The address took us to the outskirts of town, to an unpaved street lined by one-story cottages, directly fronting the street so as save more space for the garden in the backyard, in typical village fashion. Just before reaching the door, we heard the radio on behind a closed and curtained window as we passed under it. It was playing Mozart's Turkish March, which was not known to me as such then but as the signal tune for Radio Free Europe. That US sponsored station in Munich broadcasted news in every language of the Soviet Bloc. It was not against the law to listen to its much-jammed programs, but it was best not to talk about it. My companion and I barely allowed a faint smile of recognition, but no words were exchanged. When a minute later the mother ushered us in the radio was already blaring out the official program from the local station. Not a word about Radio Free Europe, not ever, not with anyone. It was best not to...

My more direct contact with a forced-labor camp came in

the summer of 1953, in Várpalota, not in the coal mine but at a huge construction project closed off by a ten-foot plank fence with barbed wire at the top. I worked as a mechanic's helper in a machine shop just outside, repairing construction equipment. Sometimes we had to go on site and work with the prisoners who provided all the unskilled labor. The free workers were in an awkward position asking any work from the haggard, listless prisoners who could hardly drag themselves, who seemed to have nothing but ironic little anecdotes to keep them alive. One of them related to me the "business" that had earned him his job:

He was from the country but working in a factory in Budapest He commuted back home on Saturday afternoons to spend the night with his family. On one of his trips he carried a loaf of bread home under one arm. He got ten years for sabotage that is, trying to create a bread shortage in the Capital.

Another case: an old peasant only got five years for sabotage when he accidentally fed wheat kernels to the horses instead of oats. His being drunk at the time was considered an extenuating circumstance but no excuse. Incidentally, alcohol seemed to have played an important part in the downfall of many of the protagonists in this book; maybe even Aladár's induction into espionage would have escaped official attention if alcohol had been omitted from his initiation ceremony. Maybe, to this day, even he himself would be unaware of his special assignment and the special status it conferred upon him.

My prisoner informant also pointed out a former owner of the local jewelry store, a survivor of Nazi camps, who, when his store was nationalized, was slated to be automatically arrested for hoarding gold (thus sabotaging the Socialist economy). He managed to sneak out the back door but was soon caught hiding in the vineyards outside town. I will never forget his still rather rotund figure, listlessly lumbering among stacks of bricks, trying to look busy without doing anything. He was supposed to do ten years of that.

Apparently, by that time sabotage had become the buzzword with the AVO, replacing espionage as the crime of the day. The cloak-and-dagger world was only revealed to me in one little glimpse, whether put-on or real. But that was the whole point about espionage; appearances and reality intermingled so closely you never knew what you were looking at. Trust no one, keep your mouth shut; that was the leitmotif of the time. And what ended a budding romance for me. On a nice sunny Sunday afternoon, I decided to pay a visit to a beautiful brunette I had met on my summer job. Actually, she had even invited me to come to her home and pick her up so we could go for a walk on main street, which was the only entertainment available to young people in that pre-television age. She lived in a one-family house with a spacious porch in the back overlooking a nice, private garden. Walking in there on that balmy September afternoon I was greeted by a very peaceful sight of a gathering, mostly older people, some retired officers, judges, and déclassé elements, all basking in the pleasant sunshine. But there was something wrong with the picture. There were no glasses, no sign of any refreshments, not even water, and there was no greeting for me from any of those sitting around in the porch or in the garden, only suspicious looks, unanimous silent stare from the whole party. Finally the mother went inside to produce my girlfriend, and soon we were on our way downtown. Of course, I didn't query her about the scene, didn't even comment on it; I acted as if I had noticed nothing of that grim group. It was best... But a few days later there was a report on Radio Free Europe (overheard by my grandfather who spent every evening glued to his set) about the mother; she was denounced as an agent provocateur trying to get potential enemies of the regime to betray themselves. Needless to say the romance ended right then and thcrc, cvcn though I ncvcr found out whcthcr thc rcport was a plant or indeed true. And if it was a plant, whom was it meant to deceive? My innocuous self? I swear I never mentioned it to anyone outside of our family. It was best...

Recsk was not on the taboo list yet, not on any kind of list: it was kept secret from the outsiders, but I did hear about it even back then from a classmate who had dropped out of high school to join the border patrol division of the AVH. He was a few years older, but that obviously did not help his intelligence. On a return visit to the school, swaggering in his baggy, Soviet-style uniform, he told us about Recsk, and even the Michnyai-led break-out that had put all law-enforcement agencies on a nationwide alert. Apparently the word had got around in those circles, but not so much in the general population. Yes, you know it: it was best not to talk about such things.

Yes, it was back then. But why now? Why is it that, by and large, we still refrain from talking about the crimes committed on behalf of communism? Are we still deceived by its claim to be at the vanguard of human progress and the only true friend of the oppressed all over the world? Are we still under the spell of its utopian vision of a society free of exploitation and conflict? Or are we worried about disturbing the ghosts of Stalin's great apologists in the West such as Bernard Shaw and Jean-Paul Sartre? Or we don't want to seem uncivil, for example, to the legal authorities who participated in the 400 executions following the crushing of the '56 Hungarian uprising and who were never held to account.

At this point we should get over the old AVO slogan, "No one has to account for the prisoners; their number yes, but whether they are dead or alive is no one's responsibility."

It seems that Justice is not only blind, but the poor girl also suffers from a split personality. Some media trendsetters try to convince us that it takes moral courage to take revenge on doddering Nazis and tin-horn South-American dictators, but to go after crimes committed in the service of Communist paymasters is in bad taste and shows moral weakness. But why?

Perhaps I am missing a point somewhere, but I am still looking for answers to questions raised by this Grotesquerie, Aladár's and by my own mini grotesquerie, which I paraded here so as to show why I had been so eager to work with Aladár on his book and why I feel he has an important message, even if it is couched in irony. Maybe the point is that there is no point to any of the suffering exacted by one part of mankind on another. It just happens.

Or else, there is something behind it all; maybe not a grand plan, but some kind of a madness beyond human scale. This madness unleashed over the land came full circle in the Rajk trial in 1950. Comrade Rákosi's speech revealing the indictment was broadcast and blared out from loudspeakers all over town. My personal involvement was limited to my resentment of the delay in the start of an itinerant tightrope walker's show I was waiting to see with hundreds of other people. "Many a sleepless night I've spent unraveling this insidious conspiracy," said our Great Leader about his Minister of Internal Affairs. That sentence still rings in my ears, because it was repeated with great glee afterwards for years. But the one thing about this case that really turned the world upside down for me was a lead editorial in the leading Party organ quoting a linguistic analysis by Rákosi of the name Rajk. This Faithful Disciple of Stalin speculated that Rajk was a Serbian version of Reich, an obvious evidence of Serbian loyalty, and the German-sounding root needed no further elaboration, a clear indication of Jewish origin. I could not believe my eyes. All that talk from our Leader at a time when any kind of ethnic reference was forbidden? Zionism was not mentioned in the indictment, but Rákosi was already getting ready for an anti-Zionist campaign. It was only many years later that I found out Rajk was, unlike his accuser, not even of Jewish origin. He was simply a true believer who willingly cooperated in his show trial. A truly grotesque figure, who, like a suicide bomber, took a lot of innocent people down with him. Legend has it that he was promised a mock execution, but as the perpetrator of many such trials earlier he was probably well aware of the inevitable. His story deserves special treatment, and we hope the "Grotesquerie" will strike again.

One more word about irony. Somehow Aladár's tone immediately sounded familiar to me, his style reminding me of something I had read in my youth. And then it came out in one of his stories that his main contribution to the cultural life of the camp was his recitation of Jenő Rejtő's books. This writer did wonderful spoofs of pulp fiction under the penname of P. Howard in the 1930's until WW II when he unfortunately perished. His books still entertain readers of all ages and backgrounds. I propose to pay tribute to that writer here whose deadpan style and dry humor I had a lot of fun reproducing in Aladár's prose in our collaboration. Following in his footsteps I piled up tongue-in-cheek clichés which are grossly at odds with the serious material on hand and yet enhancing it by contrast. Aladár is the master of the mock-serious tone that allows him to approach a serious subject without ever hitting a false note, without ever sounding preachy or pathetic. It is my hope that in this book I was able to assume his voice in English even in the portions I added at his request as connective tissue around the bare facts of his reminiscences. The translations of the other contributions were rendered faithful to the original and with permission.

My work was aided by Elizabeth Csicsery-Rónay's proofreading and helpful suggestions. Both Aladár and I wish to acknowledge her efforts on behalf of this book.

Paul Sohar

ABOUT THE AUTHORS

FERENC ALADÁR GYÖRGYEY

Born in 1925 to a prosperous family. After graduating from Pázmány/Eotvös Loránt University of Budapest in 1948 with a M.A. Degree he was arrested by the Communist secret police. He was released just a few months before the Hungarian Revolution of 1956 which opened the way to the West for him and for thousands of other refugees. He was immediately admitted into the USA where he found life-time employment at Yale University Library. His further education earned him an MLS degree at the University of Connecticut and an MA in the history of medicine at Yale. He authored three books and scores of literary and scientific articles, both in English and Hungarian. He is also responsible for the script of the successful movie: "Automania 2000." When he retired from Yale he was the Director of the Medical History section at the University's Medical Library.

GYÖRGY FALUDY

A prominent Hungarian poet who started publishing his works in the 1930's and continued till his death in 2006. Between 1956 and 1990 he lived in England and later in Canada in exile, but after the demise of Communism he went back to Budapest.

GYULA ILLYÉS (1902-1983)

The undeclared poet laureate of Hungary, especially in the years following WW II.

ZOLTÁN NYESTE

A mechanical engineer, also left Hungary in 1956, lived in Germany for a few years before coming to the US. Died in 2001 in Hungary. Also published a book about his experiences at Recsk. Was an active member of the Hungarian community in the US.

PAUL (Pál) SOHAR

Domiciled in the US since 1957, has published nine books of poetry in translation, such as "Dancing Embers," selected poems by Sándor Kányádi (Twisted Spoon Press, 2002). His own poetry and translations have seen print in more than 200 magazines in the US, UK and Canada. He first appeared with Synergebooks as the translator of "The Curious Moon", a children's story in verse, also by Kányádi. His latest poetry translation volumes include "Silver Pirouettes", Faludy poems published by TheWriteDeal (2012) and "In Contemporary Tense", more poems by Sándor Kányádi (Iniquity Press, 2013). His own poetry can be found in a prize-winning book; "The Wayward Orchard" (Wordrunner Press, 2011).

CPSIA information can be obtained
at www.ICGtesting.com
Printed in the USA
BVHW042133171019
561449BV00008B/93/P